PLAYING WITH MATCHES

ALSO AVAILABLE FROM LAUREL-LEAF BOOKS

PLAYING WITH MATCHES
BY BRIAN KATCHER

Copyright © 2008 by Brian Katcher
Interior illustration © 2008 by Cole Gerst/option-G

All rights reserved. Published in the United States by Laurel-Leaf, an imprint of Random House Children's Books, a division of Random House, Inc., New York. Originally published in hardcover by Delacorte Press, an imprint of Random House Children's Books, in 2008.

Laurel-Leaf and the colophon are trademarks of Random House, Inc.

Visit us on the Web! www.randomhouse.com/teens
Educators and librarians, for a variety of teaching tools, visit us at www.randomhouse.com/teachers

The Library of Congress has cataloged the hardcover edition of this work as follows:

Katcher, Brian.
Playing with matches / Brian Katcher.
p. cm.
Summary: While trying to find a girl who will date him, Missouri high school junior Leon Sanders befriends a lonely, disfigured female classmate.
ISBN: 978-0-385-73544-5 (trade)—ISBN: 978-0-385-90525-1 (Gibraltar lib. bdg.)—ISBN: 978-0-375-84882-7 (e-book)
[1. Dating (Social customs)—Fiction. 2. Friendship—Fiction.
3. Beauty, Personal—Fiction. 4. High schools—Fiction. 5. Schools—Fiction.
6. Disfigured persons—Fiction. 7. Missouri—Fiction.] I. Title.
PZ7.K1565Pl 2008
[Fic]—dc22
2007027654

ISBN: 978-0-385-73545-2 (pbk.)

RL: 6.0
Printed in the United States of America
10 9 8 7 6 5 4 3
First Laurel-Leaf Edition

For Sandra

ACKNOWLEDGMENTS

I'd like to thank my editor, Claudia Gabel, who made this possible. None of this could have happened without you. I'd like to thank Barri, Margo, Heidi, and Elaine, who helped me knock this story into shape. I'd especially like to thank my wife, Sandra, who put up with her husband's neurosis and believed in me, even when I didn't.

1

ANOTHER DAY IN PARADISE

"So I was reading this Vonnegut novel," I said to Samantha. "The main guy figures out that the number of people he's killed and the number of women he's slept with are the same."

Samantha didn't look up from her newspaper, as if she hadn't heard me. I went on.

"It was seventy-two."

Samantha pointedly turned a page. Every morning, we would repeat this ritual. She would sit at a cafeteria table, bottle of water to her left, low-fat bran muffin to her right, copy of the *St. Louis Post* in front of her. I would sit opposite and talk at her until she could no longer concentrate.

I continued my literary review. "So do you think that number's kind of high?"

Samantha folded her paper with a sigh. "For what, Leon? Killing people or sleeping around?"

"Either."

Samantha always reminded me of a splinter of flint. She was narrow, hard, and angular. At seventeen, she was already a little old lady, with rimless glasses, short hair, and an enormous nose. Her breasts didn't sag, of course; she didn't really have any.

"Leon, how would I know? Why do you always want to discuss things like this?" She returned to her paper. The first-hour bell wouldn't ring for a few minutes, and I looked around the cafeteria for a distraction.

The Zummer High lunchroom was immense. Early-morning sunshine streamed pleasantly over us, thanks to some slanting windows near the ceiling. Now that spring was here, the windows turned the cafeteria into an unbearable greenhouse. At one end of the room, a poorly painted dog declared GO ZUMMER BULLDOGS! On the opposite wall, a portrait of General Montgomery Zummer glared at us over the soda machines. He'd once slaughtered many Indians on this very spot, back when St. Christopher, Missouri, was still just a frontier outpost.

Around us, teenagers poured into the school, back from spring break. A sea of white faces. Suburban students, all dressed in the same clothes, telling the same stories, sharing the same hive mind. If there was one thing more depressing than a suburban high school, it was a suburban high school in Missouri.

I turned back to Samantha. "You know, it's the same with me, Sam. I've killed and slept with the same number of people."

She didn't look at me. "A nice, round number, Leon?" She drew a zero in the air with her finger.

"It's bound to change."

Samantha took a swig of Evian. "Who are you planning on killing?"

I shoved the rest of her bran muffin into my mouth. Samantha had guessed my number correctly. Zero was the number of times I'd had sex. And the number of dates I'd had since the fall. Here it was, just after spring break of my junior year. I hadn't had a date since Angie Herber and I had made out after the homecoming game. She gave me the "just friends" speech the next day.

Why did every girl want to be my friend? They didn't even want that; Samantha was the only girl who came close to being my friend. Or my only friend who came close to being a girl.

The warning bell rang. Actually, it wasn't a bell but a long droning buzzer that grated on my nerves like an early-morning car alarm.

Students began to lumber to class. Samantha neatly separated her recyclables, grabbed her books, and walked away.

"Hey, Samantha," I hollered. "What's your number?"

She turned and indicated a digit with her middle finger.

Older high schools are architectural wonders, with the ornate exteriors, wooden trim, and murals by long-dead alumni. Newer schools are marvels of the twenty-first century, with gleaming metal fixtures, air-conditioning, and toilets that flushed.

Monty Zummer had been built in the 1960s. That meant blocky. Ugly. Cramped. Three generations of Zummer students had attended what was essentially an enormous bomb shelter. We used to joke that a busload of mental patients was accidentally delivered to MZH and it took them two weeks to realize they weren't in an asylum. The asylum served better food.

I stopped by my locker to get my stuff for chemistry class. There were almost two thousand students at this school, and half of them were female. So how come whenever I asked a girl if I could have the privilege of paying for her food and entertainment she always said no? Aside from the fact she didn't want to kiss me.

When I was in junior high, I was a nerd. The kind of guy everyone picked on. The last one chosen for teams in gym class. Now, after years of struggle, I'd succeeded in becoming an unknown. And when no girl knew you existed, odds were they wouldn't be receptive when you tried to get them horizontal.

Of course, my looks didn't exactly make girls turn their heads and drop their pants. At only five foot six, I had to look up at many of the girls at school. Puberty had come and gone without leaving me so much as a chest hair or a whisker. And my face . . . Some guys are just born handsome. I had a mug that looked like it should be hanging in a post office somewhere, with the title WANTED FOR SHOPLIFTING AND CREDIT CARD FRAUD.

Instead of wavy brown hair, I had stringy locks the color

of old hay. When I wore a hat, I looked like a scarecrow. I'd inherited my father's generous ears but not his noble nose. I was stuck with my mother's petite button nose.

And then there were my eyes. Some guys had steely blue orbs that, despite any physical shortcoming, could just freeze a woman in her tracks and hypnotize her with their raw power. I had two beady brown eyes that, no matter how hard I tried to look mysterious and cool, always seemed to say "It wasn't me who just farted."

I kicked my locker shut. Three billion women in the world, and the universe couldn't spare one for Leon Sanders.

"Excuse me?"

Female voice! I swirled, waiting to see whatever gorgeous teenage queen wanted my attention.

Disappointed wasn't the word. I was . . .

Okay, disappointed *was* the word.

Her name was Melody Hennon. Everyone in school knew Melody. At least, everyone recognized her.

Like at any school, some people at Montgomery Zummer were universally shunned. That girl in the wheelchair. The guy with leukemia who was obviously going to get his own page in the yearbook before graduation. The retarded kids from the resource room. And Melody.

Sometime in her youth, Melody had been in an accident. A fire. I didn't know the details; she hadn't started at Zummer Elementary until the third grade.

The flames had eaten away most of Melody's face and left her with no ears whatsoever. She didn't have much of a nose either, just the bony ridge over her misshapen nostrils. Her lips still remained: puffy, clownlike masses of tissue covering the teeth she never showed the world. She usually wore a scarf around her head, hiding the scant fuzz that poked out here and there from her withered scalp. Only by looking directly into her eyes–those sad gray eyes under her grafted-on eyelids–did you realize you were looking at a human face. And no one ever looked Melody Hennon in the eyes.

She was staring at me with what I supposed was an expectant look on her face. Unconsciously, I stepped back. Then I realized I'd jumped back, so I quickly stepped forward. Then I was too close, so I stepped back again. It was the first time I'd ever danced with a girl.

Melody's eyes narrowed. She was showing disgust, pain, or amusement–it was hard to tell.

"Did you say something?" I asked.

"You're standing in front of my locker," she whispered.

"Huh?" No way. Her locker wasn't anywhere near mine. That wasn't a face I had to see every day.

"That's not your locker," I told her, perhaps a bit more bluntly than I meant to.

Melody's mouth opened for a second, revealing her immaculate teeth. Then she turned and dashed away.

Jesus, she forgot where her own locker was. At least I wasn't the only one whose brain wasn't turned on that morning. As I slouched to the chemistry lab, I took a little comfort in knowing that there was one other person at this school whose number was zero.

2

IS IT HOT IN HERE, OR IS IT JUST A CHEMICAL FIRE?

High school chemistry was like the can opener on a Swiss Army knife: it was there because it had always been there, not because anyone would ever use it. When was the last time someone had to calculate the molarity of hydrochloric acid in real life?

Still, first-hour chemistry wasn't boring. Not because of the subject matter, but because I had Mr. Jackson. No one got bored in Jackson's class. Stop paying attention for a moment and you risked losing an eye.

Jackson was on his second ex-wife and his third nervous

breakdown. He had failed in life as a husband and father, and as a research scientist, and was now proceeding to fail as a teacher. Every day for a semester and a half, he stood in front of us, droning in his whiny monotone, reading out of the textbook, while we dozed. That was, until lab days. Then Mr. Jackson transformed into a 1950s mad scientist.

Strange things happened with the experiments. Chemicals caught fire. Test tubes exploded. Fifty-gallon emergency eyewash stations inexplicably opened, flooding the classroom. I still deny I had anything to do with that last incident.

Today was a mere lecture day, so students talked, passed notes, or copied each other's homework in search of that elusive C-. I sat alone at my lab table, doodling in my textbook. Before I could finish adding a mustache to Marie Curie, I was interrupted.

Jimmy and Johnny Thomson were the same height and weight as a pair of industrial refrigerators—and almost twice as smart. They were twin brothers, and the only way you could tell their bushy-haired, pockmarked faces apart was that Jimmy's broken nose had never healed quite right. Predictably, they excelled as linebackers on the Zummer High football team. It was the only place they could bust heads without being arrested.

The brothers had attached themselves to me in the seventh grade, when they'd realized I didn't mind them copying off me during tests. In return, they ensured I didn't get my clumsy ass kicked too often during PE. And they had a pool table at their house. Friendships have been built on less.

Jimmy and Johnny flopped down into the seats on either

side of me. This enabled them to copy my lab reports more easily (though they probably could have xeroxed them for all Mr. Jackson noticed). I could have put up with Jimmy's constant sinus snorting and Johnny's onion breath. What I could do without was the way they spent every science class pounding the holy hell out of each other. That day was no exception.

"Butthole!" hollered Johnny at his brother.

"Fartface!" Jimmy yelled back, and socked his brother in the arm, narrowly missing my jaw.

"Asswipe!" countered Johnny, swatting Jimmy in the back of the head. I ducked down against the table, out of the line of fire.

"Um, students . . ." Mr. Jackson addressed the class in his normal nasal voice. Good thing too; the twins would have had each other in wrestling holds in a few seconds.

There was a loud belch of static from the intercom, which always preceded the morning announcements.

"Good morning, Zummer High," said Principal Bailey, in his constipated, recorded-sounding voice. "Today is Monday, March tenth." Across the room, students continued to chat.

"Welcome back. We would like to remind all female students that tops must be worn full to the pants line. No stomach-baring shirts." Next to me, Johnny pulled up his shirt to his chest, revealing his hairy gut.

"For all students interested in trying out for the spring musical, there will be an informational meeting in the choir room after school.

"Finally, a reminder to all students with lockers numbered 5001 to 5050. New locker assignments were handed out this morning. See Ms. Anderson in the office if you have any questions. Thank you, and have a nice day."

I leaned over to Johnny. "Why did they change everyone's lockers?"

"They painted a bunch of them over spring break. The painters took all the doors off, and they lost the numbers for some of them, and no one knows the combinations. Probably just an excuse for Bailey to search our stuff."

My laughter was cut short when I realized that Melody was probably one of the refugees and I really had been standing in front of her new locker. I made a mental note to apologize to her next time we ran into each other. If her new locker assignment was permanent, that would be quite often.

Mr. Jackson opened the teacher's manual of the chemistry text. Like a bunch of zombies, we flipped our books to whatever chapter he would forget to teach us about. His shrill monotone filled the air. Ears began to rest on tables. Doodles appeared in notebooks. The muted sound of someone's hidden iPod could be heard from the back row.

I guess I was the only one who enjoyed that class. Not because of the lectures, homework, and occasional melted glassware. I enjoyed it for the same reason I never asked to be moved to a different table. At the seat diagonally in front of me sat Amy Green.

Amy. I'd known her since the fourth grade. We had once been friends of sorts; she'd even come to my tenth birthday party. Of course, back then girls were just boys who played with Barbies. But in middle school, the girls began to grow up and out (or, in Samantha's case, just up). By the time we hit high school, Amy looked like the sort of girl you'd see in a new picture frame. And with each cup size, her popularity swelled. I don't think she'd wasted a thought on me since elementary school.

All I could see from my seat was her long, long blond hair and those bare muscular arms. Still, I remembered exactly what she'd been wearing when she'd sat down: tight jeans, a blue sweater with no sleeves, and white sneakers. If someone had asked me what shirt I was wearing at that moment, I would have had to look.

I couldn't wait for the spring pep rally, when I would see Amy in her cheerleading uniform. Those tanned shoulders, those athletic legs, the way her eyes crinkled when she smiled (at other people). The slight indentations above her collarbone. The tiny scar just under her right knee.

My fantasies were rudely interrupted by the appearance of Johnny's leering face at my shoulder. "Not in a million years, Leon," he whispered.

"She wouldn't spit on you if you were on fire," echoed his brother, flashing a crooked-toothed smile at me. "But since you aren't on fire, she just might."

"Dudes," I snapped, "shut up!" It was a good thing Mr. Jackson was too clueless to notice us.

"Just trying to do you a favor," said Johnny. "She's out of your league. Besides, she's a lousy kisser." He wiggled his tongue at me.

"And she stuffs her bra," added Jimmy.

"I don't have a thing for her," I lied.

"Why not, are you gay?"

Since I was trapped between them, it was impossible to turn away.

Johnny flung his huge arm over my shoulder in what he must have assumed was a friendly gesture.

"Want some advice, Leon?" he whispered.

"No."

"I've seen you around chicks. You're about as subtle as a boner in church."

Jimmy leaned in from the other side. "I remember when you tried to ask out Laura. Christ, why didn't you just ask for her used panties?"

I thought back to the incident that had happened after school the week before. Laura had turned me down, but I wasn't *that* forward, was I?

Jimmy inhaled a wad of snot from somewhere in his nasal cavity and visibly swallowed it. "If you wanna get to know Amy, tone it down. Be friendly. Be cool."

"And don't be yourself," added Johnny.

"Shut up!" I hissed, loudly enough for Mr. Jackson to glance in our direction.

Be subtle? This from a guy who showed me his butt the first time we met. In truth, maybe I was kind of . . . abrupt. It wasn't easy for me to talk to girls. How could I start a conversation?

It probably had a lot to do with junior high. I guess after three straight years of being insulted and picked on every day, I took it for granted that no one liked me. That any girl

I asked out would turn me down. It had been years since anyone had gone out of their way to torment me, but inside I would always be twelve years old, with the other kids laughing at me the second the teacher's back was turned. Maybe that was why I was seventeen and had dated only four girls, three of them from other schools.

Chemistry couldn't have lasted longer than fifty minutes, though time tended to slow down in there. Eventually, the bell buzzed. Students walked, ran, or in the case of the Thomsons, brawled out the door. I stayed. Amy was still there, talking to one of her friends. I guess Mr. Jackson was there too, frantically trying to think of something to teach the next class, but he could be ignored.

Be subtle. Could Johnny and Jimmy have been right for the first time in five years? If I just played it cool, maybe Amy would notice me again. Why wouldn't she?

Because you're Leon Sanders, vice president of the Key Club, Computer Club secretary, and Monty Python enthusiast.

It was true. Even without all that middle school popularity crap, the only reason a guy like me should approach Amy was to leave a burnt offering at her temple.

I started to gather my stuff. Why couldn't I be really cool? Why could I never just talk to girls? Why not right now? Maybe my worries were all mental. Amy was probably as friendly as she had been in the fourth grade, and would happily talk to me if I just made the effort.

Slowly, slowly, I approached her.

It's now or never. Go talk to her.

Amy and her disciple were deep in conversation about a

new cheerleading routine. I waited until there was a pause in the discussion.

"Hi," I said, my voice sounding several octaves higher than normal.

"Er, hi," Amy replied, probably wondering why I hadn't made an appointment with her social secretary.

"How's it going?" Even as I spoke the words, I was aware of how forced they sounded. As opening lines went, it ranked right down there with *What's your sign?* and *Wanna see a dead body?*

"Fine, I guess."

"Yeah, I'm fine too...." Long, awkward pause. Amy shifted uncomfortably in her seat. I felt about as welcome as a persistent panhandler.

I babbled a goodbye and scurried off. Maybe if I snuck in with the bell for the rest of the year, Amy wouldn't notice me. A mere human like me couldn't just strike up a conversation with an angel like her.

So much for listening to the Thomsons. If I was going to take romantic advice from two guys who got nostalgic over their greatest farts, then I deserved to be embarrassed.

3

THANKS, I'M HERE ALL WEEK!

I jogged to my locker with the acidic feeling in my stomach that told me that, once again, I'd done something unbelievably moronic. When would it stop? Back when I was a junior high nerd, my father had told me that by the time I reached high school, it would all be behind me. What a load of steaming fatherly crap! I was just another scrawny, average-looking face in the crowd. No popular kids had gone out of their way to talk to me since the year before, when Jimmy had convinced a bunch of us to grab our crotches during the group sophomore class photo. And even that was a mixed reception.

Why couldn't I casually talk to a girl like Amy? Other guys could. Of course, they were generally better looking, richer, funnier, and more athletic.

As if on cue, Dylan Shelton muscled his way down the hall. Dylan was one of those guys who had no choice but to be popular. A guy that handsome and athletic could have saved comic books in plastic bags and discussed the plot holes in *Star Wars* and still had flocks of admirers. While I'd been getting kicked and tripped in seventh-grade PE, Dylan had already become captain of the flag football team. Now he was starting quarterback for the MZH football team. The sort of guy Amy would allow to talk to her.

That wasn't why I resented Dylan. I could never forget that time when I was twelve. Walking home from school. The punches. The insults. The spit in my face . . .

"Excuse me. . . ." There came a mumbled voice from behind me.

"What!" I bellowed, directly into Melody Hennon's scarred face.

Most girls would have either stepped back or kicked me in the nuts for treatment like that. Melody simply blinked for a long moment. I was surprised to notice that her eyelids bore no scars. Maybe they were artificial.

"Sorry," I grunted, moving away from her new locker.

She didn't answer; she simply opened her locker and grabbed a binder. I tried not to stare.

Now, we were trained at an early age not to gape at people who were "different." How did you look at a human monstrosity? How did she face that in the mirror every morning?

It wasn't like she could just pretend nothing was wrong, like she could have if she had been missing an ear or just had one bad scar. Her entire face, her entire head, looked like something you'd see in a low-budget wax museum. Her normal eyes and perfect teeth only accented her ugliness.

The world is a cruel place, anyone can tell you that. But I think only people like Melody could truly cite examples. I still cringed when I thought of the names she'd been called in elementary school. Every time a new horror movie came out, the other kids would make it a point to call her by the name of the monster. Freddy Krueger. Leatherface. Gollum. The Thing. They'd wait until she was just in earshot on the playground, then scream in mock horror, pretending Frankenstein had escaped from the movie screen and come to get them.

I guess I shouldn't say "they." By fifth grade I was already on the fast track to loserville, and more than once I insulted Melody before anyone could start making fun of me.

Now that we were all a little older and, theoretically, more mature, we replaced our insults with a stony silence. When Melody passed us in the hall, we averted our eyes. When we were obliged to talk to her, we were brief and to the point. Not that we didn't like her personally; it was just that she was something we'd rather not think about. There was nothing we could do to help her (aside from making an effort to be her friend, which no one was willing to do).

Melody shut her locker and sighed. There was pain in that sigh, of someone who'd had all she could take that day. And it was only 8:57 a.m. I had to say something.

I remembered a joke Ryan Kelly had told me in sixth grade.

"So this pirate walks into a bar with a steering wheel sticking out of his pants. The bartender says, 'Hey, you got a steering wheel in your pants,' and the pirate says, 'Aargh! It's drivin' me nuts!' "

Melody blinked once, and I was afraid I was adding to my socially inept reputation. Suddenly, she giggled. Melody had a pleasant laugh, like something you'd hear from the host of a children's program.

"You don't know how much I needed a laugh this morning." She then turned and walked off. As I gathered up my books, I smiled a little. I couldn't remember the last time anyone had laughed at one of my jokes.

The Buick had been my father's. He had given it to me as a sixteenth-birthday present, though I think he'd really just wanted an excuse to buy the pickup truck he'd always desired. At any rate, the car was the same age as me, had no air-conditioning and bad shocks. But she was all mine.

I walked out to the parking lot with my pal Rob Franklin, who I sometimes drove home. Rob was one of about ten black students at Monty Zummer High. He was tall, had a permanently sour expression, and could make a series of cracking noises with his joints. This had made him popular on the elementary school playground but had proven ineffective in the pursuit of women.

I'd known Rob since kindergarten. The fact that he didn't bring up the time I cried during *The Wizard of Oz* proved the depth of our friendship.

My car started on the second try and we were off into the sterile wilderness that was St. Christopher, Missouri.

"You drive like old people screw," commented Rob.

"Hey, Rob, can I ask you a serious question?"

He shrugged. Looking at Rob's wrathful expression, you'd think I had just insulted his mother. He wasn't mad, however; his mouth just naturally formed a frown, and his eyes always scowled. It made strangers nervous, but once you got to know him, you realized he disliked everyone equally.

"Rob, how come I can't ever get a date?"

Rob fiddled with the radio.

"You want the truth?"

"Of course not."

"Tough. You're a dork, dude."

I turned off the radio. "I told you I didn't want the truth."

Rob leaned back in the decaying seat. "Too bad. You follow pretty girls around like a sick dog, but you don't even bother to shave. You wear nothing but shirts with dumb sayings on 'em; you tell stupid, *stupid* jokes; and you read for fun, for Christ's sake. I can't believe you even had to ask."

I took in the harsh reality. "You really think my jokes are stupid?"

"That's not the point, Leon." He extended his arms toward the windshield. A series of crunching noises started at his shoulders and ended with his knuckles. "You spent New Year's playing Dungeons and Dragons."

"You were there!"

He twisted his neck until there was an audible snap. "Yeah, but I'm not bitching about my love life."

"Thanks for nothing."

"You're very welcome." We pulled up in front of Rob's house, an old brown split-level surrounded by dozens of concrete saints. He stooped to pick up his backpack as his spine made noises like a xylophone. "Look, don't take it too hard. It's not like you're the biggest loser in school."

"Right. I guess there's always Rick Rose or Dan Dzyan." Rick was the only guy in Zummer history who'd been suspended because of the school's no-pornography policy. Dan was a genuine head case.

Rob laughed. "Or Melody Hennon . . ."

"Melody's not a loser," I shot back without thinking. Anyone who'd laugh at my jokes was cool in my book.

Rob didn't look any angrier than usual. "Whatever. See ya tomorrow." He headed to the door.

"Hey, Rob? This guy walks into a bar carrying a big piece of highway. He says, 'Give me a drink and one for the road.' "

Rob's wrathful expression momentarily changed to one of deep pity. Then he was gone.

I gunned the gas. Was I really such a loser? I guessed certain questions were better left unanswered. *Is that thing loaded?* for instance, or *Will my head fit in there?*

It took me only five minutes to drive home from Rob's house. St. Christopher was a suburb of St. Louis. That meant you could drive thirty miles in any direction, get out of your car, and not see any sort of change. Just another Wal-Mart, another McDonald's, and another Jiffy Lube. My dad remembered when St. Christopher had been its own little town, but long before I was born, St. Louis had engulfed it, along with St. Charles, O'Fallon, Wentzville, Lake St. Louis, and a dozen or so other small cities.

I pulled up to my home, a one-story house that was identical to every other one in Oakridge subdivision. I used to joke that I had to count the houses to find mine, but until the trees Dad planted took off, that had almost been the truth.

Maybe my luck would have been different if I'd lived in a big city, where there were more girls, or in the country, where there were fewer guys. Then again, girls probably had high standards in those places too.

Neither of my parents was home from work, so I grabbed a snack and headed for my room. Because I was an only child, this was the time I could be alone for a while. My folks would soon be home, pestering me about my day. Of course, I would have loved to spend this time alone with a girl. Like Amy, for instance.

I flopped down onto my bed and slurped my soda, thinking about what it would be like to have Amy–hell, to have *any* girl–here, alone. The really embarrassing thing was I wasn't thinking about sex. Well, not just about sex. I had a much darker fantasy.

In the secret dreams that I never discussed with anyone, I pictured a generic girl looking at me, smiling, and being impressed. I fantasized about someone I could talk to unashamed. A girl who would listen to me talk about the books I read, the weird movies I liked, my abortive attempts at fan fiction. Someone who could look at Leon Sanders–the actual Leon Sanders–and like what she saw. Even Rob and the Thomsons merely tolerated me, and I sure didn't open up to them.

I could almost see the fantasy girl sitting across from me at my desk. She didn't have a face, but somehow I knew it wasn't Amy. I could hear her voice.

You're fantastic, Leon. I really like you. You're special to me.

I shook my head, disgusted by my effeminate thoughts. I tried to picture Amy doing a striptease for me, but for once my heart wasn't in it. What I wanted was a girl who'd like the real, unedited Leon Sanders. The striptease could come later.

I sat up and threw my empty soda can at my wastebasket. I'd never noticed before, but I really hadn't gotten rid of anything since about fourth grade. My old gumball machine, now half-filled with rubber eyeballs, still sat on my dresser. The D.A.R.E. poster I got in sixth grade was still attached to the wall (mostly by dust) but was now flanked by two posters of Ferraris, which were flanked by two bikini babes. My bookcase was crammed with an odd assortment of Magic Tree House chapter books, Matrix DVDs, a cow skull, and *Simpsons* figurines. And last time I'd groped under my bed for a *Playboy,* I'd found Baxter, my old teddy bear. Jesus, and I had to ask why I couldn't meet a girl?

I got up and looked at a photo hung on my bulletin board next to a plastic Key Club key chain and a smutty postcard from Rob. The picture had been taken on Halloween of my eighth-grade year. Me, Johnny, Jimmy, Rob, and Samantha. Johnny and Jimmy were wearing football uniforms. Samantha was a witch (and she didn't need a fake pointy nose). Rob was a cowboy. And I was wearing a Starfleet uniform.

What girl would ever think a geek like that was special?

An hour or so later, I heard my father come home from work. Though it took me only about a minute to go down the stairs, he was already drinking milk straight from the carton, dressed only in his boxers.

"Hey, Son. How was school?"

"It sucked."

Dad put away the milk and scratched himself. I prayed that I would not inherit his gorilla-like body hair. Unlike me, Dad had been a bit of an athlete in high school. I knew that even with his middle-aged gut, he'd probably be in his seventies before I could finally beat him at arm wrestling.

We'd always been close, but it had been a while since I'd asked for his advice. Sometimes it seemed like he'd been born a hundred years ago, and nothing he could tell me would have anything to do with my problems. Still, I'd asked Rob, Samantha, Jimmy, and Johnny for help that day. Might as well ask everyone.

"Hey, Dad? When you were my age, how did you, you know, meet girls?"

Dad grinned. He loved telling stories about his youth. "Well, your uncle and I had this '72 Chrysler. We used to go driving down State Street when it was just this two-lane road. There was this burger joint where your dentist's office is now . . ."

Dad paused, apparently aware he was going off on a

tangent. "Okay. Meeting girls. You know. I never really went out of my way to meet anyone. I mean, I'd see them in class, at work, driving around..."

This was going nowhere. "Well, how did you get dates? How did you meet Mom?"

Dad had opend a can of pineapple and was shoveling forkfuls into his mouth. "You know the story. She had car trouble and I helped her. We went out to eat after."

None of this would help me land Amy. "Thanks."

Dad, realizing I needed some help, put away the pineapple. "Leon, if you go out looking to meet girls, you never will. They travel in packs, and can tell when a guy's after them. What you have to do is be their friend. Just talk. Give them a hand when they need it. Be nice to any girl, even the ugly ones. Once they think you're a nice guy, that's when to make your move."

I nodded but hadn't been listening. Standard dad advice.

"And Leon? Just be yourself. Women hate phonies."

Be myself. That was one bit of fatherly advice I was not going to take.

4

FROM THE HALLS
OF MONTY ZUMMER

The next day, after second hour, I noticed Melody neatly stacking books in her locker. When she saw me, she flashed me a shy smile. I grinned back. Once you got over the initial shock, she wasn't *that* hard to look at. She was still a freak, of course, but it wasn't like she was Frankenstein hideous. When she smiled, you noticed her eyes more, the scars less.

I remembered my dad's advice about making friends with any girl I could. It wouldn't hurt.

"Hi, Melody."

"Hi, Leon. Hey…" She hesitated for a moment. "Why couldn't Beethoven find his teacher?"

"Why not?"

"Because he was Haydn!"

I snorted. "That was about as bad as my pirate joke."

Melody looked at me for a second, as if she was deciding something.

"Leon," she said abruptly. "That's a nice shirt."

I grinned. Instead of wearing my caffeine molecule shirt, I'd fished a nice polo out of my closet.

"Thanks."

Suddenly, Melody lurched toward me, her hand out. I was backed up against the lockers and couldn't dodge. Jesus Christ, was she trying to hug me?

There was a tugging at my collar, and Melody pressed something into my hand. It was the price tag from my shirt.

I crumpled it. "I've been walking around like that all morning."

Melody toyed with the book in her hand. "Maybe no one noticed."

"You noticed. Um, thanks."

Melody laughed and walked away. Once again I was struck by her giggling. It made me forget that Amy had probably seen me with a price tag on my shirt that morning. I didn't think I'd ever noticed the way a girl laughed before.

A Zummer High riddle: Why do Eskimos wear earmuffs? Answer: So they won't hear Mr. Hamburg up in Alaska.

Mr. Hamburg, my social studies teacher, didn't scream. He didn't yell. It was just that his voice was naturally loud.

Really loud. Nobody zoned out in history class; it would have been like trying to nap while the space shuttle was taking off.

Hamburg was somewhere between forty and seventy. His hair looked like it had been combed with an eggbeater. He somehow managed to constantly maintain a three-day beard. The narrow end of his tie was always a little longer than the wide end. I knew he changed shirts, because the stains were in different places every day.

"WHEN PRESIDENT ROOSEVELT ORDERED THAT AMERICAN CITIZENS OF JAPANESE DESCENT BE ARRESTED AND INTERNED, HE VIOLATED THE CONSTITUTION." He paused to drain his third cup of black coffee that period. "CAN ANYONE TELL ME WHAT PART OF THE CONSTITUTION SHOULD HAVE PREVENTED THIS?"

No one bothered to answer. Mr. Hamburg, without fail, would call on everyone before class was over. Well, almost everyone.

"MR. STEWARD?"

Bill Steward looked around nervously, not sure of the question, not even sure if he was the one called on, probably not even sure what class he was in. Poor guy. He was nice enough, but he just didn't have a lot upstairs.

Bill did a pretty good impression of an epileptic until Mr. Hamburg called on someone else. People chuckled. I felt sorry for Bill. He had not been able to answer a question the whole year. I wondered why Mr. Hamburg insisted on calling on Bill, while he never called on . . .

I turned in my seat and took a sideways glance at Melody. I hadn't ever noticed we had a class together. Well, I had *noticed* but never really thought about it. She was like that 10 MPH sign in the parking lot. People knew it was there, but it didn't affect them.

Melody sat in the cornermost desk. She was sort of hunched over her notebook and was the only one not laughing at Bill's spaz attack. I had the urge to make a face at her across the room and crack her up.

"MR. SANDERS," bellowed our teacher, rapping my desk with his bony knuckles, "IF YOU ARE THROUGH DAYDREAMING, PERHAPS YOU MIGHT EN-LIGHTEN US?" His good eye stared me down, his glass one focused on the wall.

"Uhhhh..."

"THANK YOU, MR. SANDERS. AS FOR THE REST OF YOU, THE SEMESTER PROJECT WILL BEGIN TODAY. YOU HAVE A LIST OF POSSIBLE TOPICS. AS I MENTIONED BEFORE, YOU MAY WORK WITH A PARTNER. LET'S TAKE THE LAST FIVE MINUTES TO PAIR UP."

Crap. I hated group projects. I always got saddled with some dumb-ass and ended up having to do all the work.

To my horror, Bill was looking at me and smiling his bucktoothed, moronic grin. That was one person whose grade I did not want to be linked with.

I looked frantically around the room for anyone else to partner with. Everyone seemed to be pairing up. Everyone except Melody. She hadn't moved from her desk. From the other side of the room, I noticed her looking at me. It was funny, but at that distance, it looked as if her face was made up only of eyes, as if she had no other features.

I didn't know if Melody was smart, but unlike Bill, she'd never accidentally got a binder caught in her hair. I propelled my chair across the newly waxed floor and slammed into Melody's desk. She hadn't expected this, and I almost took off two of her fingers.

"Hey, wanna be partners?"

"Okay." Melody was no longer looking at me and was squirming in her seat.

"Tight." The bell rang.

"When should we . . ."

I was already moving toward the door. "I like to wait till the last second and then do a really half-assed job. If you want to get together during study hall tomorrow, we can choose a topic."

As I left, I noticed that Melody was still sitting in her seat, not moving. I regretted my rash behavior. Maybe she liked working alone and I'd put her on the spot. I'd just kind of assumed she'd enjoy hanging out with me. But why should she be any different? She was a girl, after all. And few girls liked spending time with me. Even outcasts like her.

The poster proudly declared WINNERS DON'T USE DRUGS. Seven people, evidently winners, stood grinning at the camera: a jock-looking guy, three pretty girls, a guy in a leather jacket (the safe, school-sponsored rebel), a handsome guy with glasses and a biology book, and the token black guy. Across their mugs, someone with a Sharpie had written *You wash your walls to erase my pens / But the Poster Poet strikes again!*

I sat in the cafeteria after school, waiting for Rob to get out of the bathroom. Zummer High was big enough that there were always about a hundred kids hanging around after school, practicing sports, meeting with clubs, or just lounging with friends. I hoped they'd all get savage diarrhea.

Maybe if I had tried harder to be an athlete, girls would notice me. Or if I'd been one of those student council jack-offs; there were always white-bread girls hanging around them. Hell, even the losers who snorted paint had chicks who cleaned up their vomit. But not me.

"I'm tired of cleaning up my own vomit!" I shouted to Rob as he exited the restroom.

"Aren't we all." We headed out the front doors, into the blistering blandness of a spring afternoon in Missouri.

I could open my passenger door only from the inside due to age or rust or something. I leaned over to pop the door, and Rob swung his lanky body into the seat next to me.

"Hey, Rob? You ever get lonely? Feel like you'll never meet anyone?"

"Are you asking me out?"

"Not with that tone of voice."

We were stuck in the daily three-thirty-five parking lot gridlock. Rob turned to me.

"Leon, you've been on this 'poor me, I can't get a date' kick for a year now. Face it, if girls don't like you today, they won't like you tomorrow."

I inched the car forward, then slammed on the brakes when someone cut me off. "Don't you ever take the bus?"

"Massa make me sit in da back. Seriously, man, don't wait for girls to change. They won't."

I saw an opening in the traffic and gunned it, narrowly avoiding the security booth. Parking Lot Pete, the middle-aged school security officer, shouted at me as I tore onto Mexico Road.

After I dropped Rob off, I thought about what he'd said. *Girls won't change.* So what was I supposed to do? Change myself?

Cleaning out my room was like going on an archaeological expedition: I'd uncovered a lot of dust, many fragments, and several dead things. Already I'd filled three bags for the trash and two boxes for storage.

As I examined what was either a putrid roll of sweat socks or a fossilized burrito, I was stunned by the flash of a camera.

"Mom! Knock it off!"

My mother was standing in my doorway with the camera, a smug smile on her face. Mom was five feet tall and in her forties, but still intimidated me. I felt like she'd caught me downloading pornography (again).

"My son's doing housework without being asked. I had to record it." Mom chucked me on the shoulder and began to help me pick up. Nonchalantly, I dropped some books on top of my stack of swimsuit issues.

"You're getting rid of your role-playing books?" Mom asked as I stacked them in a plastic tub.

"Just packing them up."

She shook her head. "I never thought you'd get rid of those. And your Star Wars figurines?"

"C'mon, Mom, I'm seventeen." I didn't mention I'd bought some of them as recently as two years ago.

Mom sat on my bed, toying with Baxter, my teddy bear. (I didn't have the heart to shove him into a box.) I removed a model airplane from my bookshelf, dusted it off, and dropped it into the trash.

"So why are you throwing out all your toys?" asked Mom wistfully. Moms. You'll always be five years old to them.

"Just getting rid of some of my old stuff. I'll be out of high school soon. I don't think I need to leave my Cub Scouts awards up."

Mom frowned and stroked Baxter's bald head. Every time I mentioned I'd be off to college in a couple of years and leaving her and Dad alone, she'd get a little sad. I don't think she liked the idea of me growing up. Suddenly, she grinned.

"What's her name?"

"Huh?" I was taking down my fifth-grade science fair certificate. It had been on the wall so long it left a faint imprint.

"This girl you like. You haven't thrown anything away in seventeen years; I thought there might be a girl involved."

I removed a stack of Pokémon cards from my storage box and pointedly dropped them into the trash. "There's no girl, Mom."

"I just meant that maybe you had your eye on someone."

"There's no girl, Mom." I think Mom liked to believe that I

had never gotten over my elementary school fear of girl germs. She never could accept that her smart, handsome, perfect son simply could not land a date. The first time Samantha came over to hang out, Mom asked me about her for weeks.

"Leon, are you sure there's not anyone on your mind?"

No way I was getting into that conversation. If I said yes, she'd hound me; if I said no, she'd worry I was gay.

I hoisted a sack of trash. "Could you take this out to the curb?"

She took it, smiled at me, and left.

I straddled my chair. Okay, I'd gotten rid of my crap. So what? My room was cleaner, but I was no cooler. What did I think would happen? That once I'd cleaned the old *Mad* magazines off the floor, there'd be room for Amy's bra? That the only thing keeping the girls' volleyball team from pouncing on me was my Albert Einstein T-shirt?

Along with my junk, I'd eradicated a little bit of my personality. What should I replace it with?

5

NICO-TEEN

The next morning I wedged my car into its assigned spot in the student lot. The guy who owned the much nicer Taurus had parked too close to me again, but I made sure I didn't smack my door into it very hard. I skipped across the parking lot with the joy I usually reserved for the dentist.

"Hey, you!"

That voice. That beautiful, husky voice. It could belong to only one person: Amy Green. I turned.

She was leaning against someone's battered Saturn. Her arms were crossed, and she had an expression of utter boredom on her perfect face. Not for the first time, I pictured her lying on a couch, being hand-fed grapes by female slaves.

"Yeah, you," Amy said when I hesitated. She was addressing me! I came. I heeled. I would have begged or rolled over if she'd asked.

Amy held out a cigarette. "Got a light?"

In my entire life, I had never had a more desperate need to produce fire. I would have banged two rocks together if I'd thought it would make a spark. But I didn't smoke and didn't carry a lighter. Even the one in my car had long since been tossed so I could hook up a portable CD player.

Amy, the human goddess, still pointed her cigarette at me. It was my one chance to start a conversation with her, and I was blowing it! Maybe I should offer to run to that convenience store that was only half a mile away.

"I'm sorry; I don't–" I froze. We weren't alone. Parking Lot Pete was wheezing his way toward us. If there was one thing Pete loved, it was catching a student smoking. He was sneaking from behind Amy, so he probably hadn't seen anything yet, but he suspected.

I made a frantic gesture with my head, but Amy must have thought I was having a spasm or something. She stepped back a pace. And Pete (his real name was Mr. Jones) was only a few cars away.

Without thinking, I snatched the butt from her hand. Pete would see if I threw it on the ground, and I wasn't sure if he had the right to make me turn out my pockets. Desperately, I crammed the cancer stick all the way into my mouth.

Amy noticed Pete before she had time to comment on

my apparent psychotic episode. Pete glared at Amy, then at me, his bald head and white uniform already soaked with sweat. I gave him a toothless smile as the burning nicotine oozed over my tongue.

"What do you have in your mouth?" asked Pete.

"Gum." I gulped and accidentally swallowed some of the dissolving tobacco.

"Yeah?" He didn't seem inclined to leave. My eyes were beginning to water as I merrily chewed my nicotine gum.

"It really is gum, Mr. Jones," said Amy. "I just gave it to him."

Pete stared me down, apparently wondering if maybe he'd made a mistake. But my mouth was producing saliva, and I had to swallow. Mistake. My delicate stomach, which could handle a dozen Twinkies or a six-pack of Dr Pepper, rejected the Camel.

I managed not to get any vomit on Amy by gallantly catching most of it on my sneakers. The only thing I'd had for breakfast was a Coke, so everything was a lovely brown.

As I leaned on my knees, retching, I heard Pete snort. "Chewing gum, eh? Come to the office. That's going to be a week of in-school suspension."

Figuring there was no point in trying to impress Amy now, I inhaled deeply and forcibly cleared my nostrils.

"I wasn't smoking," I gasped.

"What are you talking about? There's a butt right there."

I spit between my feet. "That's not a butt."

"Then what is it, smart guy?"

Stomach acid was burning my sinuses and I think I

had barf on my lips. Still, I managed to straighten up and face Pete.

"It's a hunk of food. Feel free to prove me wrong."

I couldn't be sure, but I thought Pete almost smiled. He pulled a yellow pad out of his belt and wrote me a detention slip. It was the most serious punishment he could give; for anything worse, he'd have to go through the principal, as well as a puddle of puke.

"After school today." He retreated to his booth.

Amy wordlessly passed me a bottle of Gatorade, which I chugged.

"You couldn't smoke unfiltered?" I wanted to say more, but I had to go change into my gym shoes.

Samantha didn't look up when I grabbed her water, rinsed out my mouth, and spit into the bottle.

"If you're trying to get me horny, it's not working."

"I've been chewing on Amy Green's cigarettes." I began eating Samantha's raisin muffin but decided I'd rather taste the vomit.

"You know, Leon, there's such a thing as trying too hard to impress a girl."

I wiped my mouth on a napkin and stood as the warning bell rang.

"I don't believe that for a minute."

I hurried to chemistry in hopes that Amy was waiting for me to thank me for saving her butt (and swallowing it). As it turned out, she didn't wander in until the final bell rang, and didn't look in my direction.

6

HARD WORK PAYS OFF EVENTUALLY, BUT LAZINESS PAYS OFF RIGHT NOW

God was kind to me. My study hall was right before lunch, giving me a solid hour with nothing to do. I made my way to the library, wondering if I should spend my time downloading music in the computer lab or napping behind the reference stacks.

"Hey, Sanders!" Johnny corner checked me into a bank of lockers.

"Hey, Johnny." I rubbed my shoulder.

"I heard you got busted smoking today. Someone said you got sick and threw up on Amy Green."

Goddammit! "I wasn't smoking; she was. I had to eat her cigarette so she wouldn't get caught . . . and I puked."

I could see the little gears turning in Johnny's head as he tried to decide why he should be making fun of me. I ducked into the library as he was still thinking of an insult.

The Zummer library always reminded me of a sound-stage. It was like someone had built a school library for show, not for use. It was almost always abandoned, and you got the impression that the books were just cardboard props. I'd read enough of them to know they were real, but whenever I checked out books, I felt like an extra in some movie.

I grabbed a computer and settled down for thirty minutes' worth of hard studying. Right when I logged on to an online video game site, I felt a familiar presence behind me. Melody stood next to my chair, waiting for me to notice her. I quickly stood up.

"Ah, you probably think I forgot that we were supposed to work on the project. But as you can see"–I grandly gestured at the tanks battling on the computer screen–"I'm already doing research."

Melody just stood there, staring me right in the chin, clutching her binder to her chest. She reminded me of a child lost at the shopping mall, too terrified to ask for help. I remembered how I'd railroaded her into partnering with me on the assignment.

"That was a joke, Melody. So what topic are we supposed to be writing about?" Any schmuck could write a report when he knew what the subject was.

"We have several options." Her head continued to tilt downward, until all I could see was the scarf wrapped around her scalp. I was getting a neck cramp trying to maintain eye contact.

"Okay, Melody, that's enough."

Her head jolted back up. "Wha . . . ?"

"My eyes are up here!" I crossed my arms over my chest and affected a falsetto. "You know, I'm not just a hunk of meat. You women are all alike!"

For a second I thought Melody was crying; then I realized she was trying to stifle laughter.

I grinned at her. "Now, if you're through with the peep show, let's get started." I pointed to an empty table. "And don't try to pull the chair out for me; I'm not that type of boy."

Melody neatly laid out her social studies notes, some blank paper, and the printed instructions for the project. I snatched some mostly clean paper someone had left on another table.

Melody looked down at our instructions. "We have several topics to choose from."

I blindly stabbed at the paper with one of the free golf pencils from the checkout desk.

"Let's do this one." I looked to see what I'd landed on. "*Name and date?* Hey, that's easy!"

"Leon . . ."

"Well, enough work. It's almost time for lunch. And it's taco day!"

"Leon, c'mon."

Mr. Hamburg was not what you'd call an easy grader, so I figured I should stop trying to be silly. "Okay, how do you want to do this?"

"Maybe we could meet at the public library sometime and do our research there."

I thought back to all the times I had told my mother I was studying at the library when in reality I'd been studying at the library. I shook my head.

"Well, how about here, after school?" Melody's voice took on a self-pitying tinge, as if it wasn't the work I was trying to avoid.

"Okay. Tomorrow, though. I have detention today."

Melody's hairless eyebrows rose. "Detention?" She spoke the word like most people would say "fifty-year prison sentence." "What did you do?"

"I led a walkout as a protest against human rights violations in the Congo."

Her eyes got so wide I had the irrational fear that her skin would tear. "Really?"

"No."

The lunch bell rang.

"And it's chow time!" I jumped up. "Do you eat lunch this hour?"

"Yes."

I hopped from foot to foot. "Well, move it, then! It's Mexican day!"

"Okay!" I should have realized that the excitement in her voice wasn't due to the school's greasy tacos. She followed me to the door.

"So this snake walks into a bar . . . ," I began.

"Walks?"

"Slithers into a bar. And tells the bartender he wants a beer. And the bartender says, 'No way.' And the snake asks why not. And the bartender says . . ."

We passed through the security device and into the hall. Two guys bolted past us toward the lunchroom. One of them looked right at Melody. I couldn't hear what he said to his friend, but they both laughed.

Melody's face wasn't very expressive; when you don't really have cheeks or eyebrows, it's not easy to express anything. But the hurt in her eyes was unmistakable.

"I eat in the library, Leon." The library door didn't have time to swing shut before she was back through it.

I stood alone in the hall.

"And the bartender says, 'Because you can't hold your liquor!' "

Timing is everything in comedy.

In the book *1984,* room 101 was the government torture room. At Zummer High, it was the detention room. I was probably the only one who'd ever made that connection.

Detention began at three-forty-five sharp. I could have pleaded conflict and rescheduled, but it was best to get it over with. I waited until three-forty in case Amy wanted to thank me for my parking lot heroics, then slouched my way to my one-hour prison sentence.

Room 101 was the size of a standard classroom, though utterly void of decoration. Only one poster graced the walls.

It had no images, simply the words I AM RESPONSIBLE FOR MY ACTIONS. Where the hell did the school find stupid crap like that?

There were a dozen or so students serving time that day. Kids who'd smarted off to teachers, were tardy one too many times, or rubbed Dr. Bailey the wrong way. Mr. Knight, the shop teacher, had guard duty. It was hard to ignore the fact that he was online, intently looking at some sort of sports-fandom Web site.

I found a seat and fished a book from my backpack, preparing to wait out the next thirty-six hundred seconds.

"Leon!" whispered the guy next to me. "Hey, Leon!"

I turned toward him, then jumped away. I had approached Dan Dzyan without a crucifix or holy water.

Dan was short and chunky, with longish greasy hair and acne. In the normal scope of things, he'd have been a bigger nerd than me. However, Dan did not fit into the normal scope of anything. He was *insane*.

He worshipped the devil. Some members of the lunatic fringe claimed to be Satanists, for shock value, but I think Dan actually sacrificed poultry. He'd steal frog guts from the biology lab. Mr. Hamburg refused to discuss war atrocities when Dan was in class; the constant giggling was distracting. An attempt to allow prayer in Zummer High was scrapped when it was learned *what* Dan intended to pray to.

"Leon, check this out." Dan pulled something from his folder and looked behind him, as if fearing he would be seen. I snuck a peek at whatever dirty picture he wanted to show me, and nearly puked for the second time that day.

"Christ, Dan," I whispered, turning away. "Where the hell did you get that?"

"Internet. See, this guy had a brain tumor, but he never got it checked out, so his skull rotted away. Then these maggots—"

"Hey!" barked Mr. Knight. "Shut up!"

I propped my head on my fist, too irritated even to read. Amy was the one who should be here. Hell, she should have gotten a week of in-school suspension, but I had taken the fall for her. And was she grateful? Did she say "Thanks, Leon"? Did she say "I appreciate it, Leon"? Did she say "Would you mind helping me out of this restrictive bra, Leon?"

"Hey, Leon!" whispered Dan loudly. "Leon, look at this!"

Apparently, detention wasn't punishment enough.

"Very nice, Dan," I whispered. "I've never seen a more hilarious decapitation."

"He was running from the cops and tried to clear that fence with the spikes on it."

I rubbed my forehead. Here I sat, listening to this junior Hannibal Lecter, while Amy was off with her cool friends somewhere. It probably never occurred to her that I liked her, that it would mean a lot to me if she'd just say hi once in a while.

I bet Dan never had these problems. He didn't understand human emotions. He just sat there happily smiling, looking at a picture of some guy with a drill bit through his face.

In a way I envied Dan. I feared him even more, of course, but at least he was never lonely.

7

THE ELECTRONIC BABYSITTER

Melody and I met at our lockers after school the next day. She was less shy than usual and didn't give me a chance to pretend I'd forgotten about our study plans.

She carried several books. "I went to the library yesterday, Leon. Since you wouldn't pick a topic, I thought maybe we could do television and politics."

"I call television."

"Leon, could you be serious for just one minute?"

"Possibly not."

Melody frowned. I might not have realized that earlier in

the week, but I was beginning to clue in to the subtleties of what remained of her features.

"I want to go to the Missouri Scholars Academy this summer." That was a summer school for the upward bound.

"I'm sorry, Melody," I said in a sarcastic, pitying tone. "I didn't know." I touched her arm. Her shirt didn't have sleeves and the feel of her bare skin startled me. It was so smooth compared with the roughness of the burned flesh on her face.

"I have to keep my grades up. If we're going to do this together, I need you to help."

Did girls take secret classes on the art of the guilt trip?

"Fine. But not now; I'm fried. Hey, you got a car?"

She thought for a moment. "I can borrow one. Should we meet at the library?"

"We should, but we won't. Wanna come to my house around five? We can get started on this thing, and that'll still give me time to catch the five-thirty movie."

I scouted around my bed for dirty underwear. Thanks to the recent purge, my room was pretty clean, but I had to check for stray pubes and porno. I doubted that Melody would even see my room, at any rate.

Why had I invited Melody over? Well, she was right: we did need to get to work. This way I'd be close to my TV and junk food.

I didn't want to admit that there might have been another reason. I wasn't sure I wanted to be seen with her in public. She was certainly nice, but when a guy and a girl were hanging out together, even if they were just studying, people tended to assume they were boyfriend and girlfriend. And I had a hard enough time getting dates without people thinking I had to stoop to asking out someone like Melody. She was sweet, but I couldn't risk inspiring any rumors about us.

Mom and Dad didn't usually get home from their jobs in St. Louis until around six-thirty. Hopefully Melody would be gone by then.

At exactly 5:00 an enormous thirty-year-old pickup with a cracked windshield parked in front of my house. So much for *Evil Dead II,* which came on at 5:30.

I cleared some junk off the kitchen table. When the doorbell rang, I shouted, "Come in!" but nobody did. After a few seconds the bell rang again.

Annoyed, I answered it. Melody was standing on the porch, her skinny arms full of books, papers, and binders. She was trying to ring the bell again with one finger free. I grabbed some of the stack from her.

"Did you find the place okay?"

"Yeah." As she was stacking some of the books on the table, she dropped one. When she bent to pick it up, I could no longer see her head. A strange transformation took place.

Once Melody's face was not visible, I noticed her body for the first time. More specifically, her butt. Nice, round little cheeks, not the flabby ass of the overweight, nor the bony rear of a skinny girl. Melody, shockingly, had a perfect butt. As her shirt rode up her back, I stretched in an attempt to get a better view.

Melody stood up and suddenly I was ashamed of the way I'd been checking her out. That withered prune of a face, that mutilated nose, those tiny holes where her ears had been ... What was I doing admiring her rear?

We sat at the table. "Looks like you've already been working," I said, glancing over her notes.

"A little. I've outlined the way we could go about this, if it's okay with you."

Feeling guilty about not doing my share, I read through Melody's outline. We were supposed to research how television had influenced politics from the 1950s until the present day. In two weeks we were to present our findings to the class.

We got down to business, reading through books, making notes, and being disgusted by some of the political tactics. One congressional hopeful had run ads accusing his opponent of being a notorious Homo sapiens who was married to a practicing thespian. He won by a landslide.

After about an hour of this, I noticed that Melody was talking a lot more than I'd ever heard her at school. Once we'd gotten to work, she constantly cracked corny jokes.

"Knock knock."

"Who's there?" I couldn't remember the last time I'd heard a knock-knock joke.

"Interrupting cow."

"Interrupting cow wh–"

"Moo!" Melody cracked up at her own joke. I smiled, enjoying her tinkling laughter.

My turn. "What has two legs and bleeds profusely?"

Melody frowned. "What?"

"Half a cat."

Whenever I got on a joke-telling kick, Jimmy or Johnny or especially Samantha would tell me to shut up. Melody might have just been being polite, but she always laughed.

We'd been working for about an hour and a half, and that was enough for me. "Study break, Melody. See what's on the tube." I got up to look for some snacks. Melody continued to take notes for a few minutes, then turned on the TV.

"Hey, Leon, are these your Monty Python DVDs?"

Yikes. Nothing branded a guy a geek more than being a fan of that British sketch-comedy show. Every engineer, scientist, and computer programmer in the world could recite entire Python episodes from memory. There's a reason junk e-mail is called spam.

"Uh, I haven't watched them for a while."

Melody was rooting through the video collection under the TV. Her butt was sticking up and I caught myself looking again. It was like looking at those swimsuit catalogs I'd steal from the mail before my mom saw them: not very dignified, but no one had to know.

"And you have *Blackadder*!" continued Melody. "And *Red Dwarf*! Where did you find that?"

I was surprised she recognized the last obscure show. "On eBay."

"I tried that once, but it wouldn't play on an American machine. Ooh! *Kids in the Hall*! Can we watch this?"

Though our couch was big enough for both of us,

Melody sat in my dad's easy chair. I was relieved; things would have been a little close otherwise. Grabbing a couple of sodas and some not-too-stale chips, I joined her in the living room. She pressed Play and we began watching the Canadian answer to *Saturday Night Live*.

"I used to watch this all the time with my brother," said Melody. She took a bite of a chip, coughed, and politely laid the other half on a napkin.

"Lucky. I have to watch these alone. My friend Johnny says I have bad taste."

"Isn't he the one who mooned the Charleston basketball team last year? And he says *you* have bad taste?"

She smiled. Now, when a guy says a girl has a nice smile, he usually means *You have amazing breasts*. Melody, despite her disfigured lips, really did have a nice smile. Then again, maybe I was just getting used to her. I'd stopped thinking of her as Melody the freak. Now she was just Melody.

We began talking about movies and other things we liked. We had a lot of obscure favorites in common. Normally I never talked about my favorite films, not even around my friends. None of them shared my enthusiasm for science fiction movies. Melody, however, was really into the genre. For the first time, I could talk to someone about *Stargate* and *The X-Files* without getting that pitying look.

"I watch a lot of TV," Melody admitted. Her casual tone began to fade. "Not like I have much else to do."

I chose to ignore the deeper meaning of that statement. I really did not feel like talking about how she didn't have any friends or whatever she was going to say. That wasn't part of the assignment. I always felt uncomfortable when people unloaded on me; their problems were always bigger than mine and I never knew how to respond.

"I hear you. St. Christopher is kind of one huge wasteland in that department. No clubs, no museums, no beaches, no parks. Just a lot of car dealerships," I said, trying to change the subject.

"Well, it's not just—"

Mercifully the phone rang before she could start a deep discussion. I took it in another room.

"Hi, Leon." It was my mom.

"Hey."

"Listen, your dad has to work late again. I'll be home soon. Would you like me to grab a pizza?"

"Sure. Maybe two; I have a friend over."

I could hear Mom gritting her teeth over the phone. "It's not Johnny, is it?"

"This again? I told you, there was no toilet paper and he didn't know what else to do. But no, her name's Melody."

There was a pause. "You're there with a girl?"

Instantly, I realized my tactical blunder. Mom was torn between her joy that I had a girl over and her fear of my having a girl over.

"She's just a friend, Mom."

"I'll be home soon. *Very* soon."

I returned to find Melody cleaning up the crumbs I'd left on the coffee table.

"You in the mood for pizza?"

She smiled again, and for a moment she was almost as

normal as Samantha or Johnny. Well, as normal as Samantha.

"Sure. Domino's is having their two-for-one special tonight."

"Nah, my mom's bringing some home."

Melody shot to her feet with such violence that the scarf on her head slipped a bit. She seemed to be completely bald.

"I have to go, Leon." She hurriedly began gathering her books and notes.

"Already? Look!" I pointed to the TV. "Here's the sketch where the guys have the beer-gut contest."

Melody was heading for the door, trailing papers and books.

"Slow down, Melody! Here, I'll give you a hand." *Jesus, I know no one likes hanging out with someone's mom, but damn! What happened to "We have to get to work, Leon"?*

Melody calmed down a bit and let me help her with her things.

"I don't mean to rush off like this."

"Well, we've still got plenty of time to finish the report. We'll rent a movie next time."

Melody smiled, but this time her grin upset me. She hadn't misinterpreted my friendly invitation, had she? Asking a girl over to see a movie . . . Maybe she thought I was trying to get her here alone again. I was sure no one had ever asked her out before, and it was possible she thought I wanted a date.

"And we'll invite my buddy Rob," I quickly added.

Melody's smile didn't waver as she climbed into her truck. "I'd like that, Leon."

I watched as she drove off. I hoped she really would join us on movie night sometime. With her vote, we might get to watch something besides the T and A flicks the twins always wanted.

Mom arrived fifteen minutes later with two large pepperoni pizzas. She made a lot of obvious noise, dropping her keys, fake coughing when she opened the door, just in case I needed time to get my hand off something delicate. She was annoyed when I said Melody had left, and I didn't think it had anything to do with leftover pizza.

8

SIMON SAYS "STAND UP"

The next day was Friday. I didn't get a chance to talk to Melody. Well, I didn't *try* to talk to her. I did, unexpectedly, talk to Amy.

I noticed her as I was leaving school for that afternoon. Rob had track practice, so I was alone when I saw her walking alone down the fine arts hall. It always amazed me that even here at Zummer High, she wasn't followed by flocks of photographers and autograph-seeking fans. I wasn't exaggerating either. They always say celebrities aren't nearly as attractive in real life. To me, Amy was as pretty as anyone on TV, even without professional makeup and lighting.

I hitched up my backpack and prepared to walk right on by. *Play it cool. So what if she never thanked you for saving her in the parking lot? Just keep moving.*

I suavely ignored Amy by looking directly at her and grinning like a monkey in agony. To my surprise she walked over to me.

"I never thanked you the other day," she said with a smile. And it wasn't a fast food–employee type of smile either; it was real! Her eyes and nose crinkled in an adorable way, and for the first time since elementary school, she looked like she wasn't anxious for me to leave.

"Well . . ." I shrugged, trying to act as if I swallowed contraband all the time.

"No, seriously. Parking Lot Pete's busted me twice. I might have got suspended." She continued to smile. Her teeth were as straight as bathroom tiles, though with a slight yellowish nicotine tinge.

"Didn't you see the sign out front?" I kidded. "This is a tobacco-free school zone."

She laughed. Even the most brainwashed members of the staff knew that sign was a work of purest fiction.

Amy bit her lip as if trying to remember something. She pointed at me.

"Lee-on?" she guessed.

"Right."

She nodded. "Yeah. We were in, what, fourth grade together?"

"Mrs. Pund's class."

Amy ran her hand through her wavy blond hair and leaned against a locker. "That's right. I remember when she took away your Pokémon cards."

Of course that was the memory she glommed on to. "Uh, yeah. Or remember when Johnny Thomson pulled the fire alarm?"

"Or when Caitlin Kasper threw up on the class gerbil?"

"Good times, good times."

Amy patted my arm. I felt like a leper who'd been touched by the queen.

"Thanks again, Leon."

Damn, she was going to leave. I had to think of a conversation extender, but all that came to mind was Dan's brain-maggot story.

"Listen, Amy . . ."

She was listening, so I had to say something.

"Maybe sometime . . ." *Ah, what the hell.* "Some friends and I are going to play mini golf tonight. Would you like to go?"

Amy opened her mouth and tilted her head, with a none-too-bright expression on her face. She must have been thinking of the kindest way to say no.

"Yeah, okay, Leon." She scribbled something on a piece of paper. "Give me a call later; I think I can make it."

"Cool." My voice only cracked a little.

I managed to wait till she was out of sight. Then I treated the Zummer security cameras to the first-ever shot of a guy doing a merry jig in front of the art room. My God, I had a date with Amy! Maybe she'd agreed out of boredom or pity, but at least it was an opening.

The twins had been right: all it took was a little conversation and a little tact. Except for the cigarette-eating thing. That was all Leon.

Now, if I could just get some new clothes, a new car, a new body, and a new personality by that night, I might actually stand a chance.

I was supposed to meet Rob and the twins at Andy's Mini Golf at seven sharp. When I got home from school, I showered, shaved, splashed on way too much cologne, took another quick shower, and got ready to call Amy.

I wasn't such a dweeb that I wrote down what I was going to say, but I did mentally go over it beforehand. I'd call her, joke a bit about the cigarette incident, and tell her the evening's plans. Then I'd suggest I pick her up, and we'd be all set.

Alone in my room, I braced myself for the call. *Don't be yourself.*

I dialed.

"Yes?" asked a woman, in a voice that sounded like I'd woken her up.

"Is Amy there?"

"Amy?" She yawned. "No, she left about an hour ago."

I punched Baxter in the stomach. "She left? Are you sure?"

"Yes, I'm sure. Went to the movies with some friends." There was a distinct irritation in her voice.

"Okay. Could you tell her Leon called?" I gave her my phone number.

I wrapped my hands around Baxter's neck and began to throttle him. *To the movies with friends.* If she'd even bothered to think of me, it was probably *That dork? He can just sit at home and pick his nose. Why should I care about him?*

Maybe that was a little harsh. But if she didn't want to see me, why had she gotten my hopes up like that? It would have been easier if she'd just said she didn't like me.

So here it was, Friday night, and I'd probably spend it alone with my parents. I didn't even feel like golf. After getting stood up by my dream girl, hitting a colored ball through a miniature windmill almost seemed pointless. I threw my teddy to the floor and went sulking into the living room.

Mom and Dad were sprawled out on the couch, interrupting each other's tales of how hard their day was. I thought if either of them admitted to liking their job, the other would immediately start divorce proceedings. Sometimes I wondered if I, too, was doomed to take a job I disliked and then complain about it for the next forty years. Probably.

"Hey, Leon," said my dad, munching on the chips I had left out the day before. "Are you staying in? We could play Scrabble and watch the late movie."

I wasn't feeling *that* sorry for myself.

"Thanks, but I'm meeting the guys." I ducked into the hall to grab my jacket.

Well, at least I had friends, which was more than some nerds had. Maybe I didn't exist to Amy and her crowd, but I had some good buddies. Jimmy, Johnny, Rob, Samantha . . .

and maybe one other. Someone who appreciated good books, bad television, and worse jokes.

I hesitated, then searched out the phone book. There was only one entry for "Hennon" in our school district.

"Melody? This is Leon. Listen, you up for some mini golf?"

9

SUB-PAR

"GOLF IS A GOOD WALK SPOILED."–*Mark Twain*

Andy's Mini Golf and Driving Range had been going out of business since 1988. Apparently, Andy had managed to stave off bankruptcy for yet another season, and despite the decaying Astroturf and the headless Mother Goose on hole nine, we'd go there about once a month.

The twins whaled on each other with their putters while Rob and I waited on two separate benches.

"So a neutron walks into a bar and orders a beer," I said to Rob. "And the bartender says, 'For you, no charge.'"

Rob looked at me as if I was a child-molesting telemarketer. "Is it time to tee off?"

"Actually . . ." I spotted Melody's pickup pulling into the parking lot. "I've got a friend coming. Here she is."

I was about to give them a heads-up about Melody, to warn everyone not to stare, to tell them that we'd been working on a project together and that I wanted her to feel comfortable around us. Unfortunately, at that moment the twins remembered that the word "balls" has more than one meaning.

"Hey, look, I got blue balls!" said Jimmy, laughing.

"Hey, anyone want to hold my balls?" hollered Johnny. A woman with a child in tow quickly walked away from us.

"I have to go clean my balls."

"My balls are bigger than your balls."

"*Shut up!*" Rob and I bellowed. There was a short pause. Then Jimmy hefted his putter.

"Check out my shaft."

"Calm down," said Rob, in a voice like an exhausted kindergarten teacher's. "Leon's date's here."

No! Not a date! The twins' heads swiveled just as Melody passed the frightening clown statue at the gate. Damn. I'd have to explain things later.

Melody was wearing a tight little shirt, and I found myself not looking her in the face for an entirely new reason. She wore a wool cap that covered not only her scalp but what remained of her ears.

Melody froze when she saw the four of us. She then started to advance. With each step, her head inclined downward, until she was looking at the crumbling sidewalk.

"Guys, this is Melody. Melody, this is Rob, Jimmy, and Johnny." *Dammit, Leon! This is embarrassing for her!*

When people met the disabled, the disfigured, or the mentally challenged, they reacted in one of two ways. There was the traditional *"I didn't even notice, I'm perfectly comfortable, some of my best friends are differently abled"* false sincerity.

Luckily, the Thomsons were a lot more forward.

"Hey, Melody, check out my balls!"

Well, not the best icebreaker, but it did get her to look up again.

"I'll go and get a putter."

Johnny was on a roll. "Don't forget to ask Andy to show you his baaaargh!"

I turned to see Johnny clutching his stomach and Rob unclenching his fist.

To tell you the truth, Rob and I were usually the only ones who played the full eighteen holes. Jimmy and Johnny were so ADHD that they'd get distracted and skip the back nine. More than once we'd found them fishing for coins in the wishing well or playing dodgeball out on the driving range. I hoped they'd wander off early that night; they were just uncouth enough to ask Melody about her face.

My nondate returned, defensively clutching her putter to her chest. Two hours earlier I had thought I'd be trying to score a hole in one with Amy. Now I'd be looking out for Melody while my friends thought I was on a date.

We all wrote our names on the scorecards and attempted to wring five dollars' worth of fun out of eighteen holes. True to form, the twins landed their first shots in the dry fountain next to hole five. They proceeded to hold an impromptu game of field hockey in the basin, leaving us to golf in peace.

Rob shot first. Just before he swung, he looked back and caught my eye. And winked.

Ah, hell. I'd been complaining about not having a girl-friend all month; now I showed up here with Melody. Rob probably thought I was desperate enough to date her. And there was no way I could correct him in front of Melody.

We teed off. I knew that Rob and I were pretty good golfers, so I'd make it a point not to beat Melody by too much. I'd give her some pointers, maybe miss a couple of shots on purpose.

Melody aced the first hole. I managed to knock my ball clear off the green and into the kneecap of a large burly man. He didn't say anything, but I noticed that Rob had already scurried off to the next hole.

Melody managed to knock her ball through the wind-mill and ended up with a two. I shot the six-stroke maxi-mum.

"Do you come here a lot?" Rob asked her.

She shrugged. "Sometimes with my family. Here, Leon, can I make a suggestion?"

I'd been trying to time my shot to miss the windmill blades. Melody stepped up behind me, placed her hands on my wrists, and adjusted my stance.

Melody's hands were pink and delicate. They were too small to wrap around my wrists. I could just feel the touch of her body as she stood behind me.

And then she backed away. I swung and missed the ball

completely. Something had rattled me. At the next hole, I asked her to help me again.

Melody beat the pants off us. She even aced the impossible hole where the cup is up on a little hill. Melody returned Rob's victorious high five when they both won a free game at the last hole.

While Melody collected the free passes, Rob pulled me into the shelter over the driving range. His teeth gleamed whitely out of his dark face in a rare smile.

"So do you want me to get rid of the twins?"

I thought it over. "Could you make it look like an accident?"

"Seriously, man. We can, you know, give you guys some space."

I looked to make sure Melody was still at the office. "Listen, Rob, she is not my date, okay? That's not funny."

Rob's expression quickly returned to its normal snarl. "Who's trying to be funny?"

"Just drop it." I had enjoyed Melody's company, but I didn't want Rob saying anything that she might misunderstand.

We found Jimmy and Johnny sitting in their VW van, smoking.

"Hey, so was this a pity date, or what?" hollered Johnny as we passed.

My guts knotted. I couldn't believe he could be that cruel.

Well, I *could* believe it, but still.

"I mean, c'mon, Melody," he continued. "I know Leon probably begged you, but now you'll never get rid of him."

Ah. I was the pity date.

Johnny hopped out of the van and prodded me with his stolen putter.

"Just look at that flabby ass! And these scraggly side-burns!"

Melody's thin skin was turning purple, but I didn't think it was from humiliation.

"John?" she finally asked, her hand over her mouth. "Do you know what *really* impresses girls?"

"No . . ."

"I'm not surprised."

Jimmy and Rob slapped palms as Johnny scratched his head. I followed Melody to her truck.

"Sit with me a second, Leon."

I climbed up into the towering cab with less grace than Melody.

She smiled at me. In my mind's eye, I filled in the missing parts of her face: the smirking lips, the turned-up nose, the high cheeks.

"Leon, thanks for inviting me. It, um . . . never mind."

"Huh?" Damn, was I articulate or what?

"It's just that people tend to get really nervous around me. And when you called me tonight to hang out with you and your friends . . . It's just nice when someone looks at me and sees more than this." She waved her hand in front of her face.

I felt like a dick. The only reason I'd started talking to her was to cover up my rudeness about the lockers. I'd asked to be her study partner just to avoid working with Bill. And that night, I really wanted to be with Amy.

"Hey, Melody? Only losers eat in the library. Eat with us."

I expected her to jump at the chance, but she just revved the engine. "I'm not sure if I could stand to eat with Johnny. Especially on hot dog days."

10

THE ALGONQUIN ROUND TABLE

The following Monday I didn't wake up as a billionaire play-boy secret agent, so I was forced to return to school. I didn't see Melody during study hall, and I wondered if she'd take me up on my lunch invitation.

I didn't bother trying to talk to Amy. To my surprise, she made an effort to talk to me during science.

Mr. Jackson had been trying to demonstrate a chemical reaction when he'd spilled a beaker of pungent chemicals all over his grade book. As he desperately mopped up the mess while screaming for more paper towels, Amy abruptly swiveled in her chair and paralyzed me with her smile. All thoughts of being stood up melted away. I just wanted her to keep smiling at me.

"Hey, Larry."

I was crestfallen. "That's Leon."

Amy scooted over to my table and punched me in the arm. "I know, silly. I'm just teasing. I'm sorry about Friday. Mom said you called."

"Yeah, well..." I shrugged. "You have fun with your friends?"

Amy's smile collapsed into a sneer. "My friends? Is that what Mom told you?"

Something wasn't right. I had to choose my next words carefully.

"Uh..."

"Yeah. I was with my *friends*." The sarcasm wasn't subtle.

"Um..." What had I said wrong?

She returned to her seat before I could grunt my way to asking her out again. Johnny, who'd been listening in, shook his head at me with pity. Once again, I'd felt like I was on the wrong page of the script.

That afternoon, after elbowing my way through the prison-commissary-like receiving line in the cafeteria, I forced a path through the crowd and dropped my tray at my usual table. My three tablemates, Johnny, Rob, and Samantha, were already there. Jimmy ate at a different period.

The lunchroom was really too small for the number of students, so finding a chair wasn't always easy. The unofficial seating chart had gelled the first week of school. Jocks sat with jocks, band members with band members, Mormons with Mormons. We had claimed our large circular table early on. Johnny could handle the odd freshman or transfer student who tried to horn in on us.

"Dudes," announced Johnny as I sat, "I have just figured out how to make my fortune. I'm gonna be rich before I'm nineteen!"

"How many times, Johnny?" groaned Samantha. "There's no such thing as magic beans."

Johnny ignored her. "It's a business idea. It's called Total Bastards Incorporated."

"Fits you," Rob commented.

"Thanks. Now, say you had a girlfriend," Johnny said, looking at me. He paused, then looked at Rob. "Say *you* had a girlfriend. One you wanted to break up with. But you're too much of a spineless wimp to tell her. That's where I come in. For a modest fee, you leave town and I'll break the news to her. You get to weasel right out of it!"

Samantha sighed. "So in other words, you get the money and a chance to hit on vulnerable women."

"It's not just girlfriends, you know," said Johnny defensively. "I can fire people, tell off neighbors, basically be the bearer of bad tidings."

"So much for 'don't shoot the messenger,' " I said.

Rob looked perplexed. "But even if you broke up with my girlfriend for me, she'd still be there when I got back, madder than ever."

Johnny shrugged. "If you're the type of guy who'd hire someone like me, is she really going to miss you?"

As I proceeded to snatch french fries off Rob's tray, I

wondered if Melody would show up. I honestly didn't know what outcome I wanted. If she didn't join us, I'd feel relief that I wouldn't have to look out for her and make sure we included her in our conversations. On the other hand, I'd feel a little offended if she decided she'd rather sit alone in the library.

"Um, hello?" I turned to see Melody standing behind me, her tray clutched in front of her. So this was it.

The only empty chair was between Rob and Johnny. Rob scooted over to give her room while Johnny continued to force food into his gullet.

Samantha had politely nodded to my guest, but no one else acknowledged her. Melody picked at her food. Maybe there was a reason she had lunch alone. Maybe she realized that people didn't like to look at her while they ate.

"So," I announced to no one in particular, "Melody is going to the Missouri Scholars Academy this summer."

Johnny deftly spit a wad of gristle onto Samantha's tray. "What's that?" he asked suspiciously.

"It's a summer school program," said Melody, apparently addressing her mashed potatoes. "Just extra classes in preparation for college."

Johnny instinctively distrusted people who studied when they didn't have to. "Extra school?" His eyes narrowed. "Why?"

Melody twitched; it might have been a shrug. "I like learning."

Johnny glared at her like she was eating a ham sandwich at an animal rights rally. *"Like learning?"*

Melody's head shot up, and for the first time, she looked right at Johnny. "Well, it'll give me a chance to hang out with people who aren't obnoxious and crude."

Johnny suddenly laughed, spraying Rob with bits of food. "Dude, she totally just insulted Leon!"

For the next two weeks, Melody became a fixture at our table. I'd like to say it was because my friends warmly accepted her, but I think they probably just liked the idea of talking without having to listen in return. Melody and I would work on our project during study hall, then eat together.

It wasn't long before I realized that we had more in common than a love for obscure TV. We hated the same teachers, the same politicians, and the same music. We were both good at English and had a hard time in math. We began loaning each other books and CDs.

We never did anything outside of school again. I wasn't sure why. It would have been easy enough to invite her along to the movies or for pizza. But I could never make myself pick up the phone and call her. It would have been too much like a date.

It was Buttercup Campbell who made me realize that this was a disastrous path.

Buttercup (that was her real name) was a freckle-faced, frizzy-haired, blue-eyed sophomore, whose innocence bordered on madness. To her, Zummer High was the place deep friendships were forged, teachers shared their wisdom with eager pupils, and the Zummer Bulldogs were not a train wreck of a football team. I'm not sure if she chose to ignore the fistfights, the dropouts, and the 1–9 football season, or if she was just unaware.

Buttercup was a reporter for the *Bulldog Bugle,* the school newspaper. The English department realized she was a perfect stooge who'd never try to write about anything upsetting, or even thought provoking.

She shot a candid picture of me one morning, managing to catch me with my eyes closed, my mouth open, and my hand on my balls.

"Say 'cheese'!" she said long after I'd been blinded by her flash.

"What's the scoop today?" I asked, blinking. I assumed she was getting man-on-the-street opinions on something in-depth, like *Are parking permits too expensive?* or *Who's your favorite teacher?*

Buttercup smiled, nearly blinding me again with her braces. "I'm doing an article about dating at MZH!"

"Couldn't you ask someone else?" Someone who was more of a ladies' man. Dan Dzyan or Parking Lot Pete, for instance.

Buttercup was not to be denied. "Question one: Where do you like to take a girl on a first date?"

"The Taco Barn."

"How much do you usually spend on a date?"

"Spend?"

"And how long have you and Melody been dating?"

That woke me up. "Wait! Melody and me? What are you talking about?"

The fifteen-year-old reporter gave me a sly grin. "C'mon, I see you two having lunch every day! And hanging out in the library!"

Yikes! She couldn't print something like that. Even though it had a readership of twelve, I couldn't let the paper list Melody as my girlfriend. People would see it. Maybe Melody would think I'd said it, think I secretly had a thing for her. And I wouldn't exactly be able to write a letter to the editor demanding a retraction.

"Buttercup, listen. Melody and I are just friends. Nothing more. You'll hurt her feelings if you say we're dating." Not to mention wreck whatever prospects I had. I still secretly fantasized that there was some girl out there who'd think I was neat. I didn't need the paper saying I was off the market.

Buttercup looked confused, then smiled. "You know, Melody is awful sweet, Leon."

Aargh! Why did every girl think everyone had to fall in love?

"Drop it, Buttercup." How did one go about filing an injunction against a high school paper?

She frowned. "Fine. But can I ask you a serious question?"

"Shoot."

"Do you think the lunchroom should offer more than one vegetarian option?"

11

HELL IS A
MISSOURI SHOPPING MALL

I never enjoyed speaking in front of a group. While the presentation of our television and politics report was the easiest part of the assignment, I'd be glad when history class consisted of Mr. Hamburg yelling at us again.

"Of course, some people say the real reason Nixon lost the debate was that he broke the number one rule of broadcasting." I thumbed through my notes. *"Thou shalt not be ugly on television."*

No one reacted. At the back of the room, Mr. Hamburg shook his head and wrote something in a notebook.

"And now, Melody will tell us about the role of television in modern politics." Gratefully, I sat down.

Melody, much to my surprise, was quite an engaging speaker. She didn't mumble, read too fast, or say "you know" every other sentence. Of course, she held her notes directly in front of her face, making eye contact impossible. Maybe she just didn't want anyone looking at her face.

So Buttercup thought we were dating. Then again, Buttercup also believed in the tooth fairy. It was just a case of a romantically minded girl thinking we made a nice couple. I was sure no one else had jumped to the same conclusion.

It wasn't that I didn't like Melody. Hell, she was almost a friend. But I had a hard enough time fitting in at Zummer High. I didn't want to be known as the guy who had to date Melody. It had been five years, and I still sometimes thought of her as the object of playground ridicule. Even if she could quote entire episodes of *Family Guy*.

Melody finished her speech, and the class applauded like trained seals. As she was sitting down, she smiled and winked at me. I glanced around to make sure no one had noticed.

Enough was enough. The project was over. There was no reason for us to hang out during study hall anymore. I'd fallen behind in my online video games anyway. Of course, I didn't want to be a jerk and avoid her. Since she ate with us now, it wouldn't be as awkward to invite her along next time we went to shoot pool or something.

When class ended, Melody walked with me to the door.

"Good job, Leon."

I grunted. "At least it's over."

"Yeah. Hey, Leon, are you busy this weekend?" She was flipping through the book in her hand.

"Why?"

"I was wondering if you'd like to get together Friday. There's a production of *A Midsummer Night's Dream* at the university." Her voice was apologetic, like she was asking a huge favor.

Shakespeare on the weekend? No way. "Maybe some other time, Melody."

She closed her book and looked at me.

"Okay. But ... never mind."

I knew better than to ask, but it was obvious there was something on her mind.

"What?"

Melody gave me a shy smile. "It's my birthday Friday."

Uh-oh. "Happy birthday!"

"And, well, I'd really like to see this, and I'll have to go with my parents otherwise."

Well, there was no way I could condemn her to a fate like that.

"Ah, hell, birthdays only come once a year. I'll just work on that Mid East peace plan some other time."

In English class last semester, we had to read part of a story about this Italian poet who went to hell. What stuck with me the most was the description of the souls of the damned: walking in endless circles, only dimly remembering that they were once human.

I'm not sure why, but I'd remember that every time I went to the mall.

Mid Rivers Mall was huge, though not so huge that there was anything interesting in it. One bookstore, one video game store, one music store. Everything else was clothes. Around me, consumers marched in their never-ending pursuit to *buy, buy, buy*!

I was there to get Melody a birthday present. So what? It was her seventeenth birthday. You bought people presents. Of course, I'd never been much of a gift giver. The fake severed arm I'd gotten for Rob the year before was the only present I could remember buying for a friend.

I thumbed through my wallet. Forty-three dollars. Every cent I had, plus a "don't tell your mother" advance on my allowance from Dad.

So what was I supposed to get her? Perfume or bath stuff was way too personal, and a gift certificate was too generic. No way would I attempt to pick out any kind of clothes.

I decided to get her a DVD. We liked a lot of the same movies, and it was a simple enough gift that no one could read anything into it. No card, no sappy sentiment.

After my purchase, I still had nineteen dollars. I was heading over to the food court when I ran into Amy. As usual, it surprised me that her presence wasn't announced by a choir of angels.

She was wearing a halter top. Her arms, shoulders, stomach, and back were all on display. For a long moment, I relished the sight. I'd never seen so much of her skin at once, at least not in real life. I could even ignore that her eye makeup had gotten blobby, that her hair hung limp and loose around her face, and that she obviously hadn't shaven her pits in a few days.

"Hey, Leon, help me take these to my car." She thrust two large clothing bags at me. No "please." No polite request. Just an order like you'd give to a hotel bellboy.

Amy grabbed the rest of her purchases, and I followed her. My eyes were firmly fixated on the bare spot between her naked shoulder blades. I wanted to grab her from behind, bury my face in her neck, feel that blond hair cascade over my face, touch that soft skin.

"Nice day, isn't it?" I squeaked.

"Whatever."

Amy had a cigarette lit the second we hit the parking lot. The wind was blowing toward us and I caught a face full of smoke.

Her car was a lot newer than mine. Amy unlocked the doors with the remote, then dropped her bags onto the ground. Without a word, I began loading everything into the backseat. Maybe she'd at least tip me.

"Amy, could I . . . ?" She was already in the front seat. She dropped the cigarette out the window and started the car.

"You're welcome," I muttered, turning away.

"Leon!"

My head shot back around. Amy was leaning out the car window, smiling at me.

"You're still mad at me for standing you up last week, aren't you?" Her voice was slightly mocking, as if I was unreasonably upset.

Of course I'm angry, you bitch! Just because I'm not a football player or the class president doesn't mean you can blow me off like that! Did it ever occur to you that I have a life? That maybe I had other things to do? The world doesn't revolve around you, Amy Green. You're no better than me.

"Of course not, Amy." I was leaning on the edge of her door. It was pretty hot out and the metal was singeing the flesh on my hand, but I didn't jolt away.

She patted the seat next to her. "Get in the car, Leon."

I expected Amy's car to smell like peaches and body lotion, but it actually stank of smoke and stale fast food. There were burn holes in the upholstery and ashes all over the seats.

"Leon, you're a nice guy. And I didn't mean to just blow you off the other day."

A cooler guy would have shrugged, as if she was barely worth getting upset about.

"It's okay, Amy. It doesn't matter."

She squeezed my shoulder. I felt a shock run through my body.

"Leon, when you called my home, what did my mom tell you?"

I thought back. "That you'd gone out with some friends."

The smile vanished from her face. "Well, that's not true. My dad came in from out of town and took me to dinner."

Why was she telling me such a bogus story? Her mom wouldn't have lied to me.

"You see, Leon, my parents split up last year. It got pretty bad there at the end." Amy pulled a cigarette pack out of her purse, but it was empty. She threw it onto the floorboard.

"At any rate, Mom acts like Dad never existed. She won't talk about him, not even to me. She should have told you I was out with him, but instead she lies to a complete stranger. It really pisses me off sometimes."

I fought the urge to drape my arm around her bare shoulders in a friendly gesture. At least she had ditched me for a semilegitimate reason.

"I'm sorry, Amy."

"Nothing to do with you." Amy stared at the steering wheel, her face blank. "But I'm not as self-centered as you might think. And I really didn't mean to cancel on you like that."

Press the advantage? "Well, maybe I could give you a call."

She shook her head. "Leon, I'm not really dating anyone right now. My parents are still fighting over alimony and visitation, all that crap. You don't want to get involved."

Actually, the idea of an emotionally fragile, needy Amy appealed to me. I pictured her crying with her head in my lap. *Just let it all out, Amy. Just tell Leon all about it.*

With an inner sigh, I returned to reality. "I just meant, if you ever need to talk, give me a ring. I'm a good listener."

Amy reached over and hugged me (a sisterly embrace, but still). "Maybe I will."

Exit Leon, stage right. I waved as she pulled out of the lot.

So Amy was my friend. And Melody was my friend. Samantha was my friend (whether she liked it or not). So many girls were my friends. It was like I was a homosexual who still liked women and had no dress sense. Which isn't like being a homosexual at all, I guess.

• • •

"Hey, Mom, I'm home! Did you . . ."

Mom looked up from the novel she was reading. "Have you been smoking, Leon?"

"No!" Mom's eyes bore into me. "I, uh, was hanging out with a smoker. That's probably what you're smelling."

"I see."

I opened the fridge door to avoid Mom's accusing gaze. No one could smell your sins like a mother. It was disturbing.

"So, Leon," she continued, in a milder tone, "I got an interesting letter from your school today."

I dropped the soda I was grabbing. "It was all Johnny's idea!" I babbled. "He swore it was water based and would wash right off!"

"What? I'm talking about the school newsletter. What are you going on about?"

"Nothing. Newsletter, you say?"

She scowled at me, then laughed and shook her head. "Yes. So the spring formal is next month, I see."

I took a swig of my soda. "So?"

"I was just thinking that if you're going, we probably should see about a tux for you."

I crushed my can before remembering it wasn't empty. "Mom, I'm not going."

She handed me some paper towels. "You say that every time there's a dance. Leon, someday you're going to wish you did more in high school than hang out at the Taco Barn."

Mom didn't understand me at all. She honestly believed

I was alone by choice. Of course, I didn't think she had the slightest idea how unpopular I was when I was in junior high.

"Mom, drop it. There's no one for me to take. *No one*. Understand?"

"Fine." She smiled. "Oh, Melody called. She said to pick her up at six-thirty this Friday, unless you wanted to have dinner first." With a smug grin, she returned to her book.

12

"IF WE SHADOWS
HAVE OFFENDED . . ."

Melody lived in one of the few remaining agricultural belts in our school district. In other words, way out in the sticks. It wasn't easy trying to read her directions and drive on the narrow two-lane road at the same time.

This was not a date. I was picking up a friend to see a show and maybe grab a bite to eat. Just the same as I'd do with Rob, or Johnny, or Samantha.

Of course, Johnny always said a successful date included the three Fs: film, food, and . . .

A deer ran across the road and I nearly rolled my car trying to avoid it.

Melody had informed me that her family owned a couple of horses, and therefore I would not be able to drive past the heavy iron gate, which now barred my route to her driveway. "Just honk your horn," she had advised me. "My dad will open it for you."

I sounded the horn, the one part of the Buick that didn't cry out "I'll fail within the year!" There was a moment of silence, and a figure emerged from the distant house.

Melody's father was a handsome guy. Rugged, a country boy through and through. He had the leathery skin, the big hands, and the muscular frame of someone who did physical labor for a living. He was dressed in faded jeans and a work shirt that appeared as if he'd actually worked in it. And he was smiling at me.

I wondered why that seemed so odd to me. Probably because I'd never had a girl's father smile at me before. Sure, they'd shoot me a manly grin, but their eyes always said, "So you're the punk who's going to take my princess, my baby girl, my reason for living, and try to feel her up like some common streetwalker." If you've ever dated a teenage girl, then you know the look.

Melody's father unlatched the gate and waved me through. Keeping a careful eye on the two chestnut horses that warily watched me from near the driveway, I drove up to the house.

After I parked the car, I was struck with one of those moments that don't seem awkward until you lived it. There I was at the house, but Melody's father was still coming back up the driveway. Should I go ahead and knock or wait for him? Which way would make me look less like a tool?

Melody's mother solved my dilemma by opening the front door. "You must be Leon," she said warmly. "Please, come in."

I was escorted into a well-lit, rustically decorated living room. Most of the furniture was made from hand-hewn wood. Antique farm implements decorated the hearth of a stone fireplace. A shotgun hung over the mantle. In the corner sat an old, well-used piano.

"Melody's still getting ready," said Mrs. Hennon, directing me to a sofa. "May I get you something to drink?"

"Sure." Melody's mother was quite attractive, a middle-aged woman who'd taken good care of herself and was still slender and firm. I wondered if maybe Melody would have been that pretty had she not had her accident. Then I felt guilty for thinking it. Why did I always obsess about Melody's disfigurement? I didn't find Samantha attractive at all, but I didn't constantly worry that people thought we were an item.

Melody's mother smiled. "I'll be right back. Have you met Melody's brother? Tony!" she called into the kitchen. "Come in here and keep Leon company."

Now, obviously, the last thing in the world I wanted to do was meet Melody's brother, and I knew the feeling was probably mutual. When Tony emerged from the kitchen, I was sure.

Tony was about thirteen years old, spiky-haired and unkempt, with the typical junior high chip on his shoulder. He scowled at me, grunted a hello, and positioned himself in front of a video game system. The customary awkward silence fell.

I felt I should try to start a conversation. "So, Tony . . . ," I began.

"Yeah?"

"You go to Zummer Junior High?"

"Yeah."

"Nice." Tony never looked up from the screen. I drummed my fingers. Where the hell was Melody's father?

I heard him come in the back door a few seconds later. "Leon," he said as he entered the living room and grabbed my hand. "It's nice to meet you." His grip was crushing.

Mrs. Hennon returned from the kitchen with a glass of soda. As I took a sip, they stood there, grinning at me. Obviously I was the first guy to come pick up their daughter. Melody's first date.

This would have been a bad time to mention I found their daughter horribly unattractive.

Okay, maybe not *horribly*, but this was still not a date.

Melody's parents kept smiling at me. I kept taking nervous gulps of my soda in an effort to cover the lack of conversation. If this had been a sitcom, I could have accidentally said something grossly inappropriate or sat on the family Chihuahua or something. Anything to cut this tension!

"Ready to go, Leon?" Melody had appeared from down the hall. She was wearing a blouse and a skirt; apparently, this was a dressier occasion than I had prepared for.

"Nice to meet you, Mr. and Mrs. Hennon," I managed to squeak as I hustled her out the door.

"Be back by eleven," cautioned her father, the familiar distrust already edging into his voice.

• • •

It was not nearly late enough for the campus of the University of Missouri–St. Louis to be deserted. Students still walked the quad, laughing, shouting, holding hands. I looked forward to the not-too-distant future, when I'd join them as a freshman.

We'd just sat through a semiamateur production of *A Midsummer Night's Dream*. I didn't get a lot of it and kept having to whisper "What's that guy doing?" to Melody. There was a funny bit about a guy with a donkey head, though, and some of the actresses wore very low-cut dresses, so the production wasn't a complete wash. Melody seemed to enjoy herself.

I'd wanted to hurry out to my car right after the curtain call. (Actually, I'd wanted to leave much earlier, until Melody explained it was only the intermission.) Melody asked if we could go for a walk. I didn't like what that implied, but it was her birthday, and we didn't have to be back until late.

We didn't say much as we wandered past darkened classroom buildings, noisy dorms, and silent parks. It was a warm spring night, the first time in months that you could go for a walk and not be miserably cold. When we reached the quad, Melody stopped.

"Leon, thanks for a great birthday."

I wasn't sure why she was thanking me; we had paid for our own tickets.

"Sit down, Melody. I'll give you your present."

"Oh, Leon, you didn't have to get me anything!" She sounded so grateful I wondered if I should have gotten her something better. Or nothing at all.

We sat on a concrete bench and I pulled the unwrapped DVD from my inner jacket pocket.

"*The Twilight Zone*? I love this!" She scanned the list of episodes on the back of the case.

"Well, I had a feeling." More like a random, shot-in-the-dark guess.

"Thank you. This is the best birthday ever."

"C'mon..."

"I'm serious. This is the first time I've ever done anything on my birthday, except have dinner with my family."

This suddenly felt very dateish. Out to the theater, a long walk, a special gift... If I'd been out here with any other girl, I'd have been plotting how to put my arm around her. It would be a long time before I'd do anything alone again with Melody. It was safer that way.

"So you ready to get back, Melody?"

"In a minute." She stood there staring at *The Twilight Zone: Season One*, which I'd gotten out of the half-price bin. If you only looked at her eyes, you'd think she was holding a diamond bracelet. A single tear trickled over her shortened nose.

"Hey, none of that."

She wiped her eye on her sleeve. "I'm sorry. This is all new for me."

"What is?" I gritted my teeth. Buttercup was right. Melody was going to say "Having a boyfriend," and I'd be forced to marry her rather than tell her that I could never find her attractive.

"Having a friend, Leon. I know you do stuff like this all the time, but it means a lot to me that you'd have lunch with me and take me out on my birthday. No one's ever done that."

I thought about blowing the comment off. Just telling her it was time to go back. But she needed to talk. Plus I was touched. Without much effort, I'd given her a special birthday, which made me feel kind of special.

"Melody, can I ask you a question?"

She turned and straddled the bench and looked at me directly. "You want to know about my face?"

"What face?" I blurted, in an effort to be tactful. Melody grinned at me and I decided to be frank. "Okay. Yes. What happened?"

There was a building light directly behind her, casting her in shadows. All I could really make out was the colorful bandana around her head, and her white teeth as she smiled.

"No one's ever had the guts to ask me about that."

Maybe no one had ever been that rude before. "I just–"

"No, I don't mind; it's a good question. Actually, I wish people could be more up-front about it. I'd rather just have someone ask than stare at me."

What could I say? That people didn't stare? That her scars were hardly noticeable? I couldn't lie to her.

Melody turned her head and stared into the darkness. In profile, I could see how oddly short her nose was; there was nothing beyond the bone.

"When I was four years old, a kerosene lantern exploded in my face. I don't remember it happening. But I do remember two years of surgery and hospital stays and skin grafts and being in pain and never understanding why."

I straddled the bench so I wouldn't have to twist to look

at her. She was staring down again, and I noticed a small damp pool forming on the concrete between us. I hated that she was crying. Not because it made me uncomfortable, but because my friend was hurting. I wanted to make things right. And of course, there was nothing I could do but listen.

"I didn't start public school until I was eight. I'd seen schools on TV, read about them in books. But my grafts were healing and the doctors thought I'd get infected. All I wanted to do was go to school with other kids. And at the start of third grade, I got my wish. I thought I'd finally have friends. I thought I'd finally be normal."

Melody took several deep breaths, like someone desperately trying not to vomit. She then continued as if each word caused her physical pain.

"That first day of school... I never suspected. I never knew that it wasn't my health problems that made me a freak. I never thought..."

The puddle between us grew. Impulsively, I took Melody's hand. Her flesh was hot and sweaty, and she squeezed hard. I placed my other hand on top of hers. I couldn't make the hurt go away. I couldn't erase the painful memories, no more than I could erase my own. But I could let her know, by grasping her hand, that I was there for her. That she could unload on me if it would make her feel better.

"I hated my parents so much, Leon. They never warned me. *They never warned me.* I went into that school thinking it was the greatest day of my life. By first recess I knew I'd never belong." Racking sobs interrupted her story.

"I begged Mom and Dad not to send me back. But they did. And it was the same the next day. And in fourth grade. And fifth. And tenth."

A long-suppressed rage began to boil in my gut. What kind of asshole would make fun of a girl like Melody? What kind of jerk wouldn't see how wonderful she was? And if they didn't like her, why didn't they just leave her alone? Who would do that?

The same kind of people who made fun of me, that's who. And . . . me. I was no saint; I'd hurt her too. I wondered if she remembered.

Melody looked up at me. The reflections from her tears made her face glow. "You're my only friend, Leon. Besides my brother, you're the only guy who doesn't think I'm disgusting."

"Melody, nobody–"

Her head shot up, and I could hear an angry intake of breath. "Don't say it, Leon!" she hissed, cutting off whatever empty denials I was about to make.

"What?"

"I know what you're going to say!" She pulled her hand away. "You're going to say–"

There was only one thing I could say. *"On mules we find two legs behind, and two we find before!"* I sang, remembering the old Cub Scout song. *"We stand behind before we find what the two behind be for! When we're behind the two–"*

"What?"

"You didn't know I was going to say that, did you?"

Melody plunged her face into her hands and laughed.

"God, Leon, I guess no one ever knows what you're going to say." She took a tissue out of her purse and blew her nose. "I didn't mean to spill my guts like that. *The Twilight Zone* kind of brought things back."

"Huh?"

"You know the episode where the pretty woman is in that place where everyone has pig faces and they think she's the ugly one? That she'd never belong? I could relate."

"Me too."

She gave a half laugh, half cough. "You don't know what it's like, Leon."

Melody's self-pity was wearing thin. Just a little. She wasn't the only one who knew what it was like to be alone. To have people make fun of you for no reason. Maybe her experiences had been worse, but she wasn't the queen of pain.

"Everyone feels like they don't belong sometimes, Melody." Maybe I sounded just slightly bitter.

"You?" She wiped her eyes and looked at me with a disturbing intensity. "When did you ever feel like you didn't belong?"

"A long time ago." I wasn't going to talk about it.

"Leon, what do you mean?"

I was about to shout, about to tell her to mind her own business, but I paused. No matter how bad things had been for me, they'd been worse for her. It was like bitching about a hangnail to a guy with no hands. Maybe it would be good for me to talk about this.

I swiveled on the bench until I was no longer facing her. With a deep breath, I began to relate my most painful memory.

"When I was...eleven? Sixth grade, yeah, eleven...I walked to school. Every day. Alone. I felt like hot shit after taking the bus to elementary school.

"Anyway, it must have been like November. It was cold, I remember. I was walking home, and this guy comes up and gets right in my face."

Dylan Shelton. Even though I saw his good-looking mug every day at school, he was still a seventh grader in my mind's eye. Acne-covered, bucktoothed, and much, much bigger than me.

"So he starts yelling at me, and calls me a butt pirate. I didn't even know what that meant. There were all these kids around, watching us and laughing. And I just wanted to go home. Then he shoved me and I thought, 'Hey, I'm in real trouble here!' And there were houses everywhere, but no grown-ups, of course." My words couldn't stop; the pent-up memories spewed forth.

"I told him to let me go, and he just laughed and said he was going to kick my ass. Some of the kids started laughing again, and this one guy yells, 'Kick him in the nuts!' Some kid I'd never even talked to is trying to get me beat up!"

Something hot burned in my eyes. I clenched my butt cheeks, curled my toes, dug my nails into my palms. I would not cry. Not here in public. Not in front of Melody.

"I tried to run, but he socked me in the gut. Took the wind right out of me. And he hit me again. I started crying. And the more I cried, the more he hit me, and the more the other kids laughed. There must have been like ten of them, and they were all egging him on. All I wanted to do was go home. *He just would not stop pounding me, and I hadn't done anything!*" It occurred to me that that had been the last time I had ever cried. Until now. I wasn't sobbing, but tears were flowing.

Melody was still on the bench with me, but she stayed silent.

"So I'm laying on the sidewalk with a bloody nose, and everyone just bustin' a gut. Then he spit on me. Right in my face. Let me tell you, the audience just roared. So he spits on me again. And then some of the other kids start spitting. And then they left."

I wiped my eyes. "I never told anyone. I went home, cleaned up, cried some more, and that was that. Only that wasn't that. Because for the past five years, I've had to see that guy in the hall every day. Hell, I have Spanish class with him fifth hour. And every year I see the people who laughed at me when I was hurt five, six years ago, and I hate them. I wonder if they even remember."

I faced Melody. She'd been crying again. How had this happened? One minute we were going for a walk, and suddenly I was spilling my most secret thoughts. My most painful memories.

Just like Melody had.

"Leon," she said, with the ghost of a smile, "I guess we both know how cruel and stupid people can be. But for what it's worth, I think you're amazing. You're smart and funny and handso–nice, and maybe both of us need to remember that we shouldn't *give a damn about what anyone else thinks!*"

I remembered my secret fantasies about meeting a girl who would say more or less what Melody had just said.

Someone who'd think I was neat. And she was the one girl in school who I could never date. Figured.

It was time to stop this seriousness. Guys didn't discuss their feelings. We didn't talk about what's inside us. We bottle it up, bite back the tears, and end up climbing clock towers with rifles. I attempted to change the subject.

"Melody? A bunch of us are going out to the lock and dam tomorrow. If you'd like to join us."

She sniffled loudly. Sharing time was over. "What do you do out there?"

"Wish we had something better to do."

She smiled. "My parents wanted to give me my presents tomorrow. But I'll see if I can get out of it. You ready to go?"

"Yeah."

I wasn't sure who started the hug, but we didn't stop for quite some time. We just held each other there in the dark. It was nice having someone to hold. She trusted me with her secrets; I trusted her with mine. I was glad she was my friend.

Though a small part of me was tempted to reach down and grab that great butt of hers.

13

DAMN DAM

Lincoln County Flood Control Dam #54, on a tributary of the mighty Missouri. Built in 1940, a WPA project. It basically amounted to a concrete embankment that spanned the narrow Cuivre River. A cynic would call it a stream. A small access road led across, with a gate in front that was easily circumvented.

We'd hang out there when all else failed, usually about once a month. We'd build a campfire out of driftwood. The boys would smoke convenience store cigars. Jimmy and Johnny, and sometimes Rob, would have a few beers.

Samantha would wax poetic. The twins would rage about their enemies, plotting gory revenge for imagined crimes. Rob would rant about the dreadful trends in society, from international geopolitical dealings to the price of a gallon of gas. I'd fantasize about a future in which I was rich, successful, and about a foot taller.

The twins' van had recently broken down again and Samantha's family car was elsewhere. As the only one with a currently functioning automobile, I was chauffeur for the night. It had been a quiet evening. Rob skimmed stones; Jimmy and Johnny split a six-pack; and Samantha made s'mores.

"They discovered a new moon of Jupiter this week," said Samantha, stirring the fire.

"Hum," muttered Rob. "Kinda makes you think."

"About what?"

"Well, nothing. It was just a mindless reply to the Jupiter thing."

"Oh." More silence.

"Leon, I was wondering . . . ," began Jimmy.

"Yeah?"

"Are you secretly a Colombian drug lord?"

"No." A pause. "Any particular reason you ask?"

"You keep looking over your shoulder, down the road. You'd think you were expecting to be shot."

"No. . . ." I glanced down the empty country road that led to the dam. "It's nothing." I had given Melody detailed instructions on how to find the gate. She had said she'd try to be here by eight, and it was a quarter past nine.

There was a grinding noise as a vehicle turned off the main road. Bright headlights began to flood the area.

Jimmy and Johnny quickly tossed their half-finished beers into the water. We had always laughed at the NO TRESPASSING signs, but there was still the chance the cops would show up one day to run us off.

It wasn't a police cruiser. It was an old four-wheel drive pickup, which, judging from the mud that coated it, had been driven through the Mekong Delta.

"Cool your jets, guys. It's Melody."

She pulled to a stop behind my car and made her way cautiously toward the fire. Squinting into the dark, she called out, "Hello?"

We answered her from the glow of the fire. "Hey, Melody."

"Hi, Melody."

"Hey."

"Grunt."

"Grunt."

Melody smiled shyly and looked for a seat on the mucky ground.

"Here you go," I said, directing her to a place on the log I was sitting on.

Without looking straight at me, she took a seat.

We all sat there in silence, staring at the fire, lost in our own thoughts. I kept glancing at Melody out of the corner of my eye. The scarring had caused her skin to become extra-taut over her face. This, combined with the head scarf she was wearing, gave her a skeletal appearance. She looked like the angel of death in a sweater and jeans. It was strange, but there was beauty in that. Eerie, but not hideous.

Melody turned and faced me. The skull face melted away, revealing her eyes and her smile.

Suddenly, inexplicably, I wanted to hug her again. I wanted to talk to her. About anything. Stupid TV, school, her fears, my fears. And I couldn't do it in front of my friends. I'd known them for more than half my life and had never had a deep conversation with any of them. In less than a month, I'd gotten to know Melody on a deeper level than I knew anyone else at the campfire.

"Let's take a walk, Melody."

Melody stood up so quickly she almost knocked me off the log. Rob looked at me questioningly, but everyone stayed quiet.

There was a narrow path around the river's edge. The water was stagnant, and the way was littered with empty beer cans, cigarette butts, and used condoms. I'd never gone very far in that direction.

Soon we were far enough from the campsite that all we could hear were the twins' booming laughs. Mosquitoes bit us and once I almost lost a shoe in a mud hole. The river reeked of pond scum and rot. Eventually, our way was blocked by a fallen tree.

We stood there looking at the water for a bit. It moved at a pretty good pace at this point. During dry spells you could see the top of a '76 Vega near the far bank.

Our hands found each other. Not so much a romantic gesture, but just two people taking comfort in each other's presence. Of course, I never would have tried to hold Rob's hand when I was feeling alone.

What was I doing? Melody and I had shared a little too much the night before. And now here we were, alone, in the dark, hand in hand.

As if sensing my discomfort, Melody let go. She bent down at the water's edge and skipped a rock. The splash cut through the chorus of hidden frogs. I attempted to follow suit, but my rock just sank.

It was kind of funny: even with my lack of experience, I knew I was in a perfect romantic situation. The river, the moonlight, the secrets we had shared . . . All I'd have to do was put my arm around her and we could start working on some serious mosquito bites.

We continued to toss rocks. Why couldn't Melody be pretty? Hell, I would have settled for average. But no matter how sweet she was, I couldn't get over her face.

Melody bent over to grab a rock and suddenly went rigid.

"You okay?" I asked.

"Leon!" I was shocked to hear her voice tinged with panic.

"What's wrong?" I squealed.

"Leon." Her voice was trembling. "On my ankle."

Even in the dim moonlight, I could see the black thing stuck to her leg. I prayed that it wasn't what it looked like. When it squirmed, I gave up all hope that it wasn't a leech.

Melody was starting to hyperventilate. "Get it off!" she gasped. "Leon, please!"

"Me?" The shiny black leech pulsated. A thin stream of blood ran down into her shoe.

"Please?" She was begging.

Once again, I really wished I had a cigarette lighter.

Melody wasn't looking at her leg. "Did you get it? Is it gone?"

The second I touched the little bloodsucker, it began to writhe. My hand shot away in disgust. I forced it forward and gripped the hideous creature. Melody's blood oozed over my fingers. The thing held on for a second or two, then popped off. I hurled it into the river.

"It's gone, Mel." I soaked my hands in the muddy water.

She scampered away from the river. "I'm sorry. It's just that worms and slugs ... Sorry."

"Leeches aren't exactly my favorite thing." We both shuddered, then giggled. I took her hand and squeezed it.

"We should get back," I said after a second. "I think there's some Band-Aids in my car."

"Yeah." We continued to stand there, hand in hand, eye to eye.

Suddenly, I had the strongest desire to touch Melody's face. I didn't know why. The thought used to scare me. Maybe it was because I'd just learned there were much less pleasant things to touch. Maybe I wanted to prove that I didn't find her scars repulsive. And maybe I just wanted to touch her.

I wiped my hands on my pants and then placed them on her cheeks. She jolted a little but didn't make me stop. Her skin was thin, like the flesh of a rotten tomato. I thought if I lightly pinched her, it would slide off her skull. I ran my hands over the ridges and valleys of her scars. I touched her withered forehead. I ran my hands over the nothingness where her ears once were. Finally, gently, I removed her head scarf.

She was absolutely bald. No, not absolutely. In the dim light I could tell she still had a patch of hair near her neck but kept it shaved.

My hands moved down her neck. I felt the ridge where the destroyed part of her ended and the rest of her began.

"No one's ever touched me there, Leon."

We kissed. Her lips were warm and soft and not the slightest bit unpleasant.

I could tell this was her first time. Our teeth scraped, something you quickly learn to prevent. When I opened my eyes, I realized she'd never closed hers.

"Leon."

"Melody."

We kissed again. With my eyes closed, there were no scars. And she had great lips. And a nice tongue. I didn't think about how I'd spent weeks denying I had even a passing interest in Melody. I didn't think about what this implied, about what Melody was thinking, about how I might be committing myself to her. All I knew was that I needed to be kissed. I had needed to kiss someone for a long time. I needed Melody. For that moment, nothing else mattered.

Eventually, Melody withdrew her tongue from my mouth. She placed her chin on my shoulder, rubbing her bare cheek against mine. I still couldn't feel her scars. I took her hands in mine and we stood there, swaying. It was almost like we were slow dancing in the dark.

There was a loud bang from the direction of the fire, followed by screaming. Melody jolted away from me.

"What was that?"

I could hear Samantha angrily yelling something.

"I'm guessing one of the nimrods threw that aerosol can of Cheez Whiz into the fire." It wasn't the first time that had happened.

Melody stared at me for a moment, perhaps wondering if we were going to pick up where we left off. When I didn't make a move, she smiled and started back down the path.

The explosion hadn't killed the mood, but it had put it in intensive care. I followed a step or two behind Melody. Good God, what had I just done? I'd invited Melody for a walk, removed a parasite from her leg, and made out with her!

What now? I should say something. What? *I'll call you.* No, too dismissive. *I like you, but...* Nah, no need for the deadly relationship talk. *I think you're sweet, but your facial disfigurement is a real turnoff.* No need to be Thomson-blunt.

Just before we returned to our friends, Melody took my hand and stopped me.

"Leon, I won't ever tell."

I won't ever tell. She just assumed I didn't want anyone to know what had just happened. Did she realize how right she was?

14

CAPÍTULO CATORCE: MI TÍO ESTÁ ENFERMO, PERO LA CALLE ES VERDE

Monday morning I sat in the cafeteria, desperately trying to finish the trig homework I'd forgotten about over the weekend. Samantha sat next to me, reading and occasionally smirking at my efforts.

All Sunday I had tried not to think about what had happened out at the lock and dam. Not because it had been unpleasant. It had been a little *too* pleasant. It was the kind of thing a guy could get used to if he wasn't careful. If I didn't watch myself, I could wind up in trouble.

Melody had given me an easy out. She'd said she'd never

tell anyone. No one would know I'd kissed Melody. We were just a couple of friends who had gotten caught up in the moment. *And that's all.*

Only that wasn't all. I was the first guy Melody had ever kissed. And no matter how many times she said it didn't mean anything, it did mean something. Now every time we sat across from each other at lunch, every time we exchanged jokes at our lockers, every time we saw each other, we'd remember how our tongues had touched.

I'd kissed the ugliest girl in school on purpose. What if someone found out? Girls weren't known for their ability to keep secrets.

But did I want to keep it a secret? I could go back to no dates, no girlfriend, no kisses. I could hang out with Melody and pine over Amy and be just as miserable as before. Melody was mine for the asking. But I wasn't sure if I was ready to ask just yet.

I looked down at the unreadable mess that was my homework. With any luck I'd get a D for effort.

"Hi, Leon," I heard Melody say as she crept up to our table.

"Hey." I rapidly scribbled out the final problem. I didn't trust myself to look at her. What if, here in the sterile lights of school, I still thought she was gross-looking?

"What's black and white and red all over?" Melody asked.

"Heard it," I replied, still not looking up. "Two nuns in a chainsaw fight."

"I was thinking of a newspaper, actually."

"Yeah, but . . ." I stopped when I got my first look at her. Melody had hair! Real, actual long brown hair! It was a wig, of course, but you really couldn't tell.

I didn't realize I was staring until Samantha kicked me under the table.

"Melody! You look great!"

She smiled and for once maintained eye contact. "It was my birthday present from my parents. Second-nicest thing I got. You really like it?"

"You look great."

She fluffed her hair. "I have to go get my stuff. See you at lunch."

"You look great."

I stared at her departing figure until Samantha kicked me again. She kicked hard, and I wasn't sure she really had been aiming for my shin.

"Ow! What the hell?"

She hadn't looked up from her novel. "Leon, you need to knock it off."

"Pretend I'm as clueless as you always say I am. Knock what off?"

She carefully marked her place and closed the book. "Flirting with Melody. I know you get a kick out of it when girls pay attention to you, but Melody thinks you really like her."

Was I that obvious? "Samantha, we're just friends. Melody listens to me. And strangely, she doesn't constantly remind me of how dumb and ugly I am. For some reason, I enjoy that."

Samantha eyeballed me. When she was angry, I half expected her to pull out a paddle and tell me to bend over.

"Did you enjoy running off into the bushes with her Saturday night?"

I guess it was naive of me to think the gang would assume we'd been on a nature walk.

"Mind your own business." Maybe Melody was more than a friend, but I sure didn't owe any explanations to Samantha.

"Leon." Her voice was softer. "It's not my business. But a girl like Melody isn't used to guys taking an interest in her. And next time you go drooling over Amy Green or whoever, Melody's going to feel really ugly. Don't do that to her."

Señor Lopez Lopez, my Spanish teacher, was born in El Salvador. He had fled the country in the early eighties to escape the civil war. With nothing more than the clothes on his back, he had walked all the way to Texas. He had been assaulted by Guatemalan drug runners and mugged by Mexico City cops, and nearly drowned crossing the Rio Grande. He learned English while working illegally on a California farm, whose owner forced him to work fourteen-hour days (the other option being deportation). Sr. Lopez Lopez became a citizen when a general amnesty was declared, and earned his college degree while working as a dishwasher in Los Angeles.

Every year someone made the mistake of asking him why he gave so much homework. They'd get his life story in return. After that, no one felt inclined to complain about the workload.

Sr. Lopez Lopez was reviewing the study guide for a test we were apparently having the next day. My thoughts were elsewhere. Hell, it wasn't like I could understand my teacher anyway; sometimes it was like he was speaking a foreign language.

I was pretty pissed at Samantha for sticking her gargantuan nose in my affairs, and even more annoyed because she'd been so dead-on right. I did get my rocks off on the way Melody admired me. And unless I was willing to make out with Johnny or Rob, I couldn't really say we were *just* friends anymore. I couldn't even say I really wanted to be just friends.

But not everything was black and white either. One kiss (or one night of kissing) wasn't a cause for commitment. I probably had too high of an opinion of myself. Maybe Melody was just as confused and uncertain as I was.

Of course, I wasn't exactly *un hombre amoroso*. For all I knew, Melody might be writing *Mrs. Leon Sanders* in her notebook. Sr. Lopez Lopez directed us all to do something: either break into study groups or take off our shoes and make duck noises. I was bending down to unlace when someone scooted his desk next to mine.

I turned to see the acne-free, lantern-jawed, five o'clock–shadowed face of Dylan. The guy who'd humiliated me more than anyone else in my life. The guy whose memory had caused me to cry over the weekend. And here he was, wanting to study.

On some other plane of existence, God laughed.

I'd made it a point never to acknowledge him this whole semester. Apparently, he didn't remember our past. How could you call someone a faggot and spit on him, then expect to review verb tenses a mere five or six years later?

Dylan read our instructions, his lips moving silently. "Dude, what's a subjunctive mode?"

I'd take the high road. "It's a tense you use when describing something that might possibly happen." *You stupid monkey.*

"Huh?"

"Look at any Spanish sentence. If it has the word *'que,'* then you probably should use the subjunctive mode." *Douche bag.*

"If you see what?"

"If you see the word *'que.'*"

"If you see what?"

"If you see *'que.'*"

"If you see what?"

"If you see *'que'! If you see 'que'! If you see 'que'!*"

Sr. Lopez Lopez fixed me with a wrathful gaze. "Leon!"

I suddenly realized what "if you see *'que'*" sounded like when repeated out loud.

Dylan laughed. "Dude, you totally fell for that."

"Yeah, yeah." I wanted to be even more pissed off, but that actually was pretty funny.

"How do you say 'gotcha' in Spanish?"

"Pendejo."

"Dude, I totally *pendejo!*" he said, happily calling himself an asshole.

"I couldn't agree more. Are we going to study or what?" I had a hard time not smiling.

"This is gay. When are we ever going to use this?" said

Dylan, far too loudly. I was afraid we'd invite another "When I was your age, U.S.-backed guerrillas burned my village" speech from Lopez Lopez.

"It's not too bad," I countered. "I just finished a ballbuster from Mr. Hamburg. Lucky I had a smart partner." I smiled, remembering the fun Melody and I had had writing our report . . . and the fun we'd had Saturday night.

"Who was your partner?" asked Dylan, scratching himself in two places at once.

The bell buzzed, and we gathered our things.

"Melody Hennon."

Dylan hefted his backpack. "Scarface? Ugh. You should get an A for just having to look at her all that time." He then made a gagging noise and left.

I sat there, quietly shredding the study guide. That dick wasn't any different! After all this time, he still was the same shallow, bullying son of a bitch. Nothing had changed.

One thing had changed.

I ran out of class, just in time to see Dylan enter the men's room. Bolting in, I found him approaching a urinal.

Was I really going to do this?

I grabbed his shoulder. Dylan, who'd been unzipping his fly, turned in shock.

"Um, hi, Leon?" He didn't seem sure what to make of my getting touchy-feely in the bathroom.

I ground my teeth. My stomach was jumping and I had to pee.

"Dylan," I said, my voice certainly more confident than I felt. "If you ever call Melody that again . . . if you ever call her anything again . . ."

Dylan was not smiling. He roughly shoved me back. "You'll what?"

"I'll hurt you."

And now I would repeat the sixth grade. Now I'd be in for another serious ass beating. Now Dylan would once again prove that he was big and I was small and nothing would change that. All because I didn't like him calling Melody what everyone else in school called her.

Only that wasn't what happened. He just stood there, scowling at me.

I was aware we were not alone. Other guys had entered the john. I waited for them to start screaming at Dylan to mess me up.

Nothing but tense breathing. The stench of bleach and crap. A toilet flushing in the adjacent girls' room.

Suddenly, Dylan barged past me, knocking me into the wall. But that was it. I wasn't going to spend the next hour picking my teeth up off the floor or washing toilet water out of my hair.

The tardy bell rang, and the loiterers left. I just kind of stood there.

Why had I risked my jaw like that? If Dylan had insulted Rob, or Jimmy, or me, I would have let it go. I might have even joined in. And I was sure Melody had been called worse than Scarface.

But Melody was my friend. Maybe more, but a friend all the same. And not like Rob or Samantha. She had made me cry. She had opened her soul to me. I'd never connected with anyone like that before. And if Melody trusted me with her most secret hurts, I sure as hell was not going to let anyone talk about her like she was some kind of damn cartoon character that people could laugh at.

Even if we never kissed again, I knew that for the first time in my life, I had a best friend. An ally. Someone I could stick up for, and who would stick up for me.

And who, by the way, had an amazing ass.

15

AN ARGUMENT
FOR ARRANGED MARRIAGES

The poster in the school lobby declared KISSING A SMOKER IS LIKE KISSING AN ASHTRAY. A cartoon teen coughed and hacked while a pretty cartoon girl turned away in disgust. Someone had drawn something in the smoker's mouth: either a bong or a crude sketch of the male anatomy.

It was the morning after I'd confronted Dylan, and I was a little nervous about going to school. Just a little. Still, I avoided my usual breakfast with Samantha, in case Dylan was looking for me.

I watched the hundreds of students pass me by. Dan

Dzyan, reading a copy of *The Physicians' Desk Reference* and laughing. Buttercup, snapping pictures of happy things, like the trophy case and the fire alarm. Bill, stumbling as he attempted to chew gum and walk. Amy . . .

Amy! She was walking with her chemistry lab partner, a curvy brunette named Cassandra. Amy was wearing a very short skirt, the kind that would ride halfway up her thighs when she was sitting down. She also had on open-toed sandals. From across the lobby I could see each individual red-painted toe.

I was staring. I turned and put a dollar into the soda machine so they wouldn't realize I was watching them.

Out of the corner of my eye, I saw Amy pointing to me and saying something to Cassandra. They both laughed. Apparently, Amy was nice to me only when no one else was around.

The soda machine spit my bill out like a mocking tongue. I forced it back into the slot.

"Hey, stud muffin."

That was Amy talking. It took me a second to realize she was talking to me and not the soda machine.

"Hi, Amy." It was funny; the self-confidence that had made me stand up to Dylan failed me when I tried to be suave around her.

"So I heard you were about to throw down with Dylan yesterday."

Cassandra was laughing into her hand.

"Who, uh, told you that?" I pictured Dylan waiting for me in an alley somewhere.

"Some guys on the team were talking about it. Said Dylan insulted your friend Melody, and you said you were going to bust his face."

Hey, I liked this version.

"It didn't happen *exactly* like that. . . ." I leaned against the vending machine.

Amy laughed. "No kidding, Leon. But it's nice of you to stick up for your girlfriend like that."

Crap. Defending Melody's honor was one thing. Admitting we were dating was something entirely different.

"You know," I said with forced casualness, "Melody's not my girlfriend."

Cassandra chimed in. "Don't sell yourself short. I'm sure she likes you. Just give it some more time."

Thanks, Cassie. Now Amy thinks not only that I like Melody but that I can't get her to go out with me.

I was about to explain that Melody and I were just friends when Amy's hand dashed past my head and punched the Diet Coke button. She then bent over and reached between my legs to grab the can. Her shirt was loose enough for me to see the marks her bra straps had left on her shoulders.

She took one swig, very slowly, and handed me the can before leaving. I felt like dumping the soda over my head to cool down, but settled for a drink. The taste of Amy's lipstick almost covered the bitter aftertaste of the sugar-free cola.

A wise person once said, "If you're the only one talking, then the conversation is over." Samantha had apparently never heard this. She'd spent the better part of our lunch talking about some feminist author who'd given a lecture at St. Charles Community College.

"And Ms. Wooten explained how for the past two centuries men have been subjecting women to a constant and unending–"

I raised my hand. "If we all agree that men are responsible for everything that's wrong in the world, will you stop talking?"

Samantha got huffy. "Excuse me! I've always admired Emily Wooten. If you met"–she looked over at the book next to my tray–"H. P. Lovecraft, you'd expect *us* to be impressed!"

"I think we would be impressed," said Melody. "He's dead."

I was impressed. It seemed Melody had heard of H. P. Lovecraft, the author widely regarded as the father of the "aliens keeping a guy's brain alive in a jar" story.

Johnny was picking his teeth with a fork. "So, Leon. I heard you almost got in a fight yesterday."

Melody looked at me. "Fight? You didn't tell me about that. What happened?"

Johnny, in a rare display of tact, realized Melody didn't need to know about what Dylan had said. "Ah, Leon and Rick Rose were having the old Captain Kirk versus Captain Picard debate." He mimicked someone fighting with a limp wrist.

Melody didn't push the issue. Maybe she realized she didn't want to know.

"Anyway," I said, trying to move on to another topic,

"the new Bart Axelrod movie's coming out this weekend. Anyone want to go?" Axelrod was an inexplicably popular action-movie star who always seemed to be parodying himself. I'd never forget the movie where he defeated the terrorists, saved the town, got the girl, and then played the bass at a spontaneous rock concert.

"You actually like those movies?" asked Melody. She didn't seem to want to flat out say we had bad taste.

"Oh, yeah," said Johnny sarcastically. "We never miss a showing." We all laughed, thinking of how we'd been kicked out of the theater the last time for our running commentary on Axelrod's latest masterwork.

"Count me out," said Rob. "Vanessa's coming to visit." Vanessa was one of Rob's older sisters. I'd occasionally get a rise out of him by saying how hot she was.

"Ben's coming to town," said Samantha. "We'd come along with you, but, um, you know." Ben was her boyfriend, who was a freshman at some college somewhere.

"What, are you embarrassed by us?" I joked.

"More or less."

"Oh." So that was why she'd never introduced us.

"Could we make it next week?" asked Johnny. "I got a thing."

"You know Axelrod's movies are never in the theaters that long."

"I'll go," chirped Melody. Then, realizing she'd just arranged to go to the movies with me alone, she added, "Or we can do it some other time."

Samantha shot me a glare, but what of it? Melody was

funny and smart. If I could risk my pretty face defending her, why shouldn't we see a movie together?

Besides, it wasn't like I'd ever be anything more than Amy's goofy classmate.

"It's a date, Melody."

"Melody ain't ready yet." It was Friday, and I was picking up Melody to go to the movie. Her younger brother, Tony, had answered the door.

Tony made no move to invite me in. He just stood there looking at me like I had wronged him somehow.

"Will she be long?" I asked, hoping to get away from him.

"She's in the shower."

Showering for a movie? We stared at each other. Tony tilted his head, seeming to make up his mind about something.

"Come with me," he said, his voice cracking. "I wanna have a man-to-man talk with you."

I laughed under my breath. *A man-to-man talk? With a thirteen-year-old kid in a heavy metal T-shirt? Give me a break.*

We walked along the fence that penned in the horses. Neither of us said anything for a bit.

"So what's up with you and my sister?" he finally asked.

"What's up?"

"Are you dating or what?"

How cute. He was probably going to warn me to keep my hands off her. Overprotective kid brother.

"I dunno. Why?"

He stopped. "Because I don't want you to hurt her. What are you up to?"

I suddenly felt a whole lot less condescending. "Why do you think I'd hurt her?"

"Just look at her, man! She's seventeen and you're the first guy who's ever even called her."

"Isn't that her business?"

"You don't get it, do you? No, of course you wouldn't. No one has ever been nice to Melody, ever. For years, she'd come home from school crying. She'd never let Mom and Dad know what went on, but I knew. I knew how everyone treated her. I knew the kinds of things they said behind her back . . . or to her face."

"Tony . . ."

"She never had friends. Once, some girls invited her to a sleepover. And then they . . . they . . ." Tony was gripping a fence rail so tightly that his knuckles turned white. "It's not important. Listen, Leon. Melody's not what you'd call a looker. And now you show up, taking her out on her birthday, and out to movies and stuff. Just what are you after? She's not going to hop in the sack with you just 'cause you're nice to her."

"Tony . . . Christ. Listen, man. Your sister's a nice person. I like being with her. That's all. I can't guarantee we'll fall madly in love or anything, but if I go out with her, it's because I want to. No other reason."

Melody's brother stared at me. I regretted my earlier impressions of this kid who had been forced to be the big brother to his older sister. Finally, for the first time since I'd met him, he smiled.

"Okay, Leon," he said. "Let's get back. She should be about ready."

• • •

"You have to admit, Melody, you've never seen a more realistic movie about a Green Beret turned dance instructor."

Melody toyed with a strand of her wig. "Maybe, but I pick the movie next time."

Next time?

I turned down the gravel road where Melody lived. It was dark, well past ten. We'd seen the early showing of *Sudden Fist of Death III.* (Melody hadn't seen the first two, and I feared she hadn't followed the plot.) I then treated her to the most expensive food the Taco Barn had to offer.

"I had a good time tonight, Leon."

"So did I." I meant it too. The more I hung out with Melody, the more I wanted to. It was kind of funny, but I felt totally at ease with her. More than I did with my other friends. To Samantha, I was a running gag, a living example of all that was wrong with the male race. Around the twins, I was the butt of their jokes, the weird friend they could push around just because they were bigger and more popular. Even Rob sometimes acted like we were friends because we'd always been, not because we had a lot in common.

But when I was with Melody, I could be Leon. Just Leon. I didn't worry about how I was dressed, or if I was boring her, or that she thought I was a geek. Melody liked being with me. Maybe it worked both ways. Maybe I was the only one who made her feel like more than a face.

Besides, Melody was a cheap date who didn't seem to mind that I was wearing a Church of the SubGenius T-shirt.

Next time? Probably so.

I stopped in front of Melody's gate. My engine shuddered violently to a halt.

"Good night, Leon." She waited quietly, not making a move to get out.

"I'll walk you up."

We didn't touch as we trudged through the humid night air.

"Watch your step, Leon."

"I can see."

"No, I mean, the horses are out."

I began to take more care with where I walked. In the distance, I could see a lone light on in the living room of Melody's house. Other than that, we were in pure darkness.

"I can't believe how many stars you can see out here." It was a little overcast, but you could still clearly see the Milky Way. Back in Oakridge subdivision, you could barely make out the Big Dipper.

"You should see it when it's less cloudy. C'mere." She hopped up into the bed of an old pickup that was parked in the yard. I joined her. We leaned against the cab and gazed at the heavens.

I remembered an optical illusion my dad had shown me, and lay down flat in the bed. "Melody, check this out. Lay down next to me."

She gasped. "Oh, Leon, I can't do that."

I suddenly felt like an ass and sat up. "That's not what I meant!"

She laughed. "It's not what I meant either. It's just that . . . if I lay down, my wig will get dirt in it. It's not easy to clean."

I settled back down on my back. "Then take it off."

There was a pause, and Melody slid down next to me. Her hair lay on her chest. Absently, she stroked it like a pet cat. It occurred to me that maybe she didn't like having her head uncovered, even around me. I attempted to recover from the gaffe.

"Okay, now look up at the sky. Ready?"

"Yes."

"Now pretend we're not looking at the sky. We're flying above the ocean at night, looking down at those clouds. The stars are the lights of ships."

Melody didn't say anything for a while, and I was afraid that maybe I was the only one who could picture the night sky like that. Suddenly, she grabbed my wrist.

"Oh, my God, Leon, you're right! It's like we're flying!"

We lay there for a while, stargazing, holding hands. Slowly, slower than the stars moved across the sky, our faces turned toward each other.

We were there all alone, just the two of us. We stared at each other, knowing we were going to kiss. But we waited, savoring the anticipation. The knowledge that we were close and about to become closer.

Right when I found her lips, we were startled by a glaring light that stunned us like deer on the highway. Ten feet away, Melody's father stood, shining a high-powered flashlight at us. Even blinded by the beam, I could tell he was not smiling. The honeymoon certainly hadn't lasted.

16

A PAINFUL BOWL CONDITION

When you first start dating a girl, you do the traditional things: movies, dinner, long walks, and long conversations. After she lets you kiss her, things get less formal: hanging out with friends, going to the mall, cheap stuff like that. Once you realize that the sight of your nacho-stained shirt and mismatched socks won't send her screaming for the exit, you can pull off the ultimate slacker date: bowling.

Pioneer Lanes dated from the days when St. Christopher was its own city. Everything was decades old: the lanes, the tables, the snack counter, the shoes, the gum under the scoring machines.

On Thursdays the place was usually empty (also Mondays, Tuesdays, Fridays, and Saturdays. Wednesday was league night). Rob, Johnny, Samantha, Melody, and I were able to get a lane right away. Bowling was the one sport I didn't profoundly suck at, so I was happy Melody agreed to join us.

"It's all in the wrist," said Rob, demonstrating. "Right down the middle, but twist at the last minute."

"Like this?" I asked.

"Better, but not quite. And more to your left."

"It's still not working."

"Put more of your arm behind it. Power is important here. Watch how I do it." Deftly picking up his soda can, he effortlessly crushed it on his forehead. I attempted to follow suit but could never quite get it as flat. My lesson ended when an overweight middle-aged woman roughly grabbed the can from me. At first I thought she was going to show us how it was done, but she just threw it into the trash. I guess she didn't want me to concuss myself.

"Who's the man?" bellowed Johnny. "Tell me, who's the man?" He had just thrown a strike on the first frame (after two "practice" shots).

"Who's up next?" The scoring machine told me nothing. Johnny had entered our names: POO, BUT, ASS, DIK, and MEL.

"Samantha," replied Rob. "Is she still in the john with Melody?"

"Yeah. What do you think they're doing in there?"

"Easy," answered Johnny. "Melody's talking about Leon."

Rob laughed. I rolled my eyes but secretly wondered if it was true. Melody and I hadn't formally announced that we were dating. But after the awkward encounter with her father the other night, I kind of figured we'd become a lot more than study buddies.

"Hey, Leon," whispered Johnny. "Here comes your girlfriend."

I turned, expecting to see Melody silently returning from the bathroom. Apparently, Johnny had been speaking ironically. At the shoe-rental counter stood Amy.

Seeing Amy at Pioneer Lanes was like, um . . . well, seeing a really pretty girl at a sleazy bowling alley. She was wearing a sleeveless sweater and tight, tight jeans. Even from across the smoky room, I could see the top of her bright blue panties poking up from the back of her pants.

She wasn't there alone. The guy who was clearly her date was grabbing a pair of size fourteens from the shoe rack.

Oh, Leon, I'm not really dating anyone right now.

The dude was wearing a jacket from Charleston West High. He was bigger than me and had a face like an angry gorilla. I began to imagine scenarios in which I could drop a bowling ball into his lap and make it look like an honest accident.

What was I getting jealous about? Guys like me never wound up with the leading lady. We were the sidekicks, the extras, the ones with few speaking parts. We didn't walk off hand in hand with the heroine as the credits started to roll. Besides, I had someone. I wasn't lonely anymore; I didn't need to dwell on Amy.

I drummed my fingers on the console, pointedly ignoring the ex–girl of my dreams.

"Leon! *Hey, Leon!*" Amy was walking over to me at a good clip.

Johnny and Rob were staring at me, impressed. It took a lot of willpower not to rush to meet Amy halfway.

She sat in the console seat next to me. "Thought that was you."

"Hey, Amy." I pondered introducing her to my friends, but that would only end in embarrassment. "Didn't expect to see you here."

"Tom wanted to take me." She gestured at her date several lanes down. He was looking at the scoring machine with deep concentration. Every so often he'd randomly hit a button, then scratch his head.

Amy reached over and tucked the tag in my collar down. "Just wanted to say hi." Her hand continued to rest on my shoulder. I felt like I was getting a mild electrical shock. I wanted to say something to prolong the conversation.

"Hello, there." The voice behind me interrupted the first lengthy physical contact I'd ever had with Amy.

"Melody!" I jumped up, causing Amy's hand to fall away. "Melody, have you met Amy?"

For the first time, I introduced Melody to someone and she didn't look at the floor. She was staring Amy down. I'd never seen her look so hostile. Amy, on the other hand, didn't seem fazed.

"Hello. Are you having a good time?" Amy spoke slowly, as if Melody was profoundly retarded.

Rob and Johnny were gaping like a couple of yokels at an accident scene. Even Samantha paused, ball in hand, to stare.

"*We* are having a fine time," Melody replied pointedly.

Amy yawned. "That's nice. I don't care for bowling, myself." She examined her perfectly manicured nails.

"Then don't let us keep you here."

Amy bent over to get her purse, and stayed in that position for several seconds. Johnny got up for a better view. By the time I realized I was staring down Amy's shirt, Melody had noticed. She tensed.

Amy trotted off in the direction of her date. "Nice to see you, Leon. Oh, Melody, I like your wig. You can't really tell it's not your real hair."

No one can out-cruel a girl.

Melody deflated. Her shoulders slumped; her head tilted down.

"Who wants nachos?" barked Johnny, and he and Rob ran for the snack bar. Samantha attempted to pick up a spare.

"Melody?" I took her hand. It was limp; she didn't squeeze back. Her other hand carefully adjusted her wig. Two lanes down, someone was screaming profanity at the ten pin.

"Mel, look at me."

She lifted her head. She was biting her puffy lower lip, and her eyes still faced the ground.

Once again, everything I could think of to say would sound trite. Just because I was nice to her, it didn't mean anyone else would be.

"Mel?"

"What?"

"It's your turn."

Melody straightened up. Amy wasn't the worst person she'd faced in her life. Hell, Amy probably was just trying to be friendly in her own clueless way.

I watched as Melody threw two gutter balls. When she sat down next to me, she was smiling. I draped my arm around her.

"Leon?"

"Yeah?"

"You might want to tell your little friend over there she's not supposed to bowl in street shoes."

I kissed Melody's cheek. She smelled like peaches and body lotion.

"Get a room!" bellowed Johnny as he returned with a tray of junk food.

17

PARENTAL ADVISORY

"**S**o when do we get to meet her?" asked my Mom the next day.

"Who?" I asked, knowing full well who she meant.

"Melody. The one you're always talking to on the phone. I was wondering when you were planning on inviting her over."

"You never seemed anxious to meet my friends before," I replied. Meet my parents? Introduce her to my family?

"Well, Melody probably won't leave toilet paper in our trees," my dad said, laughing.

"You have no proof that was anyone I know!"

"Yes, I'm sure it was one of your mother's friends. Listen, invite the girl over. We'd really like to get to know her."

"Why?" I was defensive.

"Well," said Mom soothingly, "if you two are dating, I think we have a right."

So Mom and Dad knew we were more than just a couple of friends. I could put this off only so long. The thing was I'd never told them about Melody's accident. They'd probably pictured her looking more like Amy.

"Listen," I said, "Melody and I are going to the basketball game this Tuesday. She's picking me up; you can meet her then. And, Dad?"

"Yes?"

"Wear a shirt, would you?"

So now I was stuck. My parents were going to meet Melody. Quite frankly, the whole idea made me uncomfortable as hell. It wasn't like I was ashamed, but, well, I'd kind of grown accustomed to the way things were. When you cared about someone, you overlooked their imperfections. It was easy to forget that to an outsider, they might not be so perfect. They might even appear weird, strange, or freakish.

Then again, maybe everyone felt that way about their parents. In the meantime, I wondered if I should mention Melody's scars before she came over.

On one hand, I never brought that up. I wanted Melody to feel that her burns didn't matter to me at all. If that was the case, why would I go out of my way to tell people? I wouldn't say to my parents "Oh, by the way, she's blond," or "I want you to know ahead of time, she's a little tall for a girl."

On the other hand, meeting Melody could be shocking for people, even the most open-minded, well-intentioned people. Ever since I started hanging out with her, I'd noticed people staring at her in a sneaky sort of way. Or staring at her in an obvious, rude sort of way. More and more I understood why she disliked going out in public.

In the end, I decided to say something beforehand, just to avoid any awkwardness. If she had been blind or in a wheelchair, I would have mentioned it. The last thing I wanted was for my folks to look startled, even for a second, when they met Melody.

"Mom, Dad," I began the next night, "there's something you need to know about Melody. Something kind of bad."

Mom and Dad exchanged a brief look. They seemed strangely nervous.

"Go on," said my dad.

"Well, she . . . listen . . ."

"Yes?" asked my mom. She looked upset for some reason.

"She was in a fire when she was little. Her face . . . well, she has some bad scars. I just wanted to give you a heads-up."

Now, was I imagining things, or did my parents look a little relieved? Why would they be relieved to know that my date had been injured as a child? What, did they think I was going to say that she had two noses or something? Or bit the heads off puppies? Or . . . or was pregnant. That was it. They thought I was going to say I had gotten her pregnant. *Parents, sheesh.*

That Tuesday, I paced nervously. Melody would be there any second. Mom and Dad had promised me they'd be on their best behavior, but I had my doubts.

"So what time is your girlfriend getting here?" asked my mom.

"Soon." I let the girlfriend comment pass. It was more or less true.

"Okay, okay." My parents were grinning at me. What horrible thing did they have planned? I had already made sure the family albums were hidden and made them swear they wouldn't bring up any childhood stories about me.

"Did I mention the basketball game starts in half an hour?" I repeated. "She won't have time to stay long."

The horn on Melody's truck blasted like an air-raid siren. "Whoops, there she is. Gotta run."

"Go invite her in." My mom was smiling, but it wasn't a request. Glumly, I obeyed.

"Hey, Leon." Melody leaned out of the cab of her truck. She was wearing makeup. Unfortunately, makeup could only accentuate or hide. It could not create features that were not there. Melody wasn't wearing her wig; her baldness was covered by a baseball cap.

"Hey, Melody. Want to come in for a minute?"

She frowned. "We really need to get going." This was obviously an excuse; the game didn't start for quite some time. I remembered when Melody had come over to work on the history project, and how she'd darted off when Mom was about to show up.

"My parents really want to meet you."

Melody took a deep breath. "Okay, Leon. Let's do it."

My parents, to their credit, didn't bat an eye when they saw Melody. Who knows, maybe they'd been expecting worse.

"Won't you come in?" asked my mother sweetly. "Leon's told us so much about you."

"Mom . . . ," I warned.

Melody, though nervous, seemed more at ease than I was. She took a seat and glanced around the room.

"Lovely place you have here," she commented.

"Thanks," said my dad. "We really like it. You wouldn't believe the work we had to do on it."

"Dad, Melody didn't come here to hear your remodeling stories."

Mom, without my noticing, had disappeared into the kitchen. She returned with a tray of snacks. *Good Lord, just shoot me now.*

"So," said my mother, obviously secretly enjoying my torment, "Leon tells us you're going to the Missouri Scholars Academy."

"Yes. Leon thinks I'm crazy, all those weeks of work in the summer."

"That takes me back," said my dad.

"Were you in the program?" asked Melody, taking the bait.

"No, I was in the military. The air force. I signed up in June and was in basic training all summer."

I buried my face in my hands. As an ex–enlisted man who never came within a thousand miles of a battle, Dad managed to bring up his military record on every occasion.

"Were you a pilot?" asked Melody, opening us up to three hours of stories.

"I was more in what you'd call intelligence."

"He was a file clerk," I groaned.

"That can be stressful work," countered Dad.

"It's true. He still wakes up some nights screaming 'Paper jam!' "

"You know," said Melody, "my father was in the army. Worked in the motor pool."

"Really?" said my dad with interest. "Where was he stationed?"

"Whoa, look at the time! We're going to be late as it is." I grabbed Melody by the arm.

"Nice to meet you, Mr. and Mrs. Sanders," called Melody as I hustled her out the door.

As soon as we were out of my subdivision, I began hammering my head on the dashboard. Melody's eyes didn't leave the road.

"Leon? Why are you doing that?"

"My parents. They swore they wouldn't embarrass me."

We stopped at a red light. "Knock it off, Leon. Embarrass you? I thought they were sweet."

"Nice of you to say. But, um, you're the first girl I've ever really brought home. I just thought they'd tone things down."

Melody laid her hand on my knee. "They didn't embarrass me. And that counts for a lot."

I smiled. "Green light, Mel."

18

HORSEPLAY

In my opinion, there was only one reason a person should climb on top of another living creature, and it had nothing to do with transportation. That was why when Melody invited me to go horseback riding, I was sure I'd end up reenacting *Brokeback Mountain* (the broke-back part, not the homosexuality).

Of course, Melody seemed to think I *could* ride a horse and since she was a girl, I couldn't show fear. (Girls are very much like bears in that respect.) Which was why I found myself, on a misty April morning, standing in the muddy pasture behind Melody's house. We'd been dating now for a couple of weeks, and I was still at the point where I wanted her to think I was macho.

Melody wore a pair of cowboy boots (encrusted with mud, which proved they were no fashion statement), worn-out jeans, a bandana around her bald head, and a light flannel shirt. I didn't care for these bulky clothes. Her loose spring clothes had shown me that her disfigurement did not extend below her neck, and my curiosity had grown. When she got back from the Scholars Academy, maybe we could go swimming....

"Leon, meet Charger." Charger was brown, with a splotch of white on his forehead. He was also big. Big enough to drag a man caught in the stirrups for miles. It could happen. I'd seen it on TV.

I tried to ignore that voice in my head telling me to express my fears to Melody.

"Hello, Charger," I said, tentatively patting his nose. "Why the long face?"

Melody laughed. "Do you know how to mount a horse?"

I decided not to make a taxidermy joke. "No."

"It's easy. Just put your left foot in the left stirrup, then swing your right leg over."

People who are good at something tend to squash everything into two steps. *Step one: build a spaceship. Step two: fly to the moon. Simple as that.*

Resigned to my doom, I put my foot into the stirrup, started to jump, panicked, and almost fell on my rear. Charger whinnied, ready, I was sure, to kick me square in the face.

Melody was laughing into her hand. For once, we were on her turf. Broken legs or not, I had to try again.

It took three attempts, but I finally made it into the saddle. Charger immediately began to walk.

"Hey! Stop! Um... whoa?"

Melody touched the horse's flank and he stopped. Then, in one fluid movement, she leapt onto the back of her horse, Samson.

My fears were momentarily forgotten when I realized how blisteringly uncomfortable a saddle was. Melody didn't seem to mind, but then again, she didn't have testicles.

Her horse sauntered over to me. "Just follow me, Leon. Dig in your heels." Samson started trotting.

Charger was much less responsive but eventually began following his equine pal. This wasn't too bad. Then, after about two minutes, Charger started wandering along his own path.

"Melody, help!" I didn't care how sissy that sounded.

"Just pull the reins," she shouted.

I tried, but a horse is a lot less responsive than a Buick. Eventually, Charger fell back into step.

"Just smack him on the rear if he won't behave," directed Melody.

I couldn't bring myself to wallop the horse. I lightly smacked him on the butt. I didn't think he noticed.

Melody led us around the pasture four or five times. She cut a striking figure in the cool spring air. From a distance you couldn't see that she didn't have much of a face. She was just a teenage girl, taking her horse out for a morning ride.

Scars or not, that was kind of hot. I almost forgot the mortal peril I was in.

We never went faster than a gallop. I told myself that was as fast as Melody ever went, but in all honesty, she and Samson probably ran like the wind and jumped hedges when I wasn't slowing them down.

After about an hour, Melody reined in her horse. Charger wandered over to them.

"How you doing, Leon?"

I grinned while gripping the reins. "I'm great. I could do this all day."

"Sure you wouldn't like a break?"

"Yes!"

Melody led us to a building at the very back of their property. It seemed to be a small barn that was no longer in use but hadn't fallen into complete disrepair. Melody gracefully dismounted. Luckily, she was tying up her horse when I jumped down, so she didn't see me land on my butt.

When both horses were secure, Melody gestured toward the barn. Apparently, we were going to take a load off in there.

This reminded me of a story. "Okay," I began as we reached the door. "There was this traveling salesman—"

Something shot out of the darkness above our heads. Melody gasped and grabbed me around the waist. Without thinking, I wrapped my arm around her shoulder.

"It's just an owl, Mel. It's okay."

She took a deep breath. "It startled me; that's all. C'mon." We separated. Almost. As my eyes adjusted to the dim light, I realized we were holding hands.

"What is this place?"

"Just an old shed. Daddy uses it for storage."

There were gaps in the walls and unmistakable signs of wild animals, but the roof was in good repair. In one corner sat an old but clean tractor. Various farm implements and tools hung neatly on the wall or lay scattered on a workbench. In another corner a few bales of hay were stacked. One had burst, covering the floor with straw. The whole place had the pleasant, mildewy smell of disuse.

"Tony and I used to play out here when we were little," said Melody, rolling a rusty tricycle with her foot.

"So far from the house?" I sat on a hay bale.

"We had to protect everyone from the terrorists that lived in the woods. At least according to Tony."

Melody seemed to remember something and went rummaging through an old crate. She eventually pulled out a shoe box and sat down next to me.

"Treasure?" I asked.

She opened the box and pulled out a filthy, naked Barbie doll.

I smiled. "Did you actually get Tony to play with that?"

She laughed. "Never. I'd play alone a lot." She held the doll on her knees and stared at it.

Feeling a tad uncomfortable, I glanced into the shoe box. There were a couple of other Barbies. One was nearly bald. I almost asked Melody if she'd given it a haircut when she was little, but then I noticed something.

Picking up the doll, I confirmed what I thought I'd seen. Someone had carefully burned the face off Barbie, leaving a melted plastic mess.

Melody was watching. "They didn't make dolls that look like me," she said bitterly, tossing her toys back into the box. She tried to stand up, but I took her hand.

"It was just something I did when I was nine. I used to pretend that Ken still loved Barbie, and that all the other dolls still thought she was great. After a couple of years of school, I don't think I opened that box again."

For a long time I looked at her. Just looked. The eyes, the wrecked skin, the single tear running down her bony nose. I thought back to elementary school: how Melody had always sat alone on the swings at recess, how we used to dare each other to run up and touch her. I wanted to go back in time. I wanted to defend her. If not then, now. To be her protector, her friend, someone who would always look out for her.

"Leon, you're the only guy who can stand to look at me."

I placed a hand on her cheek. Her skin felt fragile, though I knew from experience she was as hard outside as she was inside. Gingerly, I pressed her head to mine. We kissed.

I kissed her large lips, her scarred cheeks, her missing ears. We kissed. We held each other. Our tongues touched. We removed our jackets.

I kept waiting for Melody to tell me to stop, to push me away. But she just kept kissing me.

Without speaking a word, we moved from sitting on the hay bale to sitting on the floor, our arms wrapped around each other. It wasn't a conscious choice, but soon I was laying her down on the floor. We were side by side in the straw. My hand crept up the back of her shirt, my fingers savoring the curve of her spine. I rubbed her skin from the base of her bra to the top of her panties. She didn't stop me; she just breathed harder. Sweat rolled down her forehead.

And suddenly, I was straddling her. She lay on her back, almost hyperventilating, her eyes closed. My fingers grabbed at her shirt, clumsily fumbling with the buttons. And then her top fell open, revealing her almost naked torso.

The scars ended just below her neck. Oh, Christ, those smooth shoulders, that flat tummy . . . and her plain cotton bra. *Oh, Christ!* The clasp was in the front. I could see my hand trembling as I reached for it.

And then Melody's eyes shot open and her hand found my wrist. She smiled sadly.

"Not yet, Leon."

I was drenched in sweat. Slowly, with regret (and a little relief), I climbed off her as she closed her shirt.

"I'm sorry, Leon. I've . . . You're the only guy I've even kissed. I can't do that, not now."

"Don't be sorry. There's no rush."

"Leon? How many times have you . . . you know . . ."

I gave her a big kiss. "Melody, I wish the world thought I was as macho as you do. This is as far as I've ever been."

We snuggled for a long time, there on the floor. Our lips touched; our fingers explored. We kissed and laughed and held each other.

Wow.

Much later, we walked giggling into the afternoon sun. Melody brushed some hay out of my hair. I groaned inwardly when I realized we'd have to remount the devil horses.

To my relief, Melody untied them and let them wander free.

"Let's walk back."

Hand in hand, we walked the half mile back to the house.

So I'd almost undressed Melody. And I'd made out with her twice. And hung out with her all the time. There was no doubt anymore. She was my girlfriend.

Melody smiled at me and I squeezed her hand.

"Melody?"

"Hmm?"

"Listen. Um, the spring formal's coming up. I was wondering if, you know, you'd like to go with me?"

I knew there was no chance she'd turn me down, but I still got pleasant shivers when I saw the way she smiled.

Ah, what the hell. Melody made me feel special. She made me feel like Dylan, like one of those guys who didn't have to prove anything. She made me feel like any girl would be lucky to have me.

I liked almost everything about Melody. I could live with the one thing I didn't like.

Besides, she said she wasn't ready for that . . . *yet.*

19

DEAD MAN'S HAND

The student council weenies had plastered the school with posters advertising "Take My Breath Away," the theme for the upcoming dance. Fliers warning about the evils of drunk driving were taped on every wall. Dr. Bailey nearly had a stroke when he saw that someone had drawn swastikas on the foreheads of the models in a photographer's ad.

I was walking Melody out to the bus after school.

"Hey, Melody? How many mosquitoes does it take to screw in a lightbulb?"

She smiled. "How many?"

"Only two. The question is, how did they get in there?"

"I don't get it."

"It'll come to you."

Since that day in the barn, I'd given up all pretense that Melody wasn't my girlfriend. I held her hand when we talked. I kissed her after school. I even let Buttercup take our picture, my arm draped around Melody's shoulders. And we were going to the spring dance together.

I braced myself for the fallout. I was ready for the snide comments, the mocking laughter, the jokes about my ugly girlfriend. But the thing was they never materialized. Maybe it all happened when my back was turned, but all my clever rebuttals and insults didn't do me any good. I never had to stand up for Melody.

Even my friends approached my having a girlfriend with their usual lazy indifference. Samantha went from harassing me about using Melody to harassing me about how Melody was too good for me. Johnny, who'd once made a substitute teacher cry with a joke about her mustache, never commented on Melody's looks (just her study habits, clothes, and poor taste in guys). Even Rob accepted a Leon girlfriend with his normal snarling apathy.

Still, it wasn't like Melody was ignored. We both noticed the stares, the whispered comments, the blunt questions from children. We just pretended not to.

"So I bought my dress yesterday," continued Melody as we stepped outside among the pulsating throng of bus riders.

"I rented a tux. Nothing like having your crotch measured by a strange man."

Melody laughed. "I can't wait till next Saturday."

I had never been to a dance, and I wasn't totally excited. The tux was uncomfortable. The tickets were expensive. I could not dance, and Samantha was the only other person I knew who was going.

Then again, I thought about our trip to the shed. The promise of things to come. My big car, and the empty country roads outside of St. Christopher.

"I'm excited too, Melody. You sure I can't give you a ride home?"

She picked up her book bag. "No, I'll take the bus. Mom and I are going shopping for shoes right when I get home."

We kissed, and I watched Melody weave her way onto her bus. Even though students were crushed together and shoving, Melody walked unmolested. No one went near her; it was as if she walked in a separate reality.

Rob didn't need a ride that day, so I took the opportunity to grab a couple of books from the library. (I'd spent study hall trying to circumvent the porn filter in the computer lab.) As always, the library was almost deserted. I poked through the almost pathetic science fiction section, but there wasn't anything there I hadn't already read. I ended up checking out *Starship Troopers*. It had lasers in it.

Dan Dzyan sat at a table near the exit, staring intently at a book. I attempted to slink by. I wasn't in the mood to see autopsy photos.

Dan didn't seem to notice me; he was too absorbed in his book. He'd read something, look at his palm, then look back at the book. It was called *Divination*. He must have been teaching himself palmistry.

I lingered too long. "Hey, Leon," he growled, not looking up. "Have a seat."

I considered ignoring him but thought the better of it. I had enough going on in my life; I didn't need a voodoo curse on top of everything. Warily, I pulled up a chair.

There was an odd assortment of crap on the desk in front of Dan: a lump of wax, several sewing needles, a deck of cards, and some raw corn kernels. Dan was still staring at his hand.

"According to this, I don't have a love line." He shrugged; the news didn't disturb him. "Hey, do you know what tiromancy is?"

"What?"

"The art of predicting the future using cheese."

There was no good response to a statement like that.

"Did you want something, Dan?"

"Yeah." He picked up the cards and shuffled. "Let me tell your fortune."

The cards were from the Casino Queen riverboat in East St. Louis. "Don't you need a special deck?"

"Nah, this'll work." He fanned out the deck. "Pick a card. Not that one! No, not that one either. . . . Ah, for Satan's sake, Leon!" Dan reshuffled.

"*Now* pick a card." I grabbed the top one. The three of diamonds. Dan checked a table in the book. "No, pick another one."

Dan apparently didn't like any of the fortunes. I was nearly a quarter of the way through the deck when I pulled a card he approved of.

"The joker. That *suits* you, Leon." I couldn't tell if he was trying to be funny. He checked the book. "The joker is a holdover of the Fool in the old tarot deck. It symbolizes someone who rushes into things without thinking, insults people without meaning to, and will never find romantic happiness." He grinned. "It's like the worst card you could have drawn."

"Bye, Dan."

"Hold on. Did you know the Puritans considered the joker to be an evil card? When they burned witches, they'd use a burning joker as kindling!"

"Really?"

"Nah, I just made that up."

Talking to Dan was like listening to Sr. Lopez Lopez's language tapes: I recognized the words but didn't understand what was being said. I got up.

"Leon?" Dan was leaning back in his chair, holding the deck in one fist. "The cards don't lie. I'd be cautious if I were you. Don't do anything rash." He attempted to cut the deck with one hand, causing the cards to fly everywhere.

20

LEON TO THE RESCUE

We often make offers when we never intend to follow through. How many times have we said, *If there's anything I can do for you, just ask*? A couple of weeks earlier, when I'd told Amy she could call me if she ever wanted to talk, I never really expected her to take me up on that.

It was the Saturday before the dance. Jimmy and Johnny were grounded; Rob was out hurling pizza dough at his part-time job; and Samantha was off visiting her boyfriend. Melody was at Tony's softball game. I'd politely declined when she'd invited me.

Of course, that meant I'd sentenced myself to *a quiet evening with my parents.* Dad and I relaxed on our living room couch, watching a rented movie. Dad had picked it out, so it featured a lot of car chases and explosions (though not near as many as a Bart Axelrod feature). Mom sat nearby, working on her unending scrapbook.

The semimilitary movie made Dad remember his years serving Uncle Sam and he was well into another story.

"So then the DI–that's drill instructor–gets right in my face and calls me a worthless piece of"–Dad glanced over at my mom–"*poop.* Then he made me do fifty push-ups."

"That'll teach you to sneeze in formation," I replied. I'd heard the story a dozen times. Though my father never had anything good to say about his time in the air force, he sure talked about it a lot. Maybe after twenty years of pushing pencils in an office, he looked back on his military time as the wild and crazy days.

I wondered if I'd ever have any wild and crazy days, or if someday I'd be boring my son with stories of Pioneer Lanes and nights at the lock and dam.

The phone rang and my mom answered it. "Yes, he's here; hold on." She passed the cordless phone to me.

I pressed the receiver to my ear and was shocked to hear someone noisily blowing their nose.

"Johnny?" I asked.

I heard a hiccup on the other end, then a voice.

"Leon, this is Amy."

I sprinted to my room so fast I almost stepped in the bowl of popcorn. *Amy? Calling me?*

"Um, hi." I attempted to straighten my hair in the reflection of my computer monitor until I remembered she couldn't see me.

"I wasn't sure if this was your number. Do you have any idea how many Sanderses there are in the phone book?"

"Uh . . ." How should I respond? Laugh? Try to make small talk?

"So . . . ," said Amy after a pause. "What are you up to?" Her voice was flat, like she was talking just to talk.

"Just watching a movie with my folks." *On Saturday night. Real cool, Leon.*

"Oh." There was more silence. What did she want? Amy wasn't the type of girl who had to chat with classmates on the weekend for something to do.

"Leon," she eventually said hoarsely. "Can we talk? Do you have time?"

I pulled up my desk chair. "Of course. What's on your mind?"

"No, I mean, can you come over for a little bit? I understand if you're busy."

I was already pulling on my jacket. "Where do you live?"

I was driving nearly twice the legal speed limit. My parents hadn't even looked up when I'd babbled about having to go see a friend. Amy lived about ten miles away, and I planned to be there in five minutes.

Steering with one hand, I pulled some gum out of my glove box and pondered what was happening. Amy wanted to talk. What the hell did that mean? She had friends she could talk to, but instead she'd called me.

I was at a loss. Guys never needed to talk, and Samantha didn't exactly confide her thoughts and fears to me. And yet Amy had asked me to come over.

I remembered an episode of *Tales from the Crypt* I'd seen with Melody. A cute girl asked out her nerdish coworker, seduced him, and then sacrificed him to an alien god. It was an outlandish idea, but better than any theory I could come up with.

Amy's house was in one of those ritzy St. Christopher subdivisions that literally sprang up out of nowhere in a matter of weeks. Every house had two stories and a two-car garage. I was very aware that I was driving the skuzziest car in the neighborhood.

I pulled into her driveway and paused for one second. What would Melody think of my running off to Amy's house late at night? Amy hadn't exactly been nice to her at the bowling alley.

I swatted at the dummy hand grenade hanging from my rearview mirror. There was only one way to find out. Melody didn't have to know that I'd been here. Besides, I somehow doubted that Amy planned to meet me at the door in a skimpy negligee.

Taking a deep breath, I rang the doorbell and waited. And waited. I was sure I'd gotten the address right. Was Amy even there? I remembered the other time we were supposed to do something together. *Jesus, maybe she stood me up again.*

I jabbed the bell a second time, right when Amy opened the door. She was dressed in sweatpants and an old sweater. Her hair hung in unkempt strands down the back of her head. She was puffing on a cigarette. And yet she was still just as gorgeous as ever (after I mentally added the bikini and the suntan lotion).

"C'mon in," she mumbled.

Amy's house was at an almost German level of order. All the chairs were exactly three inches from the table. All the blinds were pulled to precisely the same level. It looked like someone had placed the doormat with a T square. Still, something was odd. There was a large blank spot along one wall, as if there'd been a second couch there recently. The walls were covered with photos, but there were weird gaps, like some were missing.

I remembered her mentioning her parents' divorce. Her father must have taken some stuff with him when he left.

Amy sat on the couch and patted the cushion next to her. I flopped down beside her, perhaps just a little too eagerly.

She exhaled a huge cloud of smoke. "Thanks for coming out. I'm sorry to call you this late. You want a soda or something?"

"No, thanks." I was aware that my leg was jiggling, and I forced myself to stop it.

Amy crushed out her cigarette and stared at the ashtray for a while. I stared at the blank TV, desperately trying to think of something clever to say to end the silence.

"Leon, are your parents still together?" Amy asked out of nowhere.

I began to see what was bothering her. "Yes."

"Do they ever fight?"

I thought about my goofy mom and dad: how they constantly bickered, finished each other's sentences, and spent a weekend alone in Branson every summer.

"Sometimes." I didn't think spats about who didn't pick up the dry cleaning were what Amy had in mind.

"Mine do. Did." She ran her fingers through her tangled hair. "I mean, all the time. Every week they'd have a big damn blowout. When I was little, they'd try to hide it. But for the past few years, it was screaming, cussing, breaking things. And they'd try to get me to take sides." Amy snorted long and loud. "And even after all that, I hate that they're divorced."

I opened my mouth to say something stupid, but she plowed on. "The bitch of it is, they still fight! It's like even though Dad lives way out in Chesterfield now, they have to make a point of calling each other up to yell at each other. That's what happened tonight. Mom called Dad up, and I could hear her telling him to go to hell from the bedroom. She doesn't even care how that makes me feel." Amy massaged her temples.

"Did you ever tell her that?"

Amy turned to me and I was surprised at how bloodshot her eyes were. "Yes. Tonight, actually. So she started yelling at me instead. Said I didn't appreciate her, said I always took Dad's side, said . . . said I didn't love her. And then she left. Drove off. I don't know where she is."

Amy's lower lip began to quiver and her face grew red. "How . . . how could she say that? I love my mom! How could she . . ." And then she was crying. It wasn't like when

Melody cried, with silent tears and internal pain. Amy went from zero to bawling in two seconds.

"Let it all out," I said unnecessarily. She was already sobbing. When I put my arm around her, she didn't pull away. She snuggled in closer.

After a few minutes she sat up, blew her nose, and reached for her cigarettes.

I laid my hand on her wrist. "Don't."

She smiled through her tears. "You can have one, if you're hungry." She leaned back and rested her head on my shoulder. I didn't move an inch. Well, I actually moved several inches, but that was strictly involuntary. I had to remind myself that Amy just wanted to talk, and if I was going to face Melody on Monday, I should remember that. So I attempted to channel the spirit of Yoda and give some advice.

"Your mom didn't mean what she said. She's just in a bad place right now, and took it out on you."

"I know that. She probably went to my aunt's house. In a couple of hours she'll come back and we'll make up. But it really hurt me, what she said. I...I didn't want to sit here alone. That's why I called you. I was scared and angry, and didn't want any of my friends to see me like that."

"Yeah." There was a tinge of bitterness in my voice. Apparently, she still didn't even consider me a friend. I scooted away.

Amy grabbed my arm and pulled me back toward her. Her eyes were wide. "Oh, God, Leon, I didn't mean it like that. Of course you're my friend. I just...I dunno. Sometimes when I try to talk to Cassie or Jennifer, it's like they don't even hear me. They just interrupt me and talk about their own problems. And you . . ." She shrugged. "Well, you did say to call you if I wanted to talk."

She still hadn't let go of my arm. "I meant it."

"Good," she said, rather dismissively.

I gave her a grin, but her explanation rang hollow. She only ever came to me when she needed someone to talk to or to eat her cigarettes. She said she'd go out with me, but then ditched me without calling and never rescheduled. She told me she didn't want to date anyone, then showed up at the bowling alley with a guy. She'd been nice to me, but she didn't think of me as a friend.

"I need to go, Amy," I said, standing.

"Wait!" Amy got to her feet so fast she upset the ashtray onto the carpet. "Don't go just yet," she said, in a somewhat urgent tone. "I don't want to sit around here alone. Would you keep me company until my mom gets back?"

Now, a couple of weeks earlier, I would have gladly kept her company. I would have been a good buddy and a good listener, and I would have gotten a good slap when I tried to kiss her. But things had changed. Melody existed.

I looked at my watch. "I dunno . . ."

Amy smiled at me and patted a spot next to her on the sofa. I obeyed. It was okay. It wasn't like the attraction was mutual; she just wanted some company.

She habitually reached for her cigarettes, then looked at me and stopped. Suddenly, she giggled.

"Leon, can I ask you a question?"

"Okay."

"Why did it take you so long to ask me out?"

"Huh?" The question blindsided me.

"You've been following me around like a puppy since like seventh grade. Why did it take you until now to ask me out?"

I couldn't face her accusing smile, so I bent down and began picking up the butts from the ashtray. Apparently, the Thomsons were right. I wasn't subtle. Amy had me pegged from day one.

I set the ashtray back on the table. It was time to say something. "I dunno, Amy. You're kind of hard to approach."

To my surprise, she laughed. "Me? Look who's talking!"

That threw me. "What's that supposed to mean?"

Amy stretched, and her top rode up, revealing her perfectly flat belly. She didn't pull it back down, and I had a hard time not looking her in the navel. "It means, Leon, that most of the time you act–I dunno–like you're not really there. You always have your nose in some book, you never talk to anyone, and you always hang out with the same couple of people. It's like you don't want to have any friends."

"I have friends!" I almost bellowed.

Amy wasn't impressed. "Who? Besides the twins and that Rob guy."

"There's Samantha, and Melody, and . . ." *Who? Dan?*

"See? When was the last time you tried to get to know anyone else?"

Amy was starting to irritate me. I got up and began to pace. "Amy, it's not like people really want to get to know me, okay? It's not like I'm Mr. Popular!"

She rolled her eyes. "Come off it. For some reason you

got it in your head that no one likes you. Get over yourself already."

"Thank you, Sigmund. I'm sure everyone's just dying to hang out with me."

Amy stood up and faced me. For the first time, I looked her right in the eyes. I'd always assumed they were blue, but they were actually kind of a dark gray. She smiled at me for a moment, then spoke to me almost in a whisper.

"Why wouldn't people want to hang out with you?" She stepped closer to me. "Because you're smart?" And still closer. "Because you can be funny?" She backed me into the wall. "Because you're *cute*?" She lowered her eyes, looking a little embarrassed.

I should've complimented her back, but I had to get confirmation. "You really think I'm cute?"

She adjusted my collar and eyed me critically. "Well, you could use a haircut and some new clothes. But yeah, I think you're pretty cute." Her hands moved down my arms and gently took my fingers. "Maybe I'm not easy to talk to either. But I kind of wish you'd asked me out earlier. I might have said yes. I could use someone like you right now."

Both of us were looking at the floor. The only sound was our breathing. We were close; I could feel the top fringes of Amy's hair touching my head. And closer still.

What was going on? Amy had called me cute. She was holding my hands. With each breath, we moved a little closer. Our noses passed each other.

But we weren't going to . . .

We were.

All the years of fantasy did not measure up to the real thing. Her lips were just as smooth and welcoming as I'd dreamed, her tongue just as probing. I could feel the sweat on her cheeks; I could taste the chalky residue of nicotine. How could this really be happening?

Something was pushing me back. The universe wouldn't allow it. Leon Sanders should not be kissing Amy Green. I tried to hold on, but the mysterious force shoved me farther and farther away. . . .

It was Amy, the flat of her hand on my chest.

"You have a girlfriend," she said, half angrily, half mockingly. She punctuated each syllable with a jab to my ribs.

Girlfriend? Oh yeah, Melody. The secrets, the bonding, her shirt off in the barn. That's right. Girlfriend.

"You mean Melody? She's not my girlfriend." *Who said that? Ah, it was me.*

Amy looked at me with raw disbelief.

"Seriously," I lied. "I asked her to the dance, but it's just a friend thing."

Amy arched her thin eyebrow. "You're telling me the truth?"

"Yeah."

"Uh-huh. I think you should leave, Leon."

This was more like it. Amy was realizing she shouldn't have kissed me. I wandered toward the door.

She touched my shoulder as I had one hand on the knob. "But, Leon, after the dance, give me a call. I'd really like to see you again."

We kissed again. And again. I tried to lead her back to the couch, but she held me at arm's length.

"Mom will be back soon. But thanks for coming over. Maybe sometime you can take me for a ride in that heap of yours." She blew me a kiss. I nearly broke my nose on the door before I remembered to open it before leaving.

I walked across Amy's yard in a daze. Half of me wanted to scream at the heavens in joy, while the other half just wanted to scream at the heavens.

Amy kind of liked me! Amy had kissed me! Amy wanted to go out with me!

And I was going to have to pretend like this night didn't happen.

Right?

By the time I got home, everyone was asleep. I played a lone answering machine message.

"Leon? It's Melody. I was calling to see if you wanted to get some Taco Barn food after the game, but I guess you went out. Anyway, I got my shoes and purse for the dance today. I'm really excited. Can't wait to see you Monday."

Shit.

21

DEVIL'S ADVOCATE

Rob talked nonstop about baseball as I drove him to school that Monday. He'd been talking to me about the St. Louis Cardinals for over ten years. It didn't bother him that I'd never watched a game.

I tuned him out, grunting occasionally so he'd think I was listening. I had bigger things on my mind.

I had kissed Amy. Actually, Amy had kissed me! And called me cute and asked me out. It was exactly how I'd always pictured it (except without the baby oil and silk sheets).

I was scum. I already had a girlfriend! Someone who'd

told me her secrets. A girl who convinced me to ride a horse. A girl who let me take her top off and implied that we'd do more someday. What was I doing kissing someone else?

I should have known better than to go to Amy's house. In retrospect, I realized I'd been secretly hoping that something would happen.

Rob was pounding the dashboard, ranting about something that had gone on at the Cards/Cubs game the night before. Hopefully he'd take my frustrated growling as a sign that I agreed with him.

If only I'd asked Amy out the year before. Maybe she would have said yes. Hell, I could be taking her to the dance instead of . . .

I was suddenly horrified by the thought. I was happy with Melody! *Happy! Do you hear me? Happy!*

I turned into the MZH parking lot at fifty miles per hour, banged over a curb, nearly took out Pete's shack, and fishtailed into my space. Rob stared at me with a rare look of genuine anger.

"Sorry," I said with a shrug. "The freakin' Cubs. Always get me pissed."

"I'm taking the bus home today."

Guilt bred paranoia. When I ran into Dan that morning, he leered at me and, pointing an accusing finger, loudly whispered, "You did something bad!"

Not stopping to remember that Dan was always saying things like that, I grabbed him by the arm and hurled him into the men's room.

"How did you know?" I demanded.

Dan's temporary look of shock turned to one of glee. "You really *did* do something bad? Tell me, tell me!"

I had to get a hold of myself. I had no idea what I was going to do about Amy, but if I didn't pull it together, I was going to blurt the whole thing out. I needed to talk to someone.

Dan was rubbing his hands together in anticipation. "Did you burn down a church? Beat up a nun? Rebroadcast accounts of this game . . ."

I couldn't talk to Rob or the twins about my dilemma, and definitely not Samantha. (There were no secrets when two girls were involved.) I couldn't even tell my parents. I needed someone I didn't know very well who wouldn't give me any high-toned lectures on morality and goodness. . . .

"Did you not wash your hands before returning to work?" Dan continued to guess.

I braced myself. It was worth a shot.

"Dan, could I ask you for some advice? Some *serious* advice."

Dan stopped twitching and wringing his hands. "Um, okay."

"You can't tell anyone what I'm going to tell you. You have to promise me."

I expected a nod and maybe a handshake, but Dan clasped his hand to his chest, whispered something like *"Chthulhu fh'tagn!"* and spit into a urinal.

"That's an unbreakable oath," he said in response to my baffled expression.

"Whatever. Here's the deal, Dan. You know that Melody Hennon and I are kind of dating, right?"

"Yeah."

"Well . . . last night, Amy Green and I . . . kissed." Was I asking Dan for advice or bragging? "And I told her Melody was just my friend. She wants me to call her."

Dan looked confused for a moment, then bared his crooked fangs. "Ah, the sins of the flesh are the most subtle. We try to walk the straight and narrow path, but when we spy lady fair, with golden brow, and quaking lips, and big ol' knockers . . . Well, go on."

"So I should just tell Amy no, right? Just forget that ever happened. Right?"

Dan cleaned his ear with his pinkie. "Well, I don't have a lot of experience with the fairer sex, believe it or not. But looks to me like you have two choices. You can cheat on Melody and forever hate yourself for doing that to her. Or you can pretend last night didn't happen—I'm sure Amy's not exactly shouting it from the rooftops—and hate yourself for giving up such a hot little succubus."

"A what?"

"A hot chick."

Despite the overwhelming evidence that Dan was schizophrenic, he had pretty much cut to the quick of things.

"I guess I have to do the right thing."

"You're asking *me*?"

"Thanks, Dan." I turned to go.

"Leon? One more thing. Don't tell Melody what you did. That's playing with fire, man."

Melody stood by her locker, carefully organizing her books. I slouched in a doorway, sizing her up like a mugger.

Now that she wore a wig, she looked perfectly normal from behind. Slim figure, nice legs, pert little butt. How could I have cheated on her? We had a good thing. But as I thought that, Melody turned and faced me.

Even from down the hall, you could see how mutilated she was. She was the kind of girl who turned heads, the sort of person people talked about when she was out of earshot.

That poor thing. I wonder what happened to her. How does she live like that?

And I was her boyfriend. She made me happy. But maybe, just maybe, I was settling. Melody was the first girl who had ever really noticed me. But now Amy liked me too, and I was just going to give that up. I felt like I was cheating myself.

Melody turned and saw me stalking her. Her lips spread into a smile, and I couldn't help smiling back. Two seconds later, I was standing next to her.

"I missed you this weekend, Leon."

"I'm sorry. I had to, um, do some things."

She took my hand. I touched her delicate wrist.

"It's okay, Leon. You don't have to report in."

Great. If she had been mean and sniping, I could have forgiven myself for kissing Amy. But of course, Melody was perfectly understanding. She had no idea that the day before, I'd denied dating her.

We stood there, talking until long after the bell rang. As Mr. Jackson fumbled for his tardy slips, I thought about my girlfriend. Smart, funny, and with a nice rear end.

Amy smiled at me as I passed her table, and I winked back. Melody or not, it was nice to be noticed.

22

SAVE THE LAST DANCE FOR ME

In speech class once, Dan had given a somewhat incoherent report on the history of the straitjacket. He mentioned that American restraining jackets buckled behind the back, while British ones latched behind the neck.

I recalled this as I attempted to assemble my tuxedo. Never had I been so itchy, uncomfortable, and ridiculous-looking. A canvas straitjacket would have felt less restrictive than this thing.

I looked in the mirror. The rented clothes did little to mask the fact that I was not a tux type of guy. I looked like a contestant in one of those reality shows where they set up nerds with sexy women for comedic results.

Dad knocked on the bathroom door, then came in.

"Leon, you look great."

"I look stupid."

He sat down on the toilet lid. "Yeah, you do. I think you have to be Sean Connery to look good in one of those things."

Dad was nothing if not truthful.

"Listen, Son, there's something we need to talk about."

I knew what he was going to say. I braced myself for the awkward speech.

"I know you and Melody have been seeing each other for a while, and I know this dance will be special for both of you."

I recombed my hair, being sure not to make eye contact.

"And, well, I know you'll be out late, and I know, um, well, you know..." I hadn't seen him this uncomfortable since he'd gone for his colonoscopy.

"Dad, I promise we won't—"

He cut me off. "Son, I'm not saying you should or you shouldn't. But, um..." He suddenly froze, unable to continue. "Just take these!" He thrust a package at me and hurried out of the bathroom.

I removed the small box from the drugstore bag. A month earlier, I never would have needed protection. And now, that night, with Melody...would I actually have a chance to use them? Maybe that night would be the night.

Did I really want Melody to be the first girl? I might not get another chance for years. Then again, after making out with Amy, maybe I was selling myself short. We'd smiled at each other during chemistry all week but never talked. And that was what I needed to keep doing. No more talking to Amy. No more thoughts about those kisses and how she wanted to go for a ride. I had to forget about her–which would be impossible to do without a head injury or electro-shock equipment.

Mom insisted on taking several dozen pictures of me. To her, it was like I was on my way to my coronation as pope rather than a high school dance.

"Leon, are you sure you can't stop by here with Melody? I'd really like to get your picture together." I thought Mom had always regretted not having a daughter, someone she could dress up in lace and ribbons. The best she could hope for was to see my date all dolled up.

"Mom, I told you, she lives way out by Cottleville. We'll be late if we have to drive back here." Actually, I just wanted to spare Melody the inspection by my parents.

"Well, be sure to get your portrait taken." She had given me the money, so there was no way out of it.

Dad slipped me a couple of bucks. I had breath mints in one pocket and a three-pack of condoms in the other. I was off.

As I drove to Melody's, ninety percent of my thoughts centered on how to convince her to go for a long drive in the country. But that nagging ten percent kept reminding me that Amy had told me to call her.

Now, Melody wasn't one of those unattractive girls who became beautiful the second they put on their fancy prom dresses. But when she stepped into her living room, I was shocked at how nice she looked.

Her dress was green and bared her shoulders. She was wearing high heels and was now a bit taller than me. She carried a matching purse and was wearing a necklace and a bracelet (the first jewelry I'd ever seen on her). Her hair was up. It occurred to me later that you couldn't style a wig; she must have bought another one for this night. She was wearing makeup. Her scars were just as obvious, but it did bring out her eyes and lips.

"You look great, Melody." She did. I'd never seen her so pretty. Her parents stood beaming at me, and I had to make a special effort to not look her in the chest.

I strapped a corsage to her wrist and suffered while her dad filmed us. He seemed proud of his daughter, but there was a chill in the air. Perhaps he was thinking the same thing as my dad.

It was awkward to hold the car door for your date when it opened only from the inside, but somehow I managed. Melody smiled. She pulled down the visor to touch up her makeup. When she realized the mirror was gone, she used her compact.

"Leon, thanks for doing this."

One of my headlights was dead, and I had to squint to see Melody's unlit street. I almost missed the significance of what she'd said.

"Wait a minute. 'Thank you'? Why are you thanking me?"

"Well, I just really appreciate this. I've always wanted to go to one of these."

I swerved to avoid a pothole. "Mel, let's get one thing straight. I'm not doing you any favors. I should be thanking you." I sure as hell didn't want her to think this was a pity date. "It's my pleasure to take my *girlfriend* to the dance."

There. I'd said it. I couldn't take that back. Sure, Amy had kissed me. She had even asked me to call her. And all week long she'd been smiling at me in chemistry. Even the twins noticed that. But Melody was the one I was with. That was just the way it was.

"Thank you, Leon. . . ."

"I'm warning you, Melody. . . ."

We both laughed. As I turned onto the main road, I slipped my hand onto the back of Melody's neck. It was unscarred and I enjoyed the smoothness. I also enjoyed the feel of her bare skin. She didn't seem to mind as I traced her shoulder blades with my fingers.

"Leon?"

"Yeah?"

"I have to be home by midnight tonight. For real."

I pulled my hand away. *Point taken.*

"But," she continued, "my parents are going out of town next weekend."

This conversation had taken an interesting turn. "Yes?"

"And Tony is spending the night with some friends."

Deep within the confines of my tux, I began to sweat.

"Yes?" My voice squeaked.

"And . . . um . . . maybe you could come by."

"I'd like that."

I jammed my foot down on the accelerator and we

zoomed off into the night. Actually, my car was incapable of zooming, but we did drive less slowly.

I felt great. What the hell had I been so uptight about? Melody was wonderful, and nothing else mattered. Screw what anyone thought. Screw Dylan. Screw Amy (well, not really). Great things were going to happen with Melody. Amy was history.

Just as soon as I danced with her once.

23

DANCIN' FOOL

The student council seemed to think that streamers and balloons could transform our gym into a magical paradise. Well, either paradise smelled like sweat and old socks, or it was still a gym.

By the time we arrived, people were already dancing. The DJ was blasting a song I didn't recognize. It was about eighty degrees. Some couples stood awkwardly talking at the foul lines. Others–those who could dance–moved to the beat at half-court.

Dr. Bailey made the rounds, separating couples who got

too close. Sr. Lopez Lopez danced rather impressively with his lovely Cuban wife. Mr. Hamburg was holding a conversation with an English teacher; his was the only voice we could hear above the noise.

Melody clutched my hand the second we walked into the gym. She didn't care for social situations. Hell, I wasn't exactly an expert myself.

Cafeteria tables festooned with ribbons were lined up by the bleachers. We made our way to a couple of empty seats. As I pulled out Melody's chair, I looked around for a familiar face.

I saw Buttercup all dressed up but still snapping pictures of people in awkward poses. Bill was there, attempting to dance with a girl who was, in my opinion, way too hot for him. I noticed Dylan with some other jocks, laughing in a corner.

Melody caught sight of Samantha and waved hello. I was horrified to see that Samantha was accompanied by a six-foot-tall animatronic Ken doll. Only when they approached us did I realize this must be her mysterious boyfriend.

"Hey, guys!" said Samantha with a wave. She was dressed fancier than I'd ever seen her, but it was a wasted effort. The formal dress emphasized her angular features, and it looked like an undertaker had applied her makeup. She reminded me of someone's unmarried great-aunt at a senior citizen's ball.

"Ben, this is Leon and Melody. I told you about them." *What did she tell him?* "Guys, this is my boyfriend, Ben."

"Hey!" He grinned. I had gone to shake his hand, but he

snapped his finger and pointed at me, leaving me with my hand stuck out like a dork. I wondered if his hair was real or just painted on.

"Nice to meet you, Ken."

"Ben."

"Sorry."

"Say, Sammy!" crooned Ben. "I've gotta go check myself in the mirror. What say you get us some punch and I'll be back, pronto!" He did the finger snap–point thing at us again. Samantha smiled in rapture as he left; then she walked off to the refreshment table.

I bit my lip to prevent myself from being a smart-ass. "He seems nice," I managed to say.

"A real dream." Melody had a twinkle in her eye. "I just hope Barbie doesn't get jealous." We both had a good laugh at Ben's expense.

"So what's Samantha doing dating Captain Hair Gel?" I asked. "I expected this guy to be a Nobel Prize–winning member of Amnesty International."

"He's good-looking. That can make up for a lot."

"Like what?"

"Oh, being superficial, for instance, or dumb. Or not be-ing able to golf."

I took her by the arm. "Let's dance."

Now, I had always assumed that dancing was something that just happened naturally, like walking or breaking wind. The second we were on the dance floor, I realized I had no idea what to do. I just kind of stood there.

I think Melody misinterpreted my awkwardness.

"We don't have to do this, Leon." Her head began the familiar downward tilt toward her toes.

"No, it's just . . . you know that stereotype that white people can't dance? I'm afraid that's my fault."

Melody placed one of my hands on her hip and I grabbed the other one. We began to try to sync ourselves to the beat.

I thought I was doing okay. I really did. But when Melody had to remind me to move quickly when the music was quick, I realized it was hopeless. I looked like this guy I saw getting Tasered on TV.

"You're doing fine, Leon."

"You really think so?"

"Yeah," she said, almost defiantly, "I do."

"Bless you for lying."

Mercifully, a slow number came on. The light show faded. For a few moments, we stood there, holding each other. Even in the semidarkness, I could trace her familiar scars. The ridge over her right eye. The way her upper and lower lips didn't connect on one side.

I pulled her close and laid my head on her shoulder. That was nice. I liked the feel of her shoulders. We snuggled closer. I kissed her neck.

Right when the song ended, I brushed her cheek. And jolted away.

"Leon? Leon, are you okay?" The music was loud again; she almost had to shout.

"I'm fine. Just got to run to the bathroom."

I rushed to the locker rooms. The reason I had to get

away was that for a moment I'd forgotten who I was dancing with. And when I went to nuzzle Melody's ear, *it wasn't there.*

I hurried to a sink and splashed some water on my face. Why had that rattled me so much? I knew she'd lost her external ears in the fire. It was just . . . just a little weird.

"You look like you've seen the devil, Leon."

I turned. "Hi, Dan."

"You *haven't* seen the devil, have you?"

"No."

Dan was looking surprisingly dapper in his black tux, with black shirt and black tie. His long hair was pulled back in a ponytail, and he hadn't drawn any visible tattoos on himself. He cleaned up nicely. Maybe his bosses were going to let him try his hand at soul acquisitions.

I combed my hair in the mirror. "Are you here with anyone, Dan?"

"When you've seen what I've seen, you're never truly alone." He glanced meaningfully over my shoulder before slithering out of the bathroom.

The conversation with Dan had taken my mind off Melody's face. *Accentuate the positive, Leon. Think about the parts your girlfriend has, not the ones she's missing.*

Suddenly, a hand grabbed my shoulder. I remembered what Dan had said about his unseen companion, and yelped. When I looked in the mirror and saw Dylan's reflection, I almost would have preferred a demon.

Dylan's hair was newly cut; he'd shaved and was wearing a tuxedo. It somehow didn't work; he reminded me of a prison inmate who'd been given new clothes upon release. He stared at my reflection with unsteady eyes.

We'd not spoken since the day I'd told him off after Spanish. I wondered if he'd forgotten the incident.

He belched and I smelled booze. He staggered a bit, then steadied himself on the sink. Maybe he wasn't angry, just drunk.

"Leon?" He seemed to notice me for the first time. "Hey, how's it going?"

"Fine. Who are you here with?"

Dylan reached into his jacket and pulled out a cheap whiskey flask. He took a slug and shuddered.

"Sonya. You know, from history class?"

Sonya, cute and athletic, was on the girls' basketball team. I reflected that if I was her date, I wouldn't be numbing myself with liquor.

"She's nice."

Dylan downed another shot. "Yeah. Do you have a date?"

"Melody Hennon," I said pointedly, remembering what he'd said about her.

Dylan had been putting the cap back onto his flask. When I said Melody's name, he paused. Then he winced.

"Uh, Leon, I . . . Sorry about what I said about her a while ago. I was just messing around. I didn't know she was your girlfriend."

Dylan looked so ashamed I had to remind myself he was the same guy who'd kicked my ass in sixth grade.

"It's okay," I said with a shrug. In an effort to appear

manly, I grabbed his flask and took a swig. Big mistake. I'd never had hard liquor before, and the ensuing coughing fit was so intense I was afraid a teacher would come to investigate.

Dylan whacked me on the back several times. "You're okay, buddy; just take a deep breath. There you go. Wipe off your mouth there. Here." He gave me a box of Tic Tacs and I ate a handful.

"Feel better?"

"Yeah. It just hit me kind of hard."

He pocketed the flask. "Get yourself a glass of punch and you'll feel fine." He placed his hand on the door. "Oh, and Amy Green asked me if I'd seen you. I think she's looking for you."

A slow song was playing when I left the restroom. I searched for Melody. To my horror, she was dancing with Dan. She didn't look frightened, though. I guessed he hadn't told her about his human-tooth collection.

So Amy was looking for me? Good. Now would be the time to prove my loyalty to Melody. I'd talk to Amy, maybe even ask her to dance, but nothing more. Our kiss had been a mistake.

I smelled Amy before I saw her. That same perfume that drowned out the gas leak in the chemistry lab. I turned.

Looking at Amy, I realized what God had in mind when he'd removed Adam's rib. This was what all women were supposed to be like.

Amy's dress was poufy and blue. While I knew nothing about these things, I could tell it was a lot more expensive than Melody's. It was also cut much lower in the front. She wore almost no makeup, just enough to accentuate her perfect features. Her hair was up; in fact, it was stacked so high that it seemed to defy gravity. Amy looked great before. Now, in her dress and makeup, she was a queen. A goddess. And suddenly, I knew that it would take a lot more than big talk for me to remember that Melody was the girl in my life.

"Hello, Leon."

Down, boy! Heel! "Hi."

"You look handsome." If she was being sarcastic, it didn't show.

"So do you! I mean–" *Damn it!*

"Do you think Melody would mind if we danced?"

Who? I glanced around the dance floor. Dan was now dancing with Buttercup, and I couldn't see Melody anywhere. Maybe she'd gone to the bathroom.

If I was stiff with Melody, I had rigor mortis with Amy. I thought back to the previous weekend, when we'd kissed and I'd lied to her about Melody. I now remembered why I had lied.

Like a man losing his eyesight, I tried to memorize every detail of what I saw. Amy's long, dangling earrings. (She could wear earrings.) The red lipstick on her perfect lips. The freckles on her shoulders . . . and lower.

We moved jerkily. I had a feeling that she was a much better dancer, but fortunately she allowed me to lead. Halfway through the song, she leaned in and whispered in my ear.

"You never called me."

So she hadn't said that on a whim. She wanted me to call her. Amy wanted me to call her!

"I'm sorry. I've been kind of..."

Amy grinned but didn't pull away. "It's okay. Are you and Melody having fun?"

"Yeah." *Fun. Lots and lots of fun.*

"You know, I kind of wish—" She suddenly stopped.

"What?"

She leaned her head into mine, until our cheeks were touching. I could feel her ear. "I'm here alone. I kind of wish I was here with you."

I flashed back to every lonely Friday night, every dance I hadn't gone to, every pathetic hour I'd spent pining over Amy. And apparently, all I'd had to do was ask. But like the dork I was, I waited. I waited until her parents were in the middle of a divorce, and then I went and got involved with Melody.

I pulled Amy just a little closer. "I wish that too." We danced in silence for a few moments. I could feel the curve of her back through the fabric of her dress.

The music ended and Amy pulled her head away. "You need to get back to Melody." There was something in her voice that implied that Melody was a pity date and I was being forced to spend time with her.

"Yeah," I sighed, with obvious regret.

We didn't separate. "Seriously. Call me. Let's get together."

"I'll do that."

We held each other for another second. Then she turned and walked away. Numbly, I searched out Melody.

Where the hell was Amy a month ago? She moves from my fantasies to reality just a couple of weeks too late.

I felt like an asshole for thinking that. Here was Melody, dressed up, for me, having a great time. And the next weekend, she was planning on letting me...

Why now, Amy? You knew I liked you. Why now?

"Leon? Are you okay?" It was Melody. She was looking at me with deep concern. I tried to smile at her, tried to see how beautiful she was, with her wig and dress and perfume. How she'd made herself beautiful for me.

I couldn't see it anymore. She was ugly again. She was the reason I couldn't have Amy. She was the one who was trapping me, the one who was keeping me from my dreams.

"I'm fine," I said, with a fake smile. "C'mon."

We danced a few more numbers, but no slow ones. We chatted with Samantha, with Dylan and his date, with Buttercup. I wanted to have fun, wanted Melody to have fun. It was like trying to enjoy the band on the *Titanic*. Letting Melody become more than a friend was the biggest mistake I'd ever made. I had been this close—*this close*—to hooking up with Amy. But I'd settled. I wound up with a girl I wasn't attracted to because I convinced myself I could never do any better. And the whole time, Amy had been waiting for me to ask her out.

When Melody and I stood for our picture, the photographer had to take three shots before he captured me with a believable smile.

I suffered through one final slow dance. Melody held me tight. I should have kissed her. I should have whispered sweet nothings into her ear canal. But I couldn't. I was actually angry with her. She'd ruined my dreams.

When the houselights came up, Dylan and Sonya cornered us.

"Hey, guys. A bunch of us are getting together at my place. Want to come?" I couldn't tell if he was being genuinely friendly or just trying to make up for insulting Melody.

"We can't," I replied before Melody could say anything. "Melody has to be back by midnight."

Dylan clapped me on the back and staggered off. I was glad to see Sonya fishing her keys out of her purse; she was driving.

I calmed down considerably on the way home. Melody didn't say anything, and I managed to decompress a little. Things were going to be okay. Things were going to be fine. Maybe I could talk to Melody later in the week. Tell her that things were getting a bit too serious. She'd said before that we could just be friends. Maybe I'd take her up on that. Of course, she'd said that long before I'd removed her shirt.

I didn't have to decide that night. The next day was Sunday; I could spend it in reflection. I could brace myself to tell Amy I couldn't see her again. Or to tell Melody . . .

As we pulled up to Melody's gate, she reached over and turned off the lights.

"We're almost an hour early, Leon."

I groaned internally. She wanted to sit here and kiss. And that felt like a chore, like something I was forced to do. I killed the engine.

"Um, Leon? There's a road that goes up to the barn. No lights. And my parents won't be mad if we're a half hour late."

Melody smiled at me. In the dark, I could see only her gleaming teeth. Her eyes were shadowed; they looked like empty sockets. She took my hand and gently placed it on her bare shoulder. I knew she expected me to lower my hand, to touch her chest.

She was about to give me what I'd always wanted, what I dreamed of more than anything. In her mind there was no reason for me to turn her down.

But I couldn't take what she was offering. I couldn't even sit here and kiss her. I couldn't lie to her for another second. She deserved to know.

"Melody." The crushed, defeated sound of my voice caused her to take her hand off mine. She turned and looked out the window at the darkness.

"What is it, Leon?" She knew what was coming.

"Melody, I had a great time tonight."

"Don't," she whispered sharply. "Don't. If you have something to say, get it over with."

I could still back out. I could grab her and kiss her and tell her she was wonderful, and she'd think she'd been imagining things.

But then I'd never be able to see Amy again.

"Melody . . . there's someone else."

I waited for the tears. The begging. Slaps, screams, sobs. There was just silence. Agonizing, long silence.

"Melody, say something."

She still didn't look at me. "You've said it all, Leon. It's that Amy girl, right?"

"Yes."

Melody smoothed her wig but didn't face me. "I thought so. That time at the bowling alley. I knew she liked you. I remember thinking it was a good thing you didn't feel the same way, or I wouldn't stand a chance."

I hated myself. I wanted to ram my fist through the windshield, to feel my knuckles break, to feel glass under my skin, to punish myself for being so weak, for hurting her like this. I wanted to stick my finger into the cigarette lighter. To crush my foot in the door.

But that wouldn't make things right.

"Melody, I'm sorry."

She didn't look at me. "Don't make this worse." She opened the door.

"Let me walk you up!"

"Don't!" she croaked. She was crying. But she didn't run. Dressed in her beautiful gown and heels, she opened and closed the gate and walked slowly up to her house. She didn't look back. I didn't drive off until I saw her front door open.

24

SUNDAY MORNING
COMING DOWN

When I woke up the next morning, I didn't remember the previous night's disaster until I saw my tuxedo crumpled on the floor of my bedroom. Then the images assaulted my brain like music from a radio unexpectedly being turned on at full volume: Dancing with Melody. Dancing with Amy. Amy telling me she wished she was my date. Melody walking silently to her house.

Shit. What now?

I pulled on some old clothes and stumbled to the bathroom. I felt sick to my stomach and I doubted that it was from that swig of Dylan's whiskey.

Mom met me in the kitchen, smiling at me as she cooked some pancakes at the stove.

"Well," she said, with a wink. "You got home awfully late."

I grunted and sat at the table. Mom scooped two pancakes onto a plate and set it in front of me.

"So how was the dance?"

"Fine."

She fixed herself a plate and sat opposite me.

"Did you get your picture taken?"

"Yeah." I picked at my food.

"Did Melody have a good time? Who all was there?" Jesus, not now. Not the third degree. Mom wanted to hear all about her son's romantic evening, his first dance, his first girlfriend. She had no idea how I'd screwed everything up, ruined Melody's first and probably only dance, and proved myself to be a shallow asshole.

"It was fine, Mom."

She wouldn't let it drop. "But what did you–"

"I said it was fine, okay! It was great! Why don't you leave me alone!"

The smile collapsed from my mother's face as she realized it wasn't shyness that was keeping me from talking. I felt like a first-class SOB. Mom watched me as I dumped my breakfast down the garbage disposal. I wanted to say something, tell her my problems, ask her for advice. But I couldn't. This wasn't her problem. Only I could solve it.

She didn't say anything as I stormed back to my bedroom. She seemed to know she couldn't help me. And that probably hurt her worse than my rudeness.

What was Melody doing now? Had she crept in and spent the night crying on her pillow? Had she stayed up all night talking to her mom as her dad and Tony loaded their shotguns? Maybe she was out on one of the horses, forcing it to run as fast as it could. Maybe she was talking to my yearbook picture, asking me why I'd been so cruel. Maybe she was still in bed.

I had to call her. It couldn't end like this. Even if it meant blowing everything with Amy, I could not lose the friendship of that strange, wonderful girl who had made me so happy.

That was the plan. But after an hour, I was still staring at my phone, like it was my opponent on some bizarre game show.

All I had to do was call her. And beg and apologize. Tell Melody I was dirt, scum, weak, horrible. She wouldn't forgive me. Not at first. But maybe after a week or so, she'd let it pass. And we'd go back to the way things were before.

There was only one problem. I wasn't sure I wanted things the way they were before.

I found myself regretting that kiss. Not with Amy, but with Melody. Back at the lock and dam. We'd been such good friends. Why hadn't I left it like that? Good friends, nothing more, not one bit of shame about kissing Amy. I could have dated Amy and still been pals with Melody.

But instead, I kissed her. Instead, I got all emotional and started telling her how I felt. I told Melody I liked her when the girl I really liked was there waiting for me.

If I called Melody now, we'd end up dating until the end of high school. Maybe longer.

Is that what I really want?

The school year would be over in a month and a half. Then Melody would go off to her scholars camp. She'd forget about me. She'd survive. When she graduated, she could take comfort in knowing she'd had a boyfriend once.

I drummed my fingers on my desk, then picked up the phone.

"Hello? Amy?"

25

NO REGRETS. REALLY.

Now, when I phoned Amy, I had told myself that this was just a friendly call. Just calling a pal. A buddy. A buddy who I'd kissed. A buddy who I would desperately like to take a shower with, but a buddy nonetheless.

"Leon! I was wondering if you were going to call me!" I could almost see her smile over the phone.

"Well, just wanted to say hi." *What are you wearing?*

"I had fun at the dance."

What did she mean by that? Was I reading too much into things?

"Me too. Hey, you busy? Want to grab something to eat?"

Totally innocent.

Over the phone line I heard water running. Dear God, she wasn't just getting out of the shower, was she? I was so distracted I almost didn't hear her answer.

"–just stepping out the door. But there's this party next Friday. Want to come with me?"

The last time I'd gone to a party, we'd played pin the tail on the donkey.

"Okay!"

"Great. See you at school."

"Yeah . . ."

Okay, so Amy had just invited me to a party. Okay, we'd kissed. Okay, I'd told Amy that Melody was just a friend. Okay, Melody's heart was broken, and I really should be calling her, apologizing, swearing that I still liked her, that she was getting upset over nothing.

Only she wasn't getting upset over nothing. I had a date with Amy Green the next weekend. That was something. And if I went to that party, then it would be over forever with Melody.

That Monday at school there was a note taped to my locker. I recognized Melody's handwriting.

Dear Leon,
We need to talk. I don't want it to end this way. Leon, I love you. Not

because you're nice to me, but because you're my best friend. I know you feel that way about me too. Amy doesn't care about you like I do. I think we can work this out.

Can we talk after school? I want to talk in private. Maybe you could drive me out to the lock and dam and we could talk again. Leon, I want to make you happy. Amy can't say that.

Melody

Ouch. The first time a girl said she loved me and it was in a note begging me not to leave her. She said she wanted to make me happy. That was what I'd always secretly fantasized about. I didn't need anything else. I didn't need—

"Hey, Leon. Whatcha reading?" It was Amy. She was wearing the same halter top she'd had on at the mall. She'd tied it at the bottom, revealing her flat belly. I hadn't noticed in the dim lights at the dance, but she had an overall tan. She'd probably been to a tanning booth. I didn't see any pale spots, so she must not have been wearing anything.

I quickly crumpled the note. *I don't need you, Amy, but, Jesus H. Christ, I want you.*

"C'mon, let me see," she teased. "Is it something dirty?"

I held it behind my back. "Maybe."

She playfully lunged for it. "Don't make me get rough with you, Leon."

"Hey, you wouldn't want me to have to eat this, would you? You know I can!"

We both laughed as the first bell rang. Amy gently shoved me. For half a decade we'd never touched; now it seemed she couldn't keep her hands off me.

"Watch it. We still on for Friday?"

"You bet." She mussed my hair, then took off down the hall. I leaned against my locker, dreamily watching her bare brown back.

As I stopped to retrieve my chemistry notes, I caught sight of a lone figure halfway down the hall. Bald, wide-eyed, and earless. Melody had seen the whole thing. She quickly turned away.

"Melody! Wait!"

She started to run and collided with Bill, causing the binder she was carrying to spill its contents all over the floor. She disappeared in a whirlwind of loose-leaf paper.

I leaned against the side of the Thomsons' van and surveyed the acres of rusted-out heaps in the salvage yard. "Every one of those cars used to be someone's baby," my father had once told me. "Every one of those cars is someone's broken heart."

Right after school I had gone home to crash, only to be immediately interrupted by a frantic call from Johnny. His van had shot craps again and he needed me to pick him up at the garage.

I hadn't been in the mood to play chauffeur. Melody had vanished; I hadn't been able to find her anywhere in school.

Maybe she'd gone home. But Johnny was stranded, and despite the years of insults, he wouldn't have left me stuck somewhere.

Johnny was pacing around the van like a father in a maternity ward. "I'm sure it's nothing," he kept saying. "Probably just the battery or something."

I looked at the pool—black oil, green antifreeze, red transmission fluid, and a bluish liquid I couldn't place—that had formed under the vehicle. "Maybe your carburetor just became disconnected from the fuel injector."

Johnny looked hopeful. "You think so?"

"No."

Mr. Garzi, the Pakistani man who ran the salvage yard, garage, and towing service, finished looking at the engine. "Okay, John. Fifty dollars."

Johnny smiled. "Really? Only fifty bucks to fix this?"

Mr. Garzi laughed. "No. I'll give you fifty bucks for the tires and radio."

Johnny whimpered. "Don't be like that. C'mon, what needs to be done?"

"Let me see. New engine, new transmission, new brakes, new U-joint, new muffler, new—"

"How much will it cost to get it running for another two weeks?"

"Two hundred."

As I drove Johnny home, he stared morosely at the estimate in his hand. "Do me a favor, Leon, and tell Jimmy the repairs are going to cost three hundred."

Normally, I would have mentioned that two hundred

was pretty cheap for fixing a van with an exhaust system made of duct tape, but my brain was elsewhere.

"Damn it!" Johnny continued. "I needed the van this weekend too. I'm taking Jessica out this Friday."

Jessica was a cheerleader for Francis Howell High. Johnny had been dating her for a few weeks.

"Yeah, and you don't want to miss two-for-one tacos at the Barn."

"Don't be a goober, Leon. I was taking her to the party at Jamal's house. I want to impress her, and now I have to ask her to drive."

That was the party Amy had invited me to. "Guess I'll see you there," I commented.

Johnny looked surprised. "Who the hell invited...I mean, Leon, good buddy, what say you and I double-date?"

"Sure, whatever."

I could see the little thoughts forming in his head. "Yeah, double-date. Jessica's pretty smart, so you and Melody can impress her with your smart talk and stuff. And you got this big old backseat here...."

There was no use putting it off any longer. Melody, of course, hadn't sat with us at lunch, but everyone had believed me when I'd said she was volunteering in the library.

"Hang on, Johnny. Melody's not coming with me." Melody wouldn't be coming with me anywhere, ever again. Not bowling, or mini golfing, or to the movies, or to her barn.

"You ought to convince her to quit wasting time studying," said Johnny, misunderstanding me. "Then she'd have more time to hang out with you. Not that being with you would be any more exciting..."

We had arrived at Johnny's house. "It's not that. We, um... we're kind of on the outs."

For the first time that day, Johnny looked at me seriously. "Since when?"

"After the dance. It wasn't working out."

"Wasn't working out" in the sense that Melody and I were best friends, enjoyed hanging out, and liked all the same things.

Johnny stared at me like a cow chewing its cud. I had to say something.

"So then Amy asked me if I wanted to go to the party with her."

I had stopped the car, but Johnny wasn't getting out. He just sat there blinking at me for a few seconds. "Oh. Okay. Well, I guess I'll see you tomorrow." He left.

I had expected him to be sarcastic or to blow off any news that didn't concern him and Jessica. Instead, he seemed rather shocked.

That was something else: I was going to have to tell everyone about what had happened. Samantha, Jimmy, Rob, my parents... and if I told them the truth, I would be the bad guy. There was no way I could make it look like the breakup was nobody's fault. I had dumped the only girl who'd ever thought I was special.

The worst thing was I could have Melody back with one phone call. All I had to do was pick up the phone and I could start to make things right.

But I wasn't going to. No matter how badly I hurt

Melody, no matter how much of a jerk that made me, it was easier to hurt her than to go through life knowing I'd passed up a chance to be with Amy Green. Maybe she'd dump me in a week. Maybe we'd end up hating each other. But right now, I held a winning lottery ticket, and all I had to do was cash it.

26

THE FIRE

The next day was Tuesday. Friday I would be taking Amy to a party. I would go to a party—a *cool* party, not like the all-night Dungeons & Dragons, Monty Python, video game marathons I usually attended. And I'd be going with the prettiest girl in school. This was what I'd always dreamed of. So when I glanced in the bathroom mirror that morning, why did I look like I'd just sat on a toilet plunger?

It was just guilt, I thought as I showered. Just guilt. Melody was a good person and I'd made her sad. Just a little guilt. Not regret. Guilt.

As I lathered, rinsed, and repeated, I resolved to talk to her. Not right away. After she'd had a chance to calm down. She could spend a couple of weeks cursing me, hating me, tearing up my love letters (well, I'd actually never written her any), and realizing what an ass I really was. Maybe then she'd be willing to talk. Other guys stayed friends with their exes; why couldn't I?

The more I thought about it, the more confident I felt. Melody's locker was right next to mine. I'd talk to her every day. Maybe she wouldn't listen. Maybe she'd beg me to take her back. Maybe I'd spend the rest of the school year in the doghouse. But after the summer, after she'd gone off to her scholars thing, she might hate me a little less. And lack of hate would be just like the close bond we'd enjoyed that spring.

That decided, I let my thoughts drift to Amy. Her full-body tan. The way she kept grabbing and poking at me. Her smile, her laugh, her legs. I began to think about what it would be like to take her to the party Friday night. Then, after, maybe I'd drive her out to the lock and dam. . . .

Downstairs, the washing machine kicked on, causing my shower to turn ice-cold. All thoughts of Amy shrank away.

When I arrived at school later that morning, I was determined to begin patching things up with Melody. The first thing I'd do was go straight to her locker and wait for her. Let her know I still cared about her, still wanted to be friends. She'd probably turn and walk away, but I wouldn't give up.

When I arrived at our locker bank, I had expected to see

a girl with a burned but oddly pretty face. Instead, I found Dan, who was busy admiring the framed picture of Jeffrey Dahmer that was now hanging in Melody's locker. I hadn't felt so disappointed since *King Kong vs. Godzilla* had been preempted for the presidential debates.

Dan smiled his Norman Bates smile at me and flashed the devil sign with two fingers. "Leon," he whispered.

"Dan. Um, what are you doing in Melody's locker?" *Please, please, let him just be storing stuff there for a little bit.*

"Melody asked me to swap yesterday."

"Did she say why?" I was feeling ill, and not just because of Dan.

"Something about hating you and never wanting to see you again." He shut his locker and made a bizarre series of hand gestures over the lock. "Oh, and she told me to give you this."

He passed me a DVD.

"*The Care Bears Movie?*"

Dan did a double take. "Whoops, that's mine. Here."

He passed me the *Twilight Zone* DVD, the one I'd given Melody for her birthday.

"You didn't take my advice, did you?" he said, sounding disappointed. "You blurted everything out the second you saw her."

I shrugged. Dan shook his head in reproach.

I stared at the movie in my hand. I'd have to search Melody out now, instead of casually meeting on neutral turf. This was going to be hard.

"You know," mused Dan, "I always kind of liked Melody."

For a second, I had the horrifying thought that Dan was going to ask Melody out and I'd have to let him. But I immediately realized she'd never agree to a date with him.

"Melody's nice," I muttered, trying to get out of the conversation.

Dan nodded. "She's been through *fire*."

Most of us had always regarded Dan as an amusement, sort of like a village idiot. I wasn't enjoying him now, however.

"Dude, that is *so* not cool!" I barked.

Dan grinned his unnerving grin again. "I don't mean she's been through *a* fire. I mean she's been through *fire*." Seeing my confused and wrathful expression, he explained further. "When something goes through fire, it's either burned up or hardened."

"Kinda like the cafeteria hamburgers."

Dan shook his head. "Melody, she went through the fire when she was a kid. She went through more fire than anyone in this school. And it made her hard. It toughened her. Made her strong. I always admired that."

I began to inch away. Dan grabbed me by the shoulder. "Then you come along. You start making her soft. Start putting out the old fire. She's not as hard anymore."

I remembered an old street preacher I had seen ranting on the corner in Kansas City. Dan strongly reminded me of him. "But now you're gone," he continued, almost in a whisper. "And she's passed back through the fire again. She's harder than she's ever been. She's almost *Unbreakable!*"

I pulled away from Dan and practically ran toward Mr. Jackson's room. Dan hollered after me. "Your fire's coming, Leon! The fire's coming for *you!*"

Dan's old locker was in the industrial arts hallway, one of the oldest wings of the school, with exposed pipes, water stains, and big metal doors. I was surprised he was willing to give up the atmosphere.

It was study hall, and I was standing by Melody's third locker of the year, hoping she'd stop by. I couldn't take the thought of her hating me so much. There had to be something of the friendship left.

When she found me standing there, she smiled. Not her full-force smile, but a smile all the same.

"Hi, Leon."

"Melody."

We stood there in silence.

"Leon, are you really going out with Amy?"

Straight to the point.

"Yes." Wasn't I?

Melody let out such a long sigh I expected her to deflate.

"I guess I know why, Leon. I always worried this would happen. Guys don't ever choose the ugly girl, except in the movies. And even there, they're not really ugly."

Where had I heard that before?

"Melody, you're not ugly."

"Don't. Please. Just answer me this: Why did you date me? Why did you make me think I was pretty and special to you?"

She said this with her eyes completely closed.

"Because you are. . . ."

"No, I'm not. If I was, we'd still be together. So if you're leaving me, if it's over, just tell me why you ever made me think you cared." Her eyes didn't open.

"Melody, I did care. I guess . . . I just think we'd be better off as friends."

She opened her eyes. "We could have been, Leon. When we started on that social studies project, I thought, 'Hey, here's a guy who likes hanging out with me! Here's a guy who enjoys spending time with me!' "

"Yeah, but—"

"But nothing!" she suddenly screamed, looking at me with raw anger. Down the hall, someone turned on a screeching table saw. She raised her voice.

"Remember how I told you we could just be friends? Remember? But you kissed me! And kept kissing me! And tried to screw me, and I *came this close to letting you*! Why would you do that if you didn't like me like that?"

"Because I'm a jerk."

Melody slammed her locker, then opened it and slammed it again. "Don't you goddamn dare! No self-pity! You got what you wanted! You got the cute girl! So do me a favor and never talk to me again! I wish I'd never met you, Leon Sanders!"

Mr. Knight stuck his head out of the shop to see what was going on. I took my cue and left.

That day, I was the one who ate alone in the library.

• • •

I lay on my bed, flipping through the previous year's Zummer High yearbook. Year after year Mom would give me money to buy the expensive thing. Then I wouldn't let her look at it, thanks to the filthy cartoons Johnny would always draw in the autograph section.

The guys who put out the yearbook were the biggest dorks in the school, and yet it was always a celebration of the popular kids. Huge candid pictures of Dylan, Amy, and the rest of the in crowd graced every other page. Aside from my microscopic class picture and some group shots, I wasn't anywhere.

Even by just looking in the index, you could tell who was a Dylan and who was a Leon:

Campbell, Buttercup: *Bulldog Bugle,* National Honor Society, Christian Teens, Young Republicans

Dzyan, Dan: Zummer Dungeons & Dragons Club

Franklin, Robert: Track, National Honor Society, Key Club

Green, Amy: Cheerleading, Sophomore Class Vice President, Softball, Tennis, Homecoming Court

Hennon, Melody: National Honor Society, Youth Scholars

Janes, Samantha: National Honor Society, Youth in Government, Young Democrats, Key Club (sec.), Students Against Drunk Driving, French Club (pres.)

Sanders, Leon: Computer Club (sec.), Key Club (VP), Chess Club, National Honor Society, Youth in Government

Shelton, Dylan: Football, Track, Baseball, Lacrosse, Wrestling

Thomson, James: Football

Thomson, Jonathan: Football

I flipped to a well-thumbed page. It was the cheerleaders' summer fund-raising car wash. Amy stood at the forefront laughing while Cassandra flipped some soapy water at her. Amy was wearing a string bikini top. The picture was grainy and out of focus, but I'd looked at it so often the yearbook naturally opened to that page.

And now Amy wanted to go out with me. I'd have thought I would have to ask Dan about selling my soul to arrange something like that. Life would be perfect, except for one small detail.

Mom's knock interrupted my thoughts. Though my door wasn't locked, she knew better than to barge into her teenage son's room unannounced.

"Come in!"

Mom was holding the cordless phone. "It's Melody," she said in a curious whisper.

Holy shit! The yearbook went flying as I lunged for the phone. Mom deftly avoided being tackled.

I glared at her until she closed the door behind her.

"Melody?"

"So you didn't even tell your mom?" She sounded resigned, like she hadn't expected any better from me.

"Melody, I'm sorry." I wasn't even sure what I was apologizing for this time. Kissing Amy, breaking up with Melody, not being honest . . . it was all running together.

"I was just watching Comedy Central. *Kids in the Hall* was on. Remember when we watched that?"

"Yeah." I seriously doubted I'd ever ask Amy to view that show with me.

"That was the first time I saw you outside of school. I had so much fun. I think that's when I started to like you."

With one hand, I flipped open the yearbook and turned to my class's pictures. The only evidence of Melody was her name in the *Not Pictured* note.

"Melody, what can I do to make this right?"

There was a sharp intake of breath over the line. "I was going to ask you the same thing, Leon. You know I'd do anything. It's bad enough you dump me, but now I'm going to have to see you every day with that . . . girl. Every day I'm going to be reminded of how I would have done anything for you. And the one thing I couldn't give you was the one thing you needed. I can't be pretty, Leon. But do you really think Amy's going to treat you as good as I did?"

"Amy treats me fine."

"I'm sure she does." Melody wasn't being sarcastic. "But remember this, Leon. I loved everything about you. I think you're amazing. And you just might find out that a girl like Amy doesn't think like that. She'll try to change you, and you'll let her, and you still won't be happy because you'll always be trying to please her. And you never had to try to please me. All you had to do was smile at me and I was happy. But I guess it didn't work both ways. Stupid me for thinking that." Her voice cracked on the last word and she didn't speak for a while. When she did, her voice trembled.

"Are you going to give up what we have? If you take me

back, I won't mention Amy again. We can go on like it didn't happen."

I scanned the faces of the sophomore class until I found Amy. Even though her photo was the same half-inch blur as everyone else's, it seemed to dominate the page. I had kissed those lips, and I would again.

"I'm sorry, Melody."

She hung up.

27

MEATLOAF WITH A SIDE OF GUILT

I had almost convinced myself to tell Amy I couldn't take her to the party the next day. I had to do the honorable thing and patch things up with Melody. Maybe not what I wanted to do, but it was the right thing.

Of course, if we always did what we *should*, then we wouldn't have wars or car alarms. The second I saw Amy sitting on the edge of my lab table, I knew I was happily going to do the wrong thing. She was wearing *short* shorts, her bare thighs pressed down on the desk where I'd taken a hundred naps.

She looked up and smiled at me. "Hey, Leon. You ready for tomorrow?"

"You bet." *Melody who?*

"Great. Pick me up around seven. I think you remember the address, don't you?" She held out her hand and allowed me to help her down from the table. There was a sweaty print where she'd been sitting.

Jimmy and Johnny stared at me, more slack-jawed than usual.

"Jesus," said Johnny when I sat down. "I thought you were full of it. You're really going out with her?"

I shrugged, as if Amy was just another of my many dates. For the first time since we were thirteen, the twins looked at me with something like respect. For once people were noticing me. It was a nice feeling.

I stood there in the lunch line, clutching my tray, afraid to enter the cafeteria. By now the twins had surely told Rob and Samantha that I had left Melody. What would they think? And what if Melody showed up?

An overweight guy behind me shoved me aside and I walked toward my usual table. What the hell, I didn't owe anyone any explanations.

Samantha was engrossed in a book, oblivious of the loud argument Rob and Johnny were having about baseball.

"Hey, Leon," said Rob as I sat down, "who's the better pitcher, Maglio or Gonzalez?"

I had no idea who either of those people was. "Maglio, hands down," I replied. Johnny snorted in triumph. Rob gave me a disgusted look.

I wasn't interested. Glancing around the cafeteria, I wondered if Melody was here. Where was she sitting? I guessed she had crawled back into the hole she had lived in before we met. Back having lunch alone in the library.

"Looking for someone?" Samantha smirked at me over the top of her novel.

"No." I reluctantly turned back to our table.

Samantha continued to stare at me. "You're looking for Melody, aren't you? Seeing where she'll sit now that you ditched her."

"No, I'm not!"

Samantha went back to her book. "Then I guess it won't matter to you that she's right over there."

My head snapped around. Samantha hadn't been lying. Head held high, eyes forward, Melody emerged from the lunch line. Even from the other side of the room, I could see the hard expression on her rough features. I remembered what Dan had told me earlier about passing through fire.

Without pausing, she strode forward. She was headed our way.

I thought back to the first time she had sat with us, just a month or so before. How she had looked at the floor, mumbled, and held her tray in front of her like a shield. That girl was long gone. Melody walked like someone who knew exactly where she was going and what she was going to do.

I felt sweaty all of a sudden. How could I face her? I never thought she'd want to sit with me after how I'd treated her. But why shouldn't she? Samantha, Rob, and Johnny had been nice to her. What right did I have to make her give that up?

Just a few yards before she reached our table, she swiveled to her right and approached another one.

Buttercup was sitting there, along with some people I didn't know. Was Melody going to sit there? Just join a bunch of strangers?

By God she was. Leaning over the shoulder of a guy who'd given me a serious wedgie in junior high, she pointed at an empty chair and said something. The guy shrugged and Melody sat. Just like that.

"Dumped her, did you?" Rob's snide remark turned me around. My trio of friends were watching me gaping at Melody.

"Um." It was all I could think of to say.

Rob shook his head. "Too bad. She was really nice."

"Too nice for Leon, that's for sure," Johnny said, chuckling.

"Guys, drop it," I snapped.

Rob couldn't resist. "Maybe I should give her a jingle."

"Yeah, but you should call her first," said Johnny, without missing a beat. They slapped fists.

I jumped up. "Shut the hell up, both of you!" Rob and Johnny stopped laughing. They didn't look hurt, just a little annoyed.

Samantha sighed and closed her book. "I think I'll go to the library," she said, and was gone.

"What the hell's your problem?" asked Johnny.

I ate in silence. When the bell rang at the end of the lunch period, I ventured one last look in Melody's direction. There she sat at another table. And she was talking. How was this possible?

As I was dumping my tray, silverware and all, into the trash, Johnny walked up beside me.

"Sorry you dumped her?" he asked sincerely.

"Nah, I just kind of feel bad."

"Don't." He placed his hand on my back. "She'll be okay."

"I hope so."

"Dude, don't sweat it." Johnny smiled and we started back to class. "Hey, remember what we used to say in elementary school when you wanted to force the other kids to do something?"

"Huh?"

"You remember. Like if you thought everyone shouldn't step on the yellow tiles. What did you say?"

"Hell if I remember."

"Think back. *If you do that, then...*"

Suddenly, it came back to me. The little fourth graders lined up behind a teacher, whispering so they wouldn't be heard. *"If you do that... then you like Melody."*

Johnny nodded. "If you can't make the basket, then you like Melody. If you can't jump the fence, you like Melody. Last one to the bus stop likes Melody."

"Why are you bringing that up?"

"Because all her life, Melody's been the butt of everyone's jokes. Now look at her. She's finally stopped thinking of herself as a punch line. You were probably the first person who ever treated her like a normal human. She's better off because of that."

I thought about that on the way back to class. Melody no longer needed me to tell her she wasn't a freak. She believed it. She didn't need me anymore.

28

JETHRO GOES TO THE CITY

I slapped on a little of Dad's aftershave and regarded myself in the mirror. Not too shabby. Not too shabby at all. In half an hour I'd be picking up Amy for the party. Picking up the hottest girl in school for the party!

I was ready. New sneakers. Clean jeans. One of my few shirts without a funny saying on it. I had money in my wallet, gas in my tank, and breath mints in reserve. After a second's hesitation, I slipped the battered pack of condoms into my pocket as well. I was prepared.

"My, don't we look handsome?" said my mother with a

smile as I exited the bathroom. I reddened under her gaze. Here I was, seventeen years old, and she still could make me feel like I was three.

"I'll be back late tonight," I told her.

"No later than midnight," she cautioned. "Is Melody coming here, or are you picking her up?"

I guessed I couldn't put off telling her. "I'm not going with Melody. I'm going with Amy Green. You haven't met her."

Mom stopped smiling. She seemed to realize finally what had happened at the dance.

"What about Melody?"

"We broke up. Mutual thing." *Liar, liar!*

Mom opened her mouth, then closed it. "Okay. Well. Have a good time, no drinking. Call us if you need a ride." Mom said that every time I drove anywhere. I wasn't sure if she meant I should call them if I was too drunk to drive or simply if my car broke down on me.

The car. As I stepped outside, I looked at the gray monster. I'd always loved the heap; it was perfect for taking five or ten of my closest friends for a ride. But now that I was taking Amy out, I wished I drove something a little nicer. I mean, the dents gave it character, and the HANG UP AND DRIVE! bumper sticker was cute, but it wasn't really classy enough for a girl like Amy.

I sort of regretted agreeing to drive Johnny and his date. I wanted to have some moments alone with Amy, and Johnny wasn't the type of guy who enhanced a romantic atmosphere.

I blared my horn when I pulled up in front of his house.

He strutted out a few seconds later, dressed in imitation designer clothes. On another guy, that might have worked. Johnny, however, looked like a farmer on his way to church. Jessica held his hand.

Johnny threw open the back door and hopped in. Jessica, obviously irritated that he didn't hold the door for her, climbed in behind him. I glanced at her in the rearview mirror. She was skinny and redheaded. Pretty, yes, but kind of gangly and awkward. Not nearly as beautiful as my date. The group dynamic had shifted. Now I was the guy who had the good-looking girlfriend.

"Hey, Leon!" hollered Johnny. "Did you hear the one about the two nuns at the sausage factory?" Jessica rolled her eyes.

"Uh, Johnny, no crude jokes tonight, okay?" What would Amy think?

"Huh? Okay."

I remembered how Johnny had told the story about the hooker at the leper colony in front of Melody and she'd laughed. I quickly crushed the memory.

My car started on the second try. Fortunately, it was making only the clunking and wheezing sounds that night, and not the ominous grinding noise. I sped off to Amy's house.

It was the first time I'd been there in the daylight. Every house in the subdivision was less than five years old. The developers had bulldozed an old-growth forest and planted these buildings. Dan described these neighborhoods as "too new to have ghosts."

Just before I could get out to ring the bell, Amy jogged out of her house. She shouted something to someone inside, then tried to pull open the car door. I had to lean over and open it from the inside.

As Amy sat down, her ponytail swung over and smacked me right in the face. I probably could have died happy right then. She kissed me, half on the mouth, half on the cheek. While I was introducing Jessica, Johnny winked at me. He was impressed.

Conversation was kind of stilted on the way over. I wasn't sure Johnny was capable of not discussing bodily functions; he just sat silently. And I still felt awkward around Amy. What did she like to talk about?

You never had trouble talking to Melody.

I tried to kill the annoying little thought, but it wouldn't shut up. By the time I managed to block it, I was driving nearly seventy.

There were about twenty cars parked in front of the small house. The *thunk-thunk* of hip-hop music rattled the windows. Clearly, the host's parents were out of town.

I parked, and hand in hand, Amy and I walked into the house. It was hard to keep the big cheesy grin off my face. People would notice when I walked into the party, and not because I had something caught in my teeth. And not because they were staring at my date's scarred face. Now I just had to make sure I didn't screw up and embarrass Amy.

You never worried about embarrassing Melody.

Festivities, it seemed, were in the basement. The second we went downstairs, we were assaulted by the stench of human bodies, smoke, and beer. The deafening music vibrated off every surface in the rec room.

There were about twenty or thirty people here, and I didn't know a soul. Everyone was dancing, laughing, and having a great time. I went to touch Amy's hand, but she had already bolted to meet some guy.

He was a huge black dude, well over six feet tall. "Jamal!" Amy shrieked as she hugged him. My fists clenched. Why was she so happy to see him?

Jamal apparently knew Johnny. They smacked hands. Johnny introduced Jessica. I waited for Amy to introduce me, but she didn't. Eventually, Jamal left to greet other guests.

Melody never ignored you around other people.

Before I realized he had gone, Johnny returned with a six-pack. Amy and Jessica each took a beer. I wasn't much of a drinker but wanted to fit in. Unfortunately, I couldn't bring myself to drink when I'd be driving, so I stuck my unopened can behind a couch. Johnny, who was already chugging his, didn't notice.

I glanced around the room. I recognized Dylan among the faces. There were several people I knew by sight but not name. Other than that, I was among strangers.

Amy said something to me, but I couldn't hear her over the music. She gestured that she was going to go say hi to some friends, and faded off in the crowd. I turned to say something to Johnny but he was gone too.

I suddenly felt out of my depth. I didn't drink; I didn't smoke; I didn't like rap; and I hardly knew anyone here.

Amy had been right: it was unhealthy that I always hung out with the same four or five people. When they were gone, I felt really self-conscious, like if I tried talking to anyone, I'd look like a nerd.

Melody never left your side when you went out. You were the one who took care of her.

Amy was on the other side of the basement, laughing with some friends. Wondering if it would come off as obsessive, I made my way toward her. Someone grabbed me from behind.

I half expected Jamal, ready to throw me out of his party for being a loser. It was Dylan.

"Dude!" he howled, raising a frothy plastic cup. "Hell of a party! Wooo!"

"Yes. Woo." I wanted to hate this guy. I wanted to remember how he'd beaten me up and insulted Melody. But all I could think of at the moment was that he was someone I knew, someone who would talk to me.

Dylan chugged most of his beer. "Dude, did I see you come in with Amy Green?"

I straightened with pride. "She's my date."

"You freakin' rock, Leon!" This apparently called for another drink. He grabbed a can out of a cooler. "But, um, weren't you dating, um . . ."

"No!"

Dylan popped the top of his beer, then shoved it at me. "You rock, Leon! You goddamn rock! Woo!" He disappeared, howling, into the crowd.

I hoped he'd end up with a football scholarship or something. The man would fit in well at college.

Rather than turn down drinks all night, I decided to carry around my beer. I'd been at the party for only ten minutes and I'd sweated through my shirt. Every time I tried to stand somewhere, someone would bang into me. It was too uncomfortable to hang out, too loud for conversation. Johnny had vanished with Jessica. I searched for Amy.

The crowd, I noticed, was moving away from the center of the room. Several couples were dancing to the vicious beat. Some moved quite well; others were too confident or too blitzed to care. The crowd shouted. Girls shrieked. Guys howled.

I realized that Amy was one of the dancers, partnered up with Jamal. He was a good dancer. Amy, not so much, but she followed his lead. I felt a twinge of misplaced jealousy. They were just dancing, after all. All I had to do was wait for the song to end and cut in.

Yeah. All I had to do. Like that was going to happen. There was no way I was going to attempt to dance in front of all these people. I simply stood on the outskirts of the crowd, hoping Amy would remember me.

You never had to try to impress Melody.

The voice in my head was so insistent that it was hard not to verbally argue. I gnawed my lip to stop my mouth from moving. If I started talking to myself, I'd end up double-dating with Dan and his voices.

More and more people joined in the dancing. Amy changed partners. I kept telling myself that the next dance I'd grab her, but I always lost my nerve. Sweaty people smashed into me. The temperature of the basement began to approach sauna levels and I started to get real thirsty. The beer was tempting, but the mental image of a cop smelling even half a can of beer on my breath scared the piss out of me.

Finally, I couldn't take it anymore. I had to get some fresh air. I toyed with the idea of asking Amy to come with me, but she was having too much fun. Screw it, if she wouldn't make an effort to be with me . . .

I fought my way upstairs and found the bathroom. The heat had caused me to sweat away any chance of needing to use it, so I ran some water and washed my face. What the hell was wrong with me? Here I was, at a party with a beautiful girl, and I was having a lousy time.

I recalled something from just one week before, on the way to the dance. Something Melody had said.

My parents are going to be out of town next weekend, Leon.

That was right now. And to be at this party, I'd given up a chance to . . .

I was locked in a bathroom, pretending to pee. My date was getting passed around the dance floor; no one here wanted to talk to me; and I was bored out of my skull. And I was here by choice. Instead of taking off Melody's clothes. Instead of seeing her whole body. Instead of becoming a man.

What the fuck had I been thinking? Just because Amy was a little prettier . . . well, a lot prettier. A whole lot. I thought of her in the halter top. The bikini picture in the yearbook. The way she kept kissing and touching me.

Just be patient. The time will come. You would have been using Melody, anyway.

Much as I didn't want to, I had to go back downstairs. I wasn't going to dance or drink, and conversation was impossible. I guessed I'd just sweat in a corner until Amy decided it was time to leave.

When I walked back through the living room, I saw that three guys from another school had turned on the video game system. Two of them forced electronic men to beat the hell out of each other while the third shouted advice.

"Hit B! No, B! Jesus, you suck!" They didn't notice me.

"Hit B and C at the same time," I suggested. On the screen, one muscleman beat the other's face into the ground.

"Tight!" shouted the victor. The loser rolled his eyes and handed the controller to the spectator.

"I'll pass. Let the new guy have a go."

I hesitated. But what harm would one game be? I grabbed the controller and began to play. The two other guys hollered advice.

Three games later I was undefeated. "So how come you're not down with everyone else?" asked my opponent, a little bitterly.

"I can't stand rap," I answered simply.

"All right, gimme a shot," said one of the other guys. "What's your name, anyway?"

"Leon."

"I'm Mike. This is Brian and Brian."

Mike and Brian No. 1 began battling, and Brian No. 2 and I shouted what they were doing wrong. Finally, I was having fun. Sitting there with three other guys, playing a game that I could have played any night, while my date danced with every other teenager in east Missouri. It never occurred to me to go back downstairs.

• • •

After saving the world from alien invasion, liberating Europe, and taking the Cincinnati Bengals to the Super Bowl, I knew I had to stop.

"Gotta fly, guys," I said, happy that I had managed to do something fun that night. I tried not to think about Melody and how we would have done a lot more than play video games.

"Take care, Leon," said Mike, without turning around. "Let's get together sometime."

I wandered back down the stairs. I noticed there were fewer people now. Apparently, some of the guests had passed through the living room without my even noticing. For a few minutes I couldn't find Amy and thought she had left without me. I found her sitting on a couch, talking to two douche bags.

They were a couple of good-looking guys from another school. They reminded me of Dylan, only without the moronic charm. They sat on either side of Amy, hanging on her every word. Something told me they weren't interested in her cheerleading stories.

Amy didn't notice me as I awkwardly stood there, and eventually I had to interrupt.

"Hey, Amy?"

She looked up. "Oh, hi, Leon. I wondered where you ran off to."

Not enough to look for me, apparently. "You about ready to go?"

One of the human piles of garbage shot me an evil look but didn't say anything.

Amy yawned. "Yeah, I guess so."

"I'll go get Johnny."

I found him standing in a corner, his tongue rammed down Jessica's throat. He disengaged just long enough to tell me he had another ride home.

Amy joined me at the top of the stairs. So did the two pricks she'd been talking to.

"Leon, you don't mind if we give Andy and Conner a ride home, do you?"

I minded.

"Sure. You live nearby?"

"Actually," said one of the asswipes, "we live out in Wright City."

"That's like twenty miles west of here," I whined.

He laughed. "Then we better hit the road."

29

NOT EXACTLY PARADISE,
BUT BY NO MEANS
AN UNPLEASANT EXPERIENCE,
BY THE DASHBOARD LIGHT

I stood next to the pump at Garzi's Gas 'n' Go, spending my last ten bucks on fuel. It had taken us half an hour to drive Dumb and Dumber out to Wright City. Amy sat turned around in her seat, talking to my passengers. All they talked about was music I didn't listen to, movies I hadn't seen, and pop stars I hated.

No one talked to me. I was a hired chauffeur.

Now we were back in St. Christopher. It was nearly two in the morning. Amy sat on my hood, talking on her cell phone.

"Okay, Mom. I'll be home in ten minutes." So much for any alone time with Leon.

Amy rummaged in her purse and pulled out her ever-present cigarettes.

"You shouldn't smoke while I'm pumping gas."

She lit up. "I'm too young to die."

I angrily shoved the pump back into the slot. I might as well not have existed tonight. Christ, was this what dates with Amy were always going to be like? Because if it was . . .

Amy slid up behind me as I was replacing the gas cap. She placed her hands on my hips and ground her chin into my shoulder.

"You're annoyed. I can tell."

If I'd been born with a spine, I might have said something. Instead, I laid my hands across hers.

"No, I'm not."

Amy snuggled closer. "What's wrong, Leon?"

"You, uh . . . kind of ignored me tonight."

She pulled back and I turned around. "I'm sorry. I guess you were bored. Why didn't you dance?"

"You know the stereotype that white people—"

"Tell you what." Amy interrupted my joke. "Next time we do what you want."

"Okay."

And then we were kissing. Hard. It wasn't like kissing Melody, or the two or three other girls I'd kissed. Amy pressed her face so hard into mine it almost hurt. She wrapped her hands around the back of my head, like she didn't want me to pull away. After a few seconds we slowed down and took it easier. She pressed her tongue into my mouth. I placed my hand on her forearm, then ran my fingers up her bicep. After a brief hesitation, I slid my hand into the armhole of her sleeveless top. She didn't stop me when I began rubbing her shoulders from inside her shirt.

After about five seconds, she pushed away and wordlessly got into the car. I wiped some drool off my chin and followed.

Okay, that was pretty nice. Who cared if Amy liked to dance or asked me to give her friends a ride? She was into *me*! At least for now.

I returned home around three, hours after my curfew. Not that it mattered; I couldn't remember my parents ever staying up to wait for me. And yet, when I walked through the door, I found my dad watching *M*A*S*H* reruns in his bathrobe.

"Dad! Didn't think you'd still be up."

He turned off the TV and stood. "Couldn't sleep," he said, obviously lying. "Where have you been? You're late."

"Sorry. I was at a party, kind of lost track of things."

Dad had a funny look on his face. "Have you been drinking?"

"Huh?"

Dad's voice was less than civil now. "You drove home. Have you been drinking?"

What was this, MADD night? "No. No, I didn't drink."

There was a brief silence, during which I could tell that Dad was smelling my breath. Then he smiled. "I'm going to have a grilled cheese. Want one?"

I nodded. The encounter had frazzled me a bit. Though

Dad had never spanked me as a child, I had the uncomfortable feeling that if I had driven drunk, he'd have whupped my ass.

Dad was buttering bread in the kitchen.

"You know," I said, getting out the griddle, "you've never waited up for me before."

"You never really went to parties before."

"Yeah."

My father tossed the sandwiches onto the stove. "Did you have a good time?"

I thought about the video game marathon I'd ended up participating in. "It was okay."

"So what's this new girl like?"

I never really felt like discussing my life with my folks, but for some reason I needed to open up that night. "She's beautiful. Blond, a cheerleader. She's great."

Dad nodded appreciatively. "So are you two dating now, or what? Hand me the spatula."

I remembered how I'd been ignored for hours. I remembered Amy's beer-soaked kisses and thought how I would gladly suffer through more nights like this if I could taste those nicotine lips again.

"I dunno, Dad. I wanted to for the longest time, but now . . ." I shrugged.

Dad didn't say anything; he just tended the food for a bit.

I continued talking without any prompting. "Dad, did you ever have a girl just turn you on so much, make you so crazy, that it didn't matter how she treated you? Like you were willing to have a crappy time just so you could be with her? Does that make sense?"

Dad scooped the sandwiches onto plates. "Oh yeah," he answered decisively. We sat down at the table.

"I mean," I continued around cheesy mouthfuls, "she's nice; she's fun; but when we went out tonight, I really didn't enjoy it. It's weird."

Dad nodded. "It happens."

"But she's wonderful! Any guy would kill to go out with her. And she likes me. I guess. So why couldn't I just enjoy it? It's not like when I–" I caught myself just in time. No need to remember *that*.

Dad finished his last bite. "Son"–he looked me square in the eye–"we all come to this point sooner or later. If this is the first time you've been messed up by a woman, it sure won't be your last. Would you like a piece of advice? You know, from someone who's been there?"

I nodded eagerly.

"Get used to it." With a grin he patted my shoulder and walked off to bed.

I sat in the dark kitchen, feeling thoroughly confused. Instead of snuggling naked with Melody, I was talking to my dad. I'd given up sex, a girlfriend, and a best friend so I could grope Amy at the gas station.

But that wasn't all Amy and I had. I remembered how she'd talked to me about her family problems. How she'd made me realize I was more popular than I thought. How she'd promised that I would get to choose what we did next.

Things would work out. They had to.

30

YOU WON'T HAVE
MELODY HENNON TO KICK
AROUND ANYMORE

"JUST SO YOU KNOW," bellowed Mr. Hamburg the following Monday, "SOME SUBHUMAN BARBARIAN DRANK THE LAST COFFEE IN THE TEACHERS' LOUNGE." His voice dropped to an ominously low volume. "And did not make a fresh pot. SO I APOLOGIZE IF I AM NOT MY USUAL JOLLY SELF."

Across the room, Melody sat in silence. Now that she'd changed lockers and lunch tables, this was the only time I saw her anymore. It had been a week since our breakup, and I didn't have the courage to try to talk to her again.

"AS I MENTIONED YESTERDAY, 1960 USHERED IN A NEW ERA IN THE POLITICAL ARENA," lectured Mr. Hamburg, as quietly as the bombing of Dresden. "MR. SANDERS? MISS HENNON? I THINK YOU DID SOME RESEARCH ON THAT EARLIER THIS SEMESTER. COULD YOU EXPLAIN?"

"Yes. . . ." I started to answer, but for the first time since Columbus' voyage, Melody volunteered to answer a history question.

"In 1960, Richard Nixon and John F. Kennedy had the first televised presidential debate. People who heard it on the radio thought Nixon did better; those who saw it on TV thought Kennedy had won. A lot of people think that was because Kennedy was handsome."

Melody turned and looked directly at me. "It goes to show, people will always choose a pretty face. Looks count for everything."

The whole class must have known that Melody was mocking me. People were staring. I had to say something.

"Kennedy was a lot more than a face. He was a great president." I glared at Melody.

"No one knew that at the time, Leon. All they knew was they had a choice between someone who was ugly and someone who wasn't, and *they made their decision*. I just hope the voters ended up happy."

Hamburg grimaced, the closest he could come to a smile. "WELL, I THINK MR. KENNEDY PROVED HIM-SELF IN OFFICE. . . ."

I refused to look at Melody again. I didn't need this crap. I wasn't going to let it annoy me.

• • •

"And then she said everyone voted for Kennedy because he was good-looking," I whined, very annoyed.

I sat on a table in the gym, talking to Rob, who was busy pressing a cotton ball to the hole in his arm. The gym was filled with about a dozen cots for the annual Honor Society blood drive. I was spending study hall passing out pretzels and juice to the donors. A few cots away Jimmy and Johnny raced to see who could bleed a pint first. Dan was harassing one of the Red Cross workers, apparently trying to buy a plasma bag. Buttercup made the rounds, snapping photos of people with needles in their arms. At the far end of the gym, Honor Society president Dave Scaff lay moaning in a most pathetic way, his face a strange shade of green.

Rob took a swig of juice and pondered. "You really think Nixon was better looking? I mean, Kennedy slept with Marilyn Monroe."

"That's not the point! Melody was talking about me!"

Rob flipped his bloody cotton ball into the biohazard bin. "So what's it matter to you?"

"I don't want her to think I'm a jerk."

"I don't see how you have much of a choice. You dumped her. She's history. Of course she's not going to like you."

I stood and began pacing. "Melody's so nice. I wish we could still, you know, be friends like before."

"Dude, no chance. You dumped her for someone hotter. But she'll live. We've all been dissed; it happens. You've got Amy, and Melody will find someone else."

I snorted at the thought of Melody on the dating scene. "Right."

Rob shot me a funny look. "Was Melody just a pity date, then?"

"Of course not!"

Rob helped himself to more pretzels. "So why do you think you're the only guy who'll ever ask her out? Melody's no hottie, but she's not gross or anything."

I felt angry, and I wished I could blame Rob. He was right. I'd been guilty of thinking of Melody as a charity case. Her life wasn't over. I'd moved on; so would she.

I peeled off a BE NICE TO ME, I GAVE BLOOD sticker and slapped it onto Rob's chest.

"Hey," he complained. "Be gentle. I'm a quart low."

"Well, thanks for giving. Remind me to mark your bottle so it doesn't turn anyone black."

Rob waited till he was halfway across the gym before shouting "Yeah, Leon, I wouldn't donate if I were you. At least until those sores heal." For the second time that day, everyone turned and looked at me.

Luckily, I was spared further embarrassment. Dave Scaff finally finished squeezing out his pint. He stood up, stumbled, and knocked his bag to the floor, where it burst in a bloody mess. Dan howled. Then he laughed.

31

SHUT UP! NO, YOU SHUT UP!

The next night I sat with Rob and Samantha at Pioneer Lanes, enjoying the sight of Amy bending over to put on her shoes. I doubted she'd like bowling all that much, but she had said it was my turn to pick what we did.

It wasn't league night, so the only other customers were a young couple with several unruly kids. I began to search the rack for the perfect ball.

"So how come we didn't see you two at the party?" Amy asked Rob and Samantha.

Rob was entering everyone's names into the scoring

machine. "I had a family thing." Those of us who knew Rob realized that this probably meant he had been grounded.

"I had better things to do," answered Samantha in her holier-than-thou tone. I doubted she'd even known about the party.

Amy was first in the bowling lineup. She looked regretfully at her long nails, then attempted a between-the-legs shot. It rolled four feet before bouncing into the gutter.

"Here," I said, "let me help you." I placed Amy's hands correctly around the ball. Putting one hand on her hip and another on her arm, I showed her the proper stance, only lingering for a few seconds. Amy tried again and this time managed to knock down the ten pin. I didn't realize I still had my hand on her upper arm until she broke free and kissed me. The moment was somewhat ruined by Rob shouting "Hands where I can see them!"

As Rob took his turn, I noticed that Samantha was looking a little down. "What's your problem?" I asked, in an attempt to be sensitive.

Samantha gave me her usual contemptuous look before explaining. "I had a fight with Ben."

Obviously, she expected us to want to know what had happened. Out of Samantha's line of sight, Rob and I did a quick rock, paper, scissors. His rock crushed my scissors, so I had to be the one who asked.

"About what, Samantha?" My voice oozed with false sincerity.

"Oh, my cousin's getting married. When I told Ben she's keeping her own last name, he made some joke. Then it got blown all out of proportion."

Amy was drying her hands with the fan thing. "You're really not going to change your name when you get married?"

Samantha had been stooping to get a ball, but froze. "If I choose to get married, I certainly will keep my own name, Amy."

With the exception of Buttercup, everyone had issues that they were overly sensitive about, that made them fly off the handle. With Samantha, it was feminism and women's rights. Even Johnny knew better than to go there. Amy, however, wouldn't let it drop.

"What about when you have kids? You're not going to do that dumb hyphenation thing, are you?"

For a second I thought Samantha and Amy would have a knockdown, drag-out chick fight right there in the alley. (Hey, a guy could dream, couldn't he?) Samantha kept her composure, however, by grabbing her ball and smashing eight pins. Too bad they weren't in her lane.

Rob stepped up and crooked his thumb at our lane, indicating that it was my turn. I ended up with a spare. When I returned, Samantha and Amy were having an animated discussion about women in the workplace.

"Do you mean to say," snapped Samantha, "that there's no such thing as sex discrimination?"

Amy shrugged. "I'm sure it happens sometimes. But instead of crying about it, people should just work harder."

Samantha was doing a good impression of her bowling ball, her eyes and mouth perfectly round. "How can you say that?"

"It's like with black people. They didn't start off having equal rights, but now they do."

Rob stood up. "I'm getting a soda. Anyone want anything?"

"Yeah," I said. "I'll have a . . ."

Rob was already walking to the snack bar. He looked angry, but then, he always looked angry.

I told Amy it was her turn. Samantha was so riled she wouldn't even talk to me. This went on most of the game. Amy and Samantha would argue politics; I'd be ignored; and Rob would laugh at us behind his hand. By the tenth frame everyone was so wound up we declined to play another game.

I helped Amy with her coat and we walked off into the warm April night.

"I don't see what the big deal is," Amy was saying. "When I get a job, I'm going to succeed on my own. And if people don't think I'm good at what I do, I'll just work harder and prove them wrong."

As we drove home, I turned the conversation to teacher bashing, a nice, neutral subject. Amy's opinions were making me uneasy somehow.

But as I kissed her that night, I tried to tell myself it wasn't important. We were only seventeen, after all. Who cared about the politics of gender discrimination? Was it really such an issue?

Amy got out and made the "call me" sign with her thumb and pinkie. I didn't drive home; I just cruised. I swung by the twins' house, but I saw Jessica's car out front. The Taco Barn was packed, and the lock and dam was empty.

I didn't mean for it to happen, but I was hardly surprised

when I found myself on the outskirts of town, in front of the familiar gate. I let the engine idle and looked across the dark yard and the silhouettes of the horses, toward the dim outline of a battered pickup. A light was burning in the living room. The front door opened and a vague figure stood in the door. Gunning my engine, I sped off.

32

BRIGHT COLLEGE DAYS

Every year, there were three signs that summer was approaching. The first was that east Missouri would experience three weeks of nice weather before it became unbearably humid. The second was that my dad would start to badger me about getting a summer job. The third sign was the recruiters.

Various colleges would set up little propaganda booths in the commons area. Any upperclassman who walked too close would be subjected to a barrage of adjectives describing the paradise that was their campus. You quickly learned not to make eye contact. Except Johnny. He'd always asked the recruiters how often he could expect to get laid at their campus. They'd never bother him after that.

One morning, about two weeks after Amy and I had started dating, I ran the academia obstacle course.

I zigged past the Washington U booth. "Sorry, I'm not a millionaire."

I zagged past the Rolla College of Engineering table. "I hear there's tons of women at Rolla, but they're both lesbians."

I scoffed at the Lindenwood recruiter. "Is it true you can still pay your tuition with pigs and cows?"

Dan was blocking the Central Christian College of the Bible station. I couldn't hear what he was saying, but the recruiter looked upset.

The Marine Corps sergeant ignored me.

I had just about run the gauntlet and was looking for Samantha when I saw Melody.

I almost missed her. Not because of the other students, or because of my usual distraction, or because her wig was obscuring her face. It was because of what she was doing.

She was leaning against the University of Missouri–St. Louis booth, talking to the recruiter, and smiling.

She wasn't alone. Buttercup, for once not taking pictures, had joined the conversation.

I'd never seen Melody go out of her way to talk to people. Even at lunch, when she sat at her new table, she didn't say a word. Not that I'd glance over at her, fifteen or twenty times, while I ate.

After the history class incident the other day, I knew better than to try to talk to her again. She obviously didn't have any use for Leon anymore.

Of course I went over and tried to talk to her anyway. If there was one thing I'd learned from Mr. Hamburg, it was that men seldom followed the sensible course of action. Granted, that usually led to wars and televised debate, but still.

Buttercup was yapping at the recruiter about how she was going to decorate her dorm. From what I heard, she was going for a rainbow theme. I wondered how she would react the first time some college guy came over and tried to take off his pants.

Melody stiffened when I approached her, but she didn't move away. And then she smiled. Just a little. We walked a few paces from Buttercup.

"Thinking about going to UMSL?" Damn, my icebreakers were forced.

"Maybe. It's close to home." Melody held my eyes. She wasn't friendly, but she wasn't too terribly hostile. That was an improvement.

"So did you catch the *Twilight Zone* marathon the other day?"

She allowed herself a laugh. "That Talking Tina episode still freaks me out."

We were having a conversation again!

"How about the one with that kid who could control people?"

Melody affected an evil voice. *"I wish you into the cornfield."* She really was smiling now. *Should I try to make peace?*

"Melody, um, you didn't have to give back that DVD."

Her smile faded. "That's what you do when...That's what you do."

"Listen, Mel, maybe we could get together sometime. Watch movies like before."

She took a quick breath. "I guess I'd kind of like that, Leon."

My God, is it working? Does she want to be friends again?
"Great!"

"How about tomorrow night?" she asked. I noticed that her hand rose to take mine, then fell quickly to her side.

"Sure...Oh, I can't. Amy wants to take me clothes shopping."

Dan had once told me that during the Spanish Inquisition, they'd rip out your tongue for making foolish remarks. Good thing I didn't live in medieval Europe.

Melody's face scrunched up like an old kiwifruit. "On second thought, Leon, you can watch it with Amy." She pronounced Amy's name like it was a curse that could make crops die.

"C'mon, Melody. How about Thursday?"

"No! Don't you get it? I'm not going to share you! I'm not going to hang out with you when it's convenient for *her*. I'm not going to sit there, remembering the dance, while you dress up for *her*! I hope she's everything you want, Leon."

Melody stomped away. I let her. Why couldn't I just let it end? Most of Zummer High wanted nothing to do with me. Why couldn't I let Melody join them?

I wanted to throttle someone. Where was that guy from Rolla?

"You broke her heart, you know."

Buttercup was standing next to me. Though the girl was incapable of not smiling, her grin was less broad than usual.

"I didn't mean to." Why did I have to explain this to everyone? What business was this of theirs?

"Of course you didn't. And she knows that."

"What did she tell you about me?"

"That you were sweet and paranoid, and the biggest dork in school. She liked that. You weren't afraid of what people thought."

Which was one of the reasons I dumped her. I was worried about what people would think.

"I didn't know you guys were friends," I said, trying to change the subject.

Buttercup shrugged, her smile growing broader. "We went mini golfing the other day. She's awfully nice."

"Yeah, I know. She–" I cut myself short. Never unburden yourself to a reporter, even one who writes for the *Bulldog Bugle*.

"Leon, why did you break up with her?"

It was almost time to go to class. I'd missed breakfast with Samantha and I didn't feel like talking anymore.

"Off the record?"

"Of course."

"Because I like Amy better. I know that makes me a son of a bitch. I know that I hurt Melody and I know that makes me scum, but that's how it is. Life isn't a fairy tale, Buttercup. People do not live happily ever after." *Right?*

Buttercup's smile didn't waver. "I don't believe that for a second. There's someone out there for everyone. I might spend my whole life waiting for Prince Charming." Her eyes narrowed and she almost frowned. "But I know if I find him, I won't let him go."

33

EVERY GIRL'S CRAZY 'BOUT
A SHARP-DRESSED MAN

If it was up to guys, human beings would still be wearing animal hides. In the winter. In the summer we'd go around naked.

In the cramped dressing room, I pulled on a shirt that cost more than a month's allowance. Ever since elementary school, I'd regarded clothes as something to keep my butt from hanging out. So why had I allowed Amy to drag me clothes shopping?

"How you doing in there?" came Amy's lilting, beautiful voice.

Well, her voice was beautiful to me. I did notice she was developing a smoker's rasp and perpetual cough.

"Just a second." The shirt actually looked kind of nice. Button-down, expensive, and no funny sayings. I modeled for the mirror.

I exited the booth to get Amy's approval. She didn't whistle or compliment me like I'd hoped; she was too busy looking at some jeans in the women's section.

"What do you think?" I called.

She glanced at me. "Nice. You should get that."

I removed the shirt and added it to the pile. This was probably the most expensive shopping trip I'd ever been on. I'd had to go to the bank and withdraw most of the money I'd been saving for a camping trip with the guys that summer.

The clerk wrapped up my purchases as I handed her the small pile of twenties. I had no idea how I was going to pay for gas that week, or that Weird Al CD I wanted. If this kept up, I might have to overcome my laziness and get a job with Rob at the pizza joint.

Why had I just spent $155.79 on a bunch of shirts and stuff I didn't care about? I used to laugh at guys like Ben, who wasted time dressing up. So what the hell was I doing in the *Gap*?

One look at Amy reminded me. A sales guy, about my age, was lurking around her, quick to show her this item or that item. He'd completely ignored me.

Amy was a girl who could have any guy she wanted *and she knew it*. And for some reason she wanted to be with me.

We'd been together for over two weeks. I'd kissed her. She seemed to like me. So of course, she'd want me to dress a little nicer. And eat at places besides the Barn. And maybe not hang out with my friends as much.

Amy pawed through outfit after outfit. The clerk kept sniffing around her. I hovered around the exit, waiting for her to be done.

She never noticed.

Unasked for, an image of Melody appeared in my mind. She never would have made me change what I wore. Or ignored me when we went out.

But then again, Melody didn't have a perfect body. Even if she'd been unscarred, Amy would have won the swimsuit competition. And the evening-gown contest. As for Miss Congeniality...

Amy joined me in the main part of the mall.

"Hey, can we stop by RadioShack?" I asked.

"Oh, Leon, do we have to?" She pouted.

"Then how about the bookstore?"

"Sure. Hey, sale at Francine's! Wait here for a minute, Leon."

A minute turned into twenty. And we never did go to the bookstore. But Amy held my hand as we went to clothes store after clothes store. And she let me kiss her when I dropped her off at home.

Everything would work out. I was sure of it.

Besides, if I didn't make the effort, I knew some other guy would.

• • •

On my third or fourth time out with Amy, I began to notice how stinky our dates were. There was the sweat of the party and the bowling alley foot odor, and now, as we strolled through the chill night air, I stank again. We had met in University City (part of St. Louis) several hours earlier. I had hoped we'd just hang out, but instead we spent three noisy hours at a dance club, listening to some lousy local band, as I sweated and was knocked around by the various headbangers. Then we ran into some of Amy's friends and I was dragged to an all-night diner, where I ate an overpriced omelet while a bunch of people I'd never met discussed people I didn't know. Finally, we all went to some dude's dorm room at Washington University, where about fifteen college students were blasting their stereo and getting ridiculously drunk on some supermarket tequila.

Now here it was, around midnight. My new shirt stank of sweat, cheap booze, and pot smoke. I felt like I'd inhaled three packs of someone else's cigarettes. We were blocks from our cars. I hadn't expected to be out this late, so I hadn't brought a jacket. For late April, it was pretty damn chilly.

Amy walked close to me, stopping to examine the various window displays we passed. While I felt like a human hair ball, Amy still managed to look like a picture you'd see in a photographer's display.

Amy was studying an outfit in the window of a vintage-clothes store. "I dunno. Kind of cute, but...what do you think?"

It amazed me that women wasted time asking men for

their opinions on clothes. "Looks great," I replied without looking.

Amy nodded, gazed for a few more seconds, and then moved on. I fidgeted. Once again, I was out with Amy and not enjoying myself. The highlight of the evening had been kissing her on the dance floor, hours earlier. Even that had been rushed. It was like kissing me was something she was supposed to do every so often, like putting change in a parking meter.

I wished I was home. I had sort of expected to get further with Amy by this point. But aside from holding hands and kissing good night, there was nothing. We were never alone long enough.

My date was looking at some titles displayed in a bookstore window. I noticed with annoyance that she was reading the cover of a book by a radio commentator I hated. The more I got to know Amy, the more I realized how little our personalities meshed.

I blew on my hands, fidgeted again, and basically, without saying it, let her know I was ready to go. She giggled, let me take her hand, and walked with me toward my car.

"You've seemed quiet lately, Leon."

"Yeah, well, I didn't have much to say." Maybe if we'd talked about something interesting . . .

"No, I mean for over a week now. Whenever we go out, you act like you're bored."

"I'm not bored."

"Leon, c'mon. You never talk when we're together." She stopped walking and looked at me. "Sometimes I think you're not having fun with me." She sounded sad, but her voice held just the slightest hint of a threat. *Other guys would enjoy being with me no matter what we did.*

"Of course I'm having fun," I asserted, but it sounded flat.

"You need to cut loose. I can't be holding your hand every time we go out."

"Holding my hand?" For the first time, I raised my voice at Amy. "I don't need anyone to hold my hand."

She looked slightly abashed. "I didn't mean that. But when we do stuff with my friends, it's like you can't wait to leave. You're allowed to talk, you know."

I pretended to be interested in a flier on a phone pole. "Maybe if people would ever discuss something interesting, I would talk."

In less than a second, Amy was staring me in the eyes. "So my friends are boring? Is that it?"

Yes. "No. I'm just not a party guy."

"I guess you'd rather hang out in a bowling alley, then? Talk about farting with Johnny or listen to Samantha wish she wasn't a girl?"

There was a long pause. On the next block, someone peeled out.

"Watch how you talk about my friends, Amy. And do you have to do that now?" She'd been about to light up again.

Amy held the unlit cigarette in her fingers. "So it's okay for you to talk about my friends, but I can't talk about yours?"

This was getting out of hand.

"Amy, I like you. All I'm saying is, I wish you wouldn't try to change me."

Amy's cigarette crumpled in her fingers. "I never tried to change you!"

That was the biggest load of BS I'd heard since my report on politics. "What about taking me clothes shopping?"

"Well, pardon the hell out of me, Leon! I had no idea your ratty jeans were such a part of you!"

"It's not just the jeans. I always feel like I'm not good enough for you, that I'm letting you down."

"I never thought that. Leon, you're great. I didn't realize you needed to be told that every two minutes."

"Listen, Mel . . . Amy."

Whoops.

It was dark and cold and lonely, and I wished we'd get mugged to cover up my enormous screwup.

"Did you just call me Melody?" Her voice was hardly audible.

"No."

Amy began to walk. Quickly, but not so fast that I couldn't follow her.

"C'mon, it was an accident."

Amy stopped in front of a McDonald's. "Leon, you better make goddamn sure you don't have another 'accident.' I saw you talking to Melody before school the other day."

"What business is that of yours?" Exactly the wrong way to answer, but I didn't think I needed an excuse.

"I thought we were . . ." She trailed off. "Forget it. I don't own you."

"Amy, c'mon. Melody and I, there's nothing going on."
Anymore.

"Bullshit! She likes you. I just didn't realize you liked her. I actually bought that 'just friends' crap."

A couple of college dudes paused at the entrance to the restaurant to watch us fight.

Now was the time for me to say I didn't like Melody. To call her ugly, or stupid, or whatever. Amy wanted blood. It was my only salvation.

"Melody's nice. Lay off her."

"Good night, Leon." She turned to go into the fast food joint.

"Amy!" I grabbed her arm. She yanked away.

"Don't you touch me!" More people were gathered around, watching us. Someone laughed.

"Amy, let's talk."

"Fine! Let's talk. Let me hear you say you're not hung up on Melody. Let me hear you say that I don't have to live up to her. Tell me you won't talk to her anymore."

Amy? Jealous of Melody?

"Listen, Amy . . ."

"I mean it, Leon! Tell me it's over between you, or it's over between us."

I paused for a second. A second too long, as it turned out.

"Goodbye, Leon."

"Amy! Melody's not . . ."

She was running. I chased her. By the time I caught up with her, she was at her car. She didn't listen when I shouted her name, and I knew better than to try to touch her right then. When she got into her car, I risked a head injury by leaning in after her.

I thought maybe she'd yell at me, but she sat still and emotionless, like an exquisite mannequin. She didn't turn toward me or make an effort to start the car. I stood up and she slammed the door.

I watched her taillights fade into the distance. (Actually, traffic was thick, so there was an awkward minute when I just stood there, two feet from her car, as she tried to merge.)

Dumb-ass! What did I go and defend Melody for? She didn't want to have anything to do with me. I should have called her every name in the book instead of jumping to her defense. I kicked the fender of a parked car in anger, then went scurrying off when the alarm sounded.

34

ZONED OUT

Shortly after I'd met Jimmy and Johnny, their parents had finished off their basement and turned it over to the twins. Mr. and Mrs. Thomson always said it was so their sons would have a place to be noisy. In truth, it was more like something you'd do for a destructive dog or an insane uncle: they had to sacrifice the basement to save the rest of the house.

Whatever the reason, it was a great place to hang out. There was a pool table, a couple of old couches, and an Xbox. Provided we didn't smoke or use drugs, the elder

Thomsons pretty much allowed us to run wild. They never asked about the stains on the rug or the head-shaped holes in the drywall.

It was Monday evening, and Rob and I were facing off against Jimmy and Samantha in a game of eight ball. Jimmy was the only one who was any good—when he wasn't reminding us of the alternate meanings of "ball," "stick," "rack," and "hole."

"Now watch this. Trick shot." Jimmy made a big show of lining up his stick. I wasn't sure what he intended, but he managed to miss the ball entirely. Somehow his pool cue ricocheted off the felt and smacked him right in the face.

"Hey, first try!" said Rob. We all applauded.

"You assholes," moaned Jimmy, clutching his bleeding nose. "That's not what I meant to do."

I managed to sink the cue ball on the next shot. Samantha began to rack the balls for another go-round.

"So where's your brother?" asked Rob, sighting his cue. He always tried to come across as a hustler. I didn't tell him he had a big streak of chalk across his forehead.

Jimmy cleared his nose. "Out with Jessica. Apparently he got tired of making out with Leon."

Samantha was still obsessively straightening the triangle. "Speaking of which, where's Amy?"

How the hell would I know? She hadn't called me for the rest of the weekend. I didn't call her. Well, actually, I did. But no one answered, and I didn't leave a message. In chemistry that day, she didn't look at me. She made it a point to ignore me.

I chalked up. "We had a fight the other day."

Several snide comments died in the air. Friends know where the line is. They might insult your looks, your clothes, your family, and your personality, but they also know when to lay off.

Samantha broke. The cue ball gently rolled into the one ball. The triangle sat undisturbed.

"What did you fight about, Leon?"

"Melody. She thinks I'm still hung up on her."

"So?" said Jimmy. "Girls are like that."

Samantha jabbed him in the ribs with her stick.

"People are like that," he immediately corrected himself. "Just tell her she has nothing to worry about."

"Well," I said, thinking about what I'd been dancing around for a couple of days, "I'm wondering if Amy might have a point." *There. I can admit it.*

Rob, Jimmy, and I all shot in silence. Samantha made three unsuccessful attempts to hit the white ball.

"Leon, I warned—" She caught herself. "So what are you going to do?"

I shrugged. "Call Amy and apologize, I guess."

"Is that what you really want?" Rob sank two balls with one shot. For a second I thought he'd broken his cue, but it was just his back popping.

"I guess. It's just that Melody...Jesus." I couldn't stop thinking about her. I even got choked up when I thought about *The Twilight Zone.*

Though the game wasn't over, Samantha hung up her cue. "I have to go. Leon..." She stood in front of me and gently took my arm. "You're not the first guy this has happened to. But if you really want to patch things up with Amy, do it soon. She's not a girl who's used to competing with anyone." She squeezed my arm and headed for the stairs.

Amy, I pondered, wasn't the only one who wouldn't wait. School ended in three weeks. Then I wouldn't see Melody again for nearly three months. When we came back to MZH as seniors, we'd be strangers.

What sort of people watched TV at three o'clock on a Tuesday morning? People who needed phone sex and drunk-driving lawyers, judging by the commercials.

I couldn't sleep. Samantha had rattled me. I guessed I'd had such a high opinion of myself that I'd secretly believed that Melody would always take me back. But once school ended, I wouldn't see her until late August. Her feelings would fade. Maybe Rob was right, she might even meet someone else.

And so what? I could grovel my way back into Amy's life; she saw *something* in me, apparently.

Then again, maybe I'd just end up being bored, with Amy trying to change me. Or more likely, she'd get bored with me. We'd dated only a couple of weeks.

Why couldn't I get a sign from God? Why couldn't he just descend from his heavenly throne for five stupid minutes and say *"Leon! Don't give up on Amy!"* or *"Melody's the one!"*

Of course, if the Lord had something to say to me, it probably wouldn't be about sorting out my love life. Which is too bad, because otherwise more teenagers would go to church.

In the meantime, I was watching infomercials in the middle of the night. Maybe I ought to just go psycho and join Dan in whatever he did.

Most stations were off the air, and I was having serious doubts about the weight-loss pills being advertised. I turned on the DVD player.

Rod Serling. It was the *Twilight Zone* DVD Melody had returned. I started an episode.

It was the one Melody had talked about back on her birthday. For twenty minutes, we heard a female hospital patient bemoaning her hideous face, but we never saw her. Then, surprise, surprise, she was actually a gorgeous woman, living on a planet of pig people. In the end, she was banished to the island of the ugly people, escorted by a handsome "mutant" guy.

Rod then beat us over the head with the obvious moral: beauty is in the eye of the beholder.

What if Amy had a pig face? Would I date her? Of course not.

What if Melody had a pig face? In a way she did. Not literally, but no one found her attractive. Even when I'd been on top of her in the barn, I'd wished she was normal.

What if they both had pig faces?

Then my choice would be easy.

"Leon?" Mom was standing in the hallway in her bathrobe. "What are you still doing up?"

"Couldn't sleep."

She joined me on the couch.

"I remember this show. Your grandma wouldn't let me watch it. She said it would give me nightmares."

Quietly, we watched part of the episode where William Shatner was tormented by the diner fortune-telling thing.

"Leon? What's bothering you?"

"Nothing. Well, something, but it's not drugs, or sex, or suicide, so don't worry."

She paused the show. "I'm always going to worry about you, whether you like it or not. Do you want to talk?"

I yawned. "No. It's something I have to deal with on my own. But, um, thanks for . . . you know, worrying."

"It's what moms do. I was pregnant with you before your grandma stopped reminding me to change my oil and check my tire pressure."

"Mom, she still does that."

"Yes," said Mom, bitterly. "And I'm sure I'll still be bugging you by the time you're my age."

I smiled at Mom, and for the first time in years, she leaned over and kissed my cheek. I winked at her and headed off to bed, hoping to get a couple of hours' sleep. I had some unpleasant stuff to do the next day.

35

DOWN IN THE DUMPS

I gazed across the Formica tabletop into Amy's blue-gray eyes. I couldn't help thinking she was the prettiest girl in the room. Of course, maybe the Taco Barn wasn't the greatest place to make such comparisons; next to this crowd of hicks, the Elephant Man would have been a looker.

It was Tuesday afternoon. I had called her earlier and asked her to meet me here. She hadn't said much since arriving. Her face told me nothing: her lips stretched in a tight line, her eyes expressionless. So cold, so distant, and so very, very beautiful. I knew I had made the right choice.

"Listen, Amy." *Sheesh, where to begin?* "I'm sorry about the other night. There was a lot I wanted to say, but it came out wrong." *God, this isn't easy.*

Amy smiled a little. I felt like she was holding my heart in her hand. "Amy, I've enjoyed being with you so much. You're a great person, and I'm sorry if you ever thought I didn't have fun with you."

"It's okay, Leon..." She moved to touch my hand. I pulled back. Then I said the word that bode disaster in any relationship talk. The dreaded word. The B word.

"But..."

"But...," repeated Amy, the smile gone.

"But"—I struggled to maintain eye contact—"we don't get along that great."

"Leon..."

"We don't, Amy. We have fun, but... we like a lot of different things. Whenever we do anything, it's either what I want to do or what you want to do. There's never anything we want to do."

I waited for Amy to say something but she kept staring me down. "Go on," she said eventually.

"I don't think we should go out anymore." I clenched my jaw.

Amy ran her tongue over her top teeth, which I should not have found erotic.

"Leon, I don't know how many guys I've dated. Probably not as many as everyone thinks. But every single one of them either cheated on me, or dumped me, or turned out to be an asshole. *Every one.*"

I sat there, stacking packets of salsa, not looking at Amy. This was hard enough without looking at those perfect lips that for a week or two I'd been allowed to kiss.

"Leon, do you know why I called you when I was sad? Why I wanted to dance with you? Wanted you to call me?"

I shrugged.

"Look at me, damn it! Because you're funny! Because you're smart. Because when I saw you hanging out with Melody and your crew, I thought that I'd finally met some-one who *didn't care what people thought*! I thought, 'Here's a guy who might want to do something besides grope me in his car all night! Here's a guy who doesn't need to be told how great he is every five seconds. Here's a guy who's got his shit together, someone I can have some fun with!'"

I flicked over my salsa pyramid. Why couldn't I hire one of Johnny's Total Bastards to do this for me?

"I guess you misjudged me, Amy."

Amy reached into her purse. I waited for the inevitable cigarette (or her pepper spray), but she pulled out some gum. "Leon, I knew you and Melody had a thing going on. And I guess that doesn't make me any better than you. But I never wanted to change you, or ignore you, or whatever the hell problem you had with me. I'm sorry you thought I was such a shallow bitch, but at least I tried. Maybe I tried to change you, but you wanted to change me too. You wanted Melody, but with my face."

"That's not true!" *That's completely true. When did Amy get so insightful?*

"Leon." She sat cracking her gum for a moment. "Maybe

someday I'll meet a guy who's not a dick. And maybe someday you'll make up your mind about what you want. But I'm sorry I met you."

"I'm sorry I hurt you."

Amy spit her gum into a napkin. "No, you're not. You're sorry *you* got hurt." She stood and took her purse.

"Leon? Is Melody going to take you back?"

I stayed seated. Amy towered over me. I remembered when she hadn't known who I was.

"I don't know, Amy."

"Good luck. Melody certainly massages that pathetic ego of yours."

I felt bad as she went, but not so bad that I didn't enjoy the sight of her legs.

So that was over. Now for the hard part.

Here was my plan: I'd corner Melody at her locker. I'd apologize. I'd tell her I'd made a horrible mistake. Tell her I was weak. I was a jerk. I was sure she'd agree with me.

But I thought she'd forgive me. I thought she cared about me enough that she'd give me a second chance. I wouldn't blow it this time.

I just didn't count on one tiny detail: Melody wouldn't talk to me.

She'd turn and walk away if she found me near her locker. She'd sit at a crowded table at lunch so we couldn't talk in private. There was no time for a protracted apology during history class, and I could never find her during study hall.

Another week went by. Jimmy and Johnny wouldn't shut

up about how we were two weeks away from being seniors. I helped Rob truck home all the crap from his locker. Even the poster vandals had stopped caring. School was almost over.

I was near panic. If I didn't mend things with Melody now, I might never get another chance. I couldn't go to her house, face her family. She'd probably slam the door in my face, anyway.

In desperation, I called her house. Her dad answered. I expected him to threaten to skin me, but he was civil, if not polite. How much had Melody told him?

"I'll go get her," he said when I asked to talk to her. There was a pause, and I could hear voices in the background. Then Mr. Hennon came back on the line.

"Leon? She's . . . She stepped out. I'll tell her you called."

Stepped out, my ass. She just wouldn't talk to me.

Things were getting desperate. If I couldn't get her to talk to me for five minutes, then I'd have to show up at her house and play my guitar under her window at night.

A fine plan, except she might sic the horses on me. Plus I didn't play the guitar.

Finally, I got a break. It was study hall, and I'd been half dozing in one of the comfy chairs in the library when I thought I heard Buttercup's voice. I looked up to see her in the periodicals section reading an issue of *Cat Fancy* magazine.

Buttercup! She was kind of friends with Melody. Maybe she could help me out.

"Buttercup?"

She smiled and patted the seat next to her. I sat.

"How you doing?"

She grinned at me. "Great. I met this guy the other day—"

"Right. Listen, I need your help."

She closed her magazine.

"Melody doesn't want to talk to you, Leon." For the first time since I met her, Buttercup was frowning.

"Five minutes with her. Help me, Buttercup. Five minutes with Melody, it's all I ask."

"Leon, you hurt her," she told me. "Melody would have forgiven you for kissing Amy if you had just come clean and said you were sorry. But you waited too long. She's moved on. She doesn't trust you anymore."

"So you won't help me?"

"You treated her like poop, Leon." Buttercup was the only teenager I knew who still said "poop."

I got up to leave. The nicest girl at Zummer thought I was an asshole. Another door shut in my face.

"Leon?" Buttercup was rolling her magazine in her lap.

"Yeah?"

"Maybe you should try to meet Melody at her work. Maybe . . . I dunno, at least there she couldn't walk away."

"Since when does Melody have a job?"

"Since last week. She's trying to earn some spending money for her scholars trip this summer. I think she works today."

36

FEAR AND IGNORANCE

The strip mall was attached to a Wal-Mart that had closed five years earlier, when they'd built the supercenter. Half a dozen businesses clung to life: cell phone shops, insurance agencies, check-cashing services, and the bookstore where Melody reportedly was working.

The front door jingled as I passed through. The place reminded me of a cave. Little book-lined tunnels ran in all directions. Cobwebs hung from the ceiling; more piles of books cluttered the floor. A few bare lightbulbs cast a dusty glow. The musty, mildewy scent that accompanies old books hung in the air. I was somewhat shocked that there was a bookstore in St. Christopher besides the Barnes & Noble. Funny that I'd never heard of this place. The Fear & Ignorance Bookstore: What was that all about?

The store seemed deserted, which suited me just fine. If Melody was somewhere in there, I could talk to her without being interrupted by a customer.

"May I help you?" I turned toward the unexpected voice. It came from behind a cluttered counter. Two beady, narrow eyes observed me from above a newspaper.

"Um, no, just looking." I was answered by a long stream of coughs.

I turned to poke through the cavernous store, then thought the better of it. "Excuse me..." I addressed whomever was behind the paper. "Is Melody Hennon working today?"

Another round of coughs. "Straight back, up the stairs."

After passing the Political Science, Psychology, and Popular Cuture (sic) sections, I found the set of wooden stairs. A short jaunt brought me to a small alcove, where a shadowy figure was shelving books.

"Melody." She turned at the sound of my voice and I saw her face. She wasn't wearing her wig; instead she had a scarf tied around her head. As I looked at her enlarged lips, her taught, mutilated skin, and her almost complete lack of ears, I couldn't help comparing them to Amy's perfect features. And I didn't care. This girl had made me happy. I wanted to be with her.

Melody looked at me for a couple of seconds, then returned to her shelving. I repeated her name.

"May I help you find something?" she asked with exaggerated politeness.

"Melody, I have to talk to you."

"Good for you. Now go away; I'm busy." She began to slam books onto the shelf.

This was not going well. I had kind of hoped there'd be some sign that she was glad to see me. Some memory of the times we'd had together.

"So how long have you worked here?" I asked, trying to get her talking.

"About a week, week and a half. And no, I have no idea what 'Fear and Ignorance' is supposed to mean." She had finished her shelving in that section and tried to push past me. I grabbed her arm.

Melody didn't resist; she simply looked at me with such wrath that I quickly let go. She stood staring at me. The laughter I had seen so often in her eyes was long gone.

"Melody, can we talk? Just five minutes?"

She leaned against a shelf full of serial Westerns. "Talk," she challenged.

"I broke up with Amy."

Melody didn't blink. She just kept staring at me. "Was there something else?" she asked eventually.

"I broke up with her because I wanted to be with you."

Melody cocked what used to be her eyebrow. "Did you?" Her tone was sarcastic.

There was a long, uncomfortable silence, broken only by the owner's coughs echoing from below.

"Oh, wait," continued Melody, "this is the part where I'm supposed to say 'Oh, Leon,' and fall into your arms, right?

The part where you kiss me and we go back to exactly how we were before. That's what you were expecting, right?"

Okay, so I'd misjudged a bit.

"Mel, I made a mistake."

"Yes. And you lost me."

"Melody, I screwed up! Can't you give me a second chance?"

"No. I'm not going to put my heart on the line again. I'm not going to wait until the next pretty face comes along so I can go through this a second time."

"It won't happen again!"

"Why should I believe that? We had a good thing going, Leon, and you chucked it as soon as someone sexy came along. I've seen the kind of person you are."

Amy hadn't exactly just appeared out of nowhere, but I knew better than to mention it. Instead, I tried the only thing I could think of. I begged.

"Melody, *pleeease...*"

"Save it, Leon. This isn't a movie. You're not allowed to run off with the cute girl only to realize it's the ugly chick you want."

For some reason that infuriated me. "You're not ugly!" My voice reverberated throughout the store.

"You're not ugly," I repeated. "You're beautiful. I know I haven't shown it, but I've always thought you were." Maybe not *always*. "Don't give up on us."

For a couple of seconds, I thought I'd reached her. At least she no longer looked as angry. "You know, you're the first person who ever made me believe that." There was a glint of warmth in her eyes. Then it passed. "But you hurt me. You hurt me in a way I can't forget."

"I could try to make it up to you."

She shook her head. "When you dumped me, I cried all night. I told my parents I wanted to be homeschooled again. I would have taken you back in a second. I would have made you think it was all my fault." She abruptly turned to the wall, took a breath, and continued.

"Leon, we were going to have sex. Maybe that didn't mean anything to you, but it meant everything to me. And after a while, I realized if that meant nothing to you, then I meant nothing to you. And we were better off apart." She looked at me almost with pity. "It wasn't easy. It hurt. But I don't want you back in my life. Not ever."

I couldn't remember ever feeling so low. It wasn't even that Melody wouldn't take me back. It was that she had trusted me and I hurt her. She had thought I was great and I treated her like she didn't matter. Thirty years from now she'd remember the guy who kissed her for the first time, and feel angry.

"So now what?"

"Now we say goodbye."

"Can I call you?" I was really grasping.

"No. Summer vacation starts in two weeks. By the time we're back, I'm sure you'll be telling some other girl how beautiful she is."

I stood there for a few seconds. "Goodbye, Melody. I'm sorry."

"Goodbye, Leon."

There was one last thing I could try. I remembered how Melody and I used to tell jokes to each other.

"A three-legged dog walks into a bar and says, 'I'm looking for the man who shot my paw.' "

Melody smiled, but it was an indulgent smile, one you'd give a kindergartner who told too many knock-knock jokes. I felt embarrassed all of a sudden and made my way down the dusty steps. Before I hit bottom I could hear the thunk of books being slammed onto a shelf.

37

GET THEE BEHIND ME, DAN!

Plunk.

Another Friday night. First Friday night in May, a week and a half left of school. Another night hanging out at the lock and dam. Another moonlit bonfire. Jimmy and Rob sat on a log, shooting the breeze. A little bit out of the firelight lurked Dan, a silhouette in the darkness. I had been kind of surprised when he had arrived with Rob.

"He just showed up at my house," Rob whispered to me. "I couldn't tell him no."

Johnny was out with Jessica, and Samantha was working. I stood away from the fire, tossing rocks into the chilly river.

Plunk.

Dan was telling one of his unending tales of the dark side of humanity. "So when the guy wakes up, he's in a bathtub filled with ice, the girl's long gone, and one of his kidneys is missing."

Rob cracked his knuckles. "I heard that story five years ago, Dan. It never happened."

"Not true," Dan insisted. "I know the guy involved."

"You know the guy who lost a kidney?" asked Jimmy.

"No. I know the guy who took it."

I didn't laugh. I was too grumpy. For the past few days, I had been a whiny bitch, and I knew it. Melody was gone; Amy was gone; I was pissed; and I wanted everyone to feel sorry for me.

Plunk.

Jimmy opened a grocery bag and passed around sodas. "You want one, Sanders?"

I didn't answer; I just grabbed a rock and threw it into the water.

Plunk.

I was pissed at myself; I knew that much. Melody had laughed at my jokes, told me her secrets, and watched my favorite shows, and I had blown it in a most spectacular manner. And I'd pissed off Amy in the process. What a loser. What a dick!

The thing about being in a bad mood was you wanted to bring everyone else down with you. It wasn't enough that your friends wanted you to be happy. You wanted them to be unhappy. It galled me that Samantha and Ben had made up, that Johnny and Jessica were probably naked some-where, and that Rob had just gotten a thirty on his ACTs. How dare they be happy?

I picked up another rock and held it in my tightened fist. A month earlier I had kissed Melody, not twenty feet from where I stood. Why hadn't I realized how happy I was? Why had I let her get away? Furious, I hurled the rock off into the darkness. It ricocheted off the NO TRESPASSING sign and pegged the sedan Rob had borrowed from his dad.

"Hey! Watch it!"

"Sor-ree!" I apologized sarcastically.

"My dad's gonna have my nuts if that gets scratched!" hollered Rob. I shrugged.

Rob got up and stood next to me. "Dude, you got to lighten up."

"Piss off."

"Seriously. I know you liked Melody, but it's all over. You got to move on. Find someone else."

"What would you know about that? When was the last time you had a date?"

It was a mean thing to say and I knew it. I hadn't seen Rob with a girl in quite some time. Zummer High wasn't ex-actly a liberal school, and not all the girls there would con-sider dating a black guy.

Rob's eyes narrowed. "You know what, Sanders? Go screw yourself. You wanna be an asshole, do it without me. I'm outta here." He hopped into his dad's car and gunned the engine. Jimmy got up from his log.

"Um, he's my ride," he said with an uncomfortable grin.

I turned away, disgusted with myself. Now that I'd chased off the women in my life, why not my friends? Why not everyone? I heard Rob's tires kick up gravel. Then there was silence.

I sat on the bank of the river and buried my face in my knees. I wished they hadn't gone. I really could have used a friend right then.

Suddenly, I screamed and jumped three feet forward, landing in ankle-deep water. A hand had gripped my shoulder from behind. Only when I realized that it belonged to Dan did my heart stop trying to bust out of my chest.

Dan didn't react to my display of terror; he just stood on the bank, looking hypnotized.

"I thought you left with the guys," I said, sloshing through the muddy bank.

He shook his head. *Great.* Now I had to give him a ride home. I stood next to the fire, trying to dry my shoes.

"Lovely night," said Dan, still standing by the river. "Full moon, shining on whatever blasphemies sneak through the darkness. Fire . . ." He crept toward the bonfire and stared intently. "Son of the morning . . . bringer of light."

I dug mud out of my shoes. "Yeah."

"One might wonder what bloated, eyeless things crawl through the primordial slime of this river. Pity we don't have dates here."

My temper was on a short fuse. "Dan, let's go home."

He ignored me. "Nothing like the soft touch of a woman. Her smooth skin . . . or her rough scars."

I shot up. Dan was standing on the opposite side of the fire. The blaze reflected redly in his dark eyes.

"Dan, shut up. Shut the hell up or I swear I'll leave you here."

He took no notice. "I warned you, did I not? Warned you of the fire?"

I stepped around the fire, toward him, but he circled away from me. His gaze held mine. The flames that flashed in his eyes seemed to come from within.

"Melody was hard; now she's harder. She'll hurt less in the future. You should be proud."

"Shut up!" I lunged at him, but he easily dodged. Slowly, slowly, we circled the fire.

"Amy's harder too. You should date more women, Sanders. You're a one-man blast furnace."

I tried not to listen. I wanted to deck him, sock him in that stupid leering mouth of his.

"And you went through the fire too, didn't you? You hurt a little less now, right? Just a little colder, a little harder?"

I lunged again and almost caught my jeans on fire.

"I know what it's like to lose someone you love. It's better this way."

I feinted left and charged right. Grabbing Dan by the lapels, I smashed him into the gravel.

"Who have you ever lost, you satanic dick? Who have you ever loved?"

The strange light in his eyes had gone out. Instead, for the first time since I'd met him, Dan looked hurt and embarrassed. He mumbled something.

"What?"

"My father."

"What are you talking about?"

He stood up and brushed himself off. Without looking at me he explained. "You asked me who I'd lost. My father. Left home when I was nine. He sends me a hundred bucks at Christmas, fifty on my birthday, and I haven't seen him in five years."

This was the first time I'd heard Dan express anything like a human emotion. But quite frankly, I was sick of hearing about other people's parents' divorces. Before I could think of a reply, his veneer of evil had returned.

"No matter." He looked back at me. His eyes were now dark and shiny. "Crying never brought him back. But the fire helped me. It cleansed and hardened me. I don't feel the pain anymore."

"Why are you telling me this?"

"I want to help you. Surrender to the fire, Leon. It burns away hopeless, useless feelings. It only hurts for a second."

"Dan . . . I don't want that. That's cold."

"Love hurts, Leon. Let the flames cauterize your feeling for Melody."

"I can't do that. I think I love her."

Dan sighed a world-weary sigh.

"Well, then what can I offer to make you happy? Thirty pieces of silver?"

"C'mon . . ."

"John the Baptist's head on a platter? Or Dr. Bailey's?"

"Let's go."

"If I offered you all you surveyed, would you bow down to me? No? Well then, what is it that you want? What would make you happy? How about . . ." He paused dramatically. "Melody's heart?"

I was horror-struck until I realized he was speaking metaphorically. "She's done with me."

"Yes. And you know why."

"Duh, I cheated on her."

He waved a chastising finger at me. "Men have been forgiven for worse. That's not why she left. She left because you told her she was ugly."

"I never said that!"

"Did you not leave her for someone prettier?"

I winced.

Dan nodded. "She's always thought of herself as ugly, but you sealed it. She trusted you and you called her ugly."

"If you're trying to cheer me up, you're doing a lousy job of it." For the observations of an insane person, Dan's were hitting close to home.

"What I don't understand is why you've given up on her."

"She won't take me back! I just said that."

"Not right off the bat, Leon. I'm sure the fire burned away all her feeling for you. But maybe not. Maybe . . ."

"Maybe what?"

"I *hear things.*"

"What? What things?"

"I heard all things in the heaven and in the earth. I heard many things in hell."

"Dan!"

"And a friend of mine mentioned that maybe Melody still likes you. Which is not to say she doesn't hate you too."

I was near the point of throwing Dan down again. "Who? Who said that?"

Dan smiled, and for once it wasn't a devilish grin. "All I'm saying, Sanders, is don't give up just yet. If you really . . ." He seemed reluctant to say the word. "If you really *love* Melody, don't count her out."

Dan walked to the riverbank and unexpectedly shook his fist at the sky. Maybe he was cursing the universe; maybe he was hating his absent father; maybe he was daring God to strike him dead. Whatever the reason, he was through talking for the night. I sat on my fender and pondered what he had told me.

38

POP GOES THE
DIHYDROGEN CHLORIDE

"Now, you'll have to be a little careful with this bit," intoned Mr. Jackson from the front of the class. He adjusted his safety glasses and turned his attention to a setup that looked like it had come from Wile E. Coyote's Acme catalog. Using a Bunsen burner, he lit a wooden splint on fire. He then held the splint to a rubber tube that protruded from the jumble of glass jars on the counter. Without warning, a loud bang ripped through the classroom. Several girls yelped in surprise. Jimmy, who'd been asleep, awoke with a snort.

Mr. Jackson launched into an explanation of how the

combustion of the gases released from the chemical mixture produced the noise. Though the man couldn't teach for anything, he certainly did know his material.

Diagonally ahead, Amy and her friends giggled in surprise. Six days had passed since she'd stormed out of the Taco Barn. When I last spoke to her, I wondered how she'd treat me. Would she be snippy, cold, belligerent? No. What she did to me was far crueler.

She treated me just like she had before that time I'd eaten her cigarette. I no longer existed for her. It wasn't that she ignored me. If she had made an effort not to notice me, at least that would have proved I was still on her mind. But now I had ceased to be. She made no point of looking away from me, not walking near me, or avoiding me. It felt like it had two months before, when I had been nothing but a piece of furniture to her. It hurt. But had I expected better?

"Okay, class," said Mr. Jackson. "Let's see if you can do it. Groups of two, everyone remember your goggles."

For most chemistry labs I worked with the twins. However, after a little disaster with some sulfur compounds had cleared the science hall for two periods, Mr. Jackson insisted they never work together again. Johnny ran off to join a couple of other jocks, while Jimmy managed to wrangle his way onto Cassandra's team. I looked around to see who'd be my partner for the last chemistry lab of the year. Amy was the only uncoupled student left, and she seemed to realize it at the same time I did.

I hoped she'd ask someone to trade partners, or tell me to find my own group, or something—anything to show we'd been more than classmates at one time. I was out of luck. Indifferently, she told me to grab the instructions and the goggles and she'd get the equipment. She might have been talking to a stranger.

Without a word we began to set up. As I linked test tubes and measured chemicals, I wondered if I should say anything. Apologize again? Ask her some generic question to start a conversation? Or just leave well enough alone? What would Bart Axelrod do?

Of course, I opened my big fat mouth. "The weather's been nice, hasn't it?"

"I guess. Check the seal on that tube there."

I couldn't believe it. I had just made a comment about the weather. Smooth. We worked another fifteen minutes in silence.

Mr. Jackson began to walk around the room with a cigarette lighter, igniting splints to see whose experiments would bang. A few loud reports echoed through the lab, but mostly there were just a few sad pops. Amy and I hurried to finish.

Johnny, whose chemicals had produced a weird whistling sound, trotted by the table as he cleaned up. "Hey, Leon," he said as he paused by our table. "The dollar theater is showing *Bloody Monday,* Friday night only. You in?"

"Miss a chance to see Axelrod's greatest masterpiece? I'm there." Romantic hell or not, this was an opportunity I couldn't pass up.

Johnny winked and walked away. When I turned back to the experiment, I was surprised to see that Amy was wearing a rather angry expression.

"I guess you'll be taking Melody," she said with a hiss. Maybe the thought of my going out with friends–friends she had begun to hang out with–set her off.

"No."

Amy wasn't looking at me. "Why not? Are you seeing someone else behind her back?" Now that Amy was acknowledging me, I longed for her to ignore me again.

"No." Someone's experiment banged and I fumbled with my chemicals.

Amy was sneering. "So just going out with the guys? Then make out with her later? Or did you dump her too?"

I slapped my hand on the table. "Melody won't talk to me, okay?"

I knew that Amy was mad at me, but I wasn't prepared for how she responded.

"Well, I'm sure you'll find someone new. Just check the burn wards."

My head snapped up. The beaker I'd been messing with slipped off the edge of the table and crashed to the floor. Someone–I thought it was Johnny–gave me a sarcastic round of applause.

For five seconds we stared at each other. Even after I'd dumped her, even after everything, I never thought Amy would make fun of *that*. There must have been something in my expression that scared Amy. Her look of mocking triumph melted rapidly away.

I stormed off to grab the oft-used broom and dustpan. I refused to look at her. That was cruel. Really, really cruel.

When I had dumped the glass shards, I found Amy

staring blankly at the experiment. Neither of us spoke as we waited for Mr. Jackson and his fire. After half a minute, Amy broke the silence.

"Okay, that was a cheap shot."

I didn't answer.

"Leon?"

I finally looked at her. Her eyes were downcast; she looked ashamed.

"Leon, I didn't mean that."

I shrugged.

"But, Leon, what did you expect..." She was interrupted by our teacher, who was halfheartedly lighting whatever gases we'd managed to produce. There was a noise like an ant farting. Jackson shook his head and moved on.

I started packing up the equipment. Amy touched my arm. I pulled away.

A lot of seniors had written on their cars with white shoe polish: *GO MZH! BULLDOGS RULE! WHERE OUT OF HERE!* (That was Dylan's.)

I sat on my hood, waiting for Rob. Just over a week till summer. I should be happy. I wanted to be happy.

I also wanted to be rich and tall. We didn't always get what we wanted.

Except this year, I'd gotten exactly what I wanted. Twice. And somehow, I managed to dump them both for the other one and end up alone.

Only you, Leon.

"Hey, Leon!"

Amy. The first time she'd called to me in the parking lot, I'd gone running like an obedient puppy.

This time... I went running like a self-assured, macho puppy.

"Hi, Amy." Even after her behavior in the lab, I still lacked the spine to ignore her. Amy had tried to apologize earlier. Now wasn't the time to focus on my own wounded pride.

Amy was chewing a wad of gum. She pulled out another piece and crammed it into her mouth.

"Did you quit smoking?"

She blew a bubble. "It's better for your health. Plus you can only cough up so much yellow phlegm before you start to think." She offered me the pack of gum and I took a piece.

"Leon, about what I said earlier..." Her ponytail whipped in the spring wind. "I didn't mean it." Amy sounded truly ashamed.

I kicked my tire. "No one expects you to like Melody."

"And I don't," she said severely. "But I shouldn't have made fun of her like that."

"Thanks." There was a pause. "So any big plans for summer?"

She sighed. "I'm going to live with my dad in Chesterfield for a while."

"Oh, boy."

We both stared at each other for a second.

"Amy? Maybe when you get back, we could–"

"No! Leon, I told you–"

"Not like that!" I objected so loudly the gum flew out of my mouth and nearly hit her. "I mean, just to hang out."

She smiled at me. "Nope. We're not friends, Leon. I don't hate you, but we're not friends."

"Yeah. Well, have fun in Chesterfield."

"You men always ask the impossible. Have fun at Taco Barn. And Leon?"

"Yeah?"

Amy put her hands on her hips and tilted her head. "Melody's a lucky girl."

"I told you, she's done with me." Or was that what Amy meant?

Amy was already walking to her car. "Are you sure about that, Leon?" she called over her shoulder.

39

MONDAY, BLOODY MONDAY

St. Christopher Cinema, one of the great old movie palaces constructed after the Depression, had been built around 1939. It boasted thirty-foot-high ceilings, elaborate murals, an orchestra pit, and a balcony (for colored patrons). You could picture the ushers helping people to their seats, soldiers on leave feeling up their girlfriends, not a cell phone to be heard. Though most two-screen theaters shut down during the VCR revolution, St. Christopher managed to stay open by showing old movies at a buck a pop.

"I'm only going to say this once, scumwad," said Johnny,

imitating Bart Axelrod's raspy voice. "Do you want popcorn?"

"Sure as a Smith and Wesson beats four aces," I replied, using Axelrod's catchphrase. Johnny and I edged into the refreshment line in St. Christopher's ornate lobby. Surprisingly, no one–not even Jessica–had opted to join us for the screening of what was generally regarded as Axelrod's only two-star movie, *Bloody Monday*.

I was having a good time in spite of myself. True, I kept flashing back to the time I'd taken Melody to see an Axelrod movie, but there was nothing I could do about that now. I would have to move on. The last thing I wanted to do was get all teary-eyed at a bad action flick.

"Hey, Leon, is that Dan and Buttercup coming out of the theater there?"

"Damn, you're right. What's up with that?" I watched in sick awe as our school's sweetest girl and most evil guy emerged from the theater hand in hand. Buttercup had mentioned something about meeting a guy. But *Dan*? This was the prince she'd been waiting for?

"Were they watching *Monday*?" asked Johnny.

I checked the schedule board. "No, some foreign film. The one with that one chick."

"Dan went to see that? Holy crap."

Buttercup spotted us and waved. For a second, I thought Dan was going to try to make a break for it; clearly he didn't like being seen coming out of a movie that didn't feature dismemberments. Realizing he was trapped, he followed his date toward us.

"John, Leon." He gave a curt nod.

"Buttercup, Dan." Johnny and I were grinning like idiots. "Did you enjoy your movie?"

"Well," said Buttercup, "I liked it, but I think Dan was bored." She pinched his cheek. She was probably the only person who could do that and not risk losing a finger.

"Next week, we rent the movie I want to," said Dan, making it clear to us that he hadn't been whipped.

"What're you watching?" I asked. "*Steel Magnolias?*"

"No," answered Buttercup, missing my jab. "Something called *Silence of the Lambs*. It sounds cute."

I opened my mouth to warn her, but changed my mind. If she really was dating Dan, then she'd have to learn some things on her own.

Buttercup and Dan left the lobby, Dan shooting me the evil eye over his shoulder. Johnny gave his ticket to the ticket taker. I waited for a few other people to pass, then followed. Maybe that made me look like a loser who went to the movies on his own, but it sure beat looking like I was Johnny's date.

Even though the film didn't start for half an hour, the theater was already filling up. Pockets of rowdy movie fans sat in the plush seats. Down in front, the seventy-year-old house musician pounded away on the old organ. The audience snapped their fingers in time to the theme from *The Addams Family*. People hollered, threw things, and made out. It was great to be young.

I plopped down in an aisle seat and threw my feet up on the seat in front of me. Johnny and I inhaled popcorn as the organist played "Monster Mash." I was about to quote some more Axelrod films when I saw something that made me choke on a kernel.

Across the wide carpeted aisle, several teenagers wrestled their way into the seats opposite mine. I recognized a few of them from our school. The girl directly on the other side of the aisle was turned away from me, but I could tell she had straight brown hair. A little too straight. I did a double take. It was definitely Melody's wig. That meant there was a good chance Melody was under it.

The organist was now playing "Take Me Out to the Ball Game" and Johnny was hollering along.

"Root, root, root for the Cardinals, if they don't win it's a shame..."

"Johnny, we gotta move."

"For it's one, two, three... huh?"

"Let's change seats."

"No way, man, the joint's packed." He saw Melody over my shoulder and quickly turned his head away.

"I see. Too late to find another place to sit. Want to change with me?"

"No, it's okay. I shouldn't hide from her."

The old organist, who some said started here as an usher in the sixties, bowed to the applause of the audience. The lights dimmed.

St. Christopher also continued the great old movie tradition of showing a cartoon before the main feature. As Bugs Bunny matched wits with Yosemite Sam, I held my palm to the side of my face and thought. Should I say hi to Melody?

She'd certainly acted like she never wanted to talk to me again. But hadn't both Amy and Dan implied that maybe I still stood a chance?

I snuck another look in Melody's direction. Her gaunt features stood out in the flickering glow of the screen. Once again, I got the impression of a skull when I saw her face in low light. The angel of death. Only now I saw more angel than death in her face. She was beautiful. Not that inner-beauty crap either. And not that she had a hot little body. I liked her face. I wanted to see her smile.

Just as the cartoon reached the surprising ending of Bugs humiliating Sam, Melody looked in my direction. Her face registered brief surprise, then lost all trace of emotion. She simply stared at me for a few seconds, like I was an acquaintance she couldn't quite place.

"Hi," I blurted out. She turned back toward the screen.

"Let it pass, Leon," whispered Johnny. "She's with people."

Bart Axelrod exploded onto the screen in a hail of gunfire. Wearing a ponytail entirely too long for the cop he was supposed to be playing, he burst into a crack house. Facing down the drug runners, he let loose more shots from his pistol than were fired during the invasion of Normandy. "Punk," he whispered at the last man standing. "I'm gonna be picking your brains out of my shoes for a week when I'm done with you."

Okay, maybe it wasn't *Citizen Kane*.

I kept trying to pretend that Melody wasn't there and enjoy the film. By the time Axelrod's black, by-the-book, older partner was killed by the head villain, I was looking in Melody's direction again. She noticed and pointedly looked away.

"Melody?" I called in a loud whisper. She frowned and shook her head. Several of her companions looked in my direction. I felt unreasonably jealous. She should be sitting with me, not them.

I sat staring at my lap, feeling sorry for myself, until I was interrupted by Johnny's moronic laughter. Axelrod was wrestling with a henchman in the back of a speeding truck. The thug had him by the throat and was trying to force his face into the road as they sped along at a zillion miles an hour.

"Now there's a stunt I've never seen in any other movies."

I nodded, not really listening. My gaze fell across the aisle and I caught Melody looking at me. She instantly turned her head away.

"Melody?" I tried again.

"Leon, no!" she almost yelled. Someone behind me shushed us.

This went on for about ten more minutes. We kept glancing in each other's direction, only to turn away when we were noticed. I felt like I was back in elementary school. It was time for action.

"Johnny," I whispered, "I'm going in."

"Eh?"

"I'm going to tell Melody I love her."

"What? Since when?" The person behind us shushed us again.

"For a while now. I just didn't realize it."

"Obviously."

"Wish me luck."

"What? You can't tell her now; we're at the movies."

"Then I'll tell everyone I love her." The idea hadn't occurred to me until then, but it was worth a shot.

"Leon! Don't even think about it!" A look of horror spread across Johnny's face.

"Think Romeo and Juliet, Johnny. Think, um, Samson and Delilah."

"Think John Hinckley," begged Johnny. "Think restraining order."

"Here I go."

Johnny sighed, dumped the remains of his popcorn on the floor, and stuck the tub over his head. "Tell me when it's over."

As I hopped up and over to Melody's seat, I suddenly had a pretty good idea of how kamikaze pilots felt: I was going to die and I didn't even care. Waiting for her to forgive me wasn't working; I had to show her I was willing to do anything to win her back.

"Melody," I said, in my normal voice.

Melody started a bit when she realized I was standing right next to her. "Leon, sit down," she ordered loudly and angrily.

"Shut up!" someone called.

I knew I should go back to my seat, but I couldn't. The problem was I couldn't think of a blessed thing to say.

But someone up above was to give me inspiration. By

coincidence or design, I had approached Melody right when Bart Axelrod was giving a passionate speech to his on-screen love. Striking a pose in full view of the packed theater, I faced Melody and mouthed the words I'd heard a dozen times.

"*Babe, take me back. I know I hurt you, honey. I know I did you wrong.*"

Melody cringed and looked like she'd very much rather be somewhere else. Her companions looked from her to me with great amusement.

"*I been a loner all my life, babe. I didn't think I needed no one. But then I seen you up onstage at Chi Chi's and I can't think about no one different.*"

Melody was blushing through her scars. Several audience members were yelling for me to sit down. Too late to stop now. I continued the monologue.

"*I loves ya, darling. I tell you, she didn't mean nothing to me.*" That got a reaction from Melody, though not exactly a happy one. "*It won't happen again, sweetcheeks.*"

Someone's half-eaten candy bar pegged me in the side of the head.

"*I could be dead in the morning. Let me know you still care.*"

By this time, everyone in the theater was watching us. Audience members shouted opinions.

"Take him back!"

"Shut the hell up!"

"Down in front!"

"Dump him; go home with me!"

"Make him beg!"

"*You're my everything. . . .*"

I suddenly made full eye contact with Melody, and I hated what I saw. She wasn't impressed. She was mortified. She looked like I was ridiculing her, which was exactly what I was doing. I had tried to impress her by being goofy, but I'd only managed to draw attention to her and make her look foolish. The thing she'd told me she hated more than anything.

There was no point in going on. Turning away, I trudged out of the theater. Audience members laughed, whistled, and pelted me with popcorn. I didn't give them the satisfaction of seeing me run.

I walked out into the cold night air and sat on the curb. She was really gone this time. Just when I thought I couldn't sink any lower, something like this happened. To top it all off, Johnny had driven me. I had to wait out in the parking lot till the movie was over. My life was in the toilet.

Only it wasn't, really. I'd had a semester I'd remember for the rest of my life. I'd won the girl of my fantasies and dumped her. I'd taken off a girl's shirt. I'd eaten a cigarette. And I'd learned that maybe, just maybe, there was something about Leon Sanders that girls liked.

I didn't turn around when the theater door opened, but I did recognize Melody's voice.

"Everyone's going to be talking about that on Monday, you know."

I still didn't turn around. "Anything to be popular."

She sat down on the concrete next to me. "Did you think making a public spectacle of me would win me back?"

"Yes." I was too miserable to think of any other reason for what I'd done.

"You're unique; I'll give you that."

We sat in silence, not looking at each other.

"Melody?"

"Yes, Leon?"

"Do I stand a chance? At all?"

There was a pause. "As a boyfriend, no."

"How about as a friend? I miss that."

"Leon, I want to hate you so much. I want to put you out of my life. I want to say you meant nothing to me. But I really did like being with you. I . . . Leon, you were my best friend. I've never had that before."

Insert knife into heart, twist.

"Could we go back like that?" I asked, afraid of the answer.

"I don't know. Could we?"

I finally looked in her direction. She was staring at me expectantly. And then it hit me: for one of the few times in my life, I knew exactly what a woman wanted.

She didn't want lame excuses for my cheating, or promises she wouldn't believe. She didn't want public displays of insanity or whining and begging. After several weeks, I finally figured out what it was she needed. I took her hand and she didn't pull away.

"Melody, I'm sorry. I'm sorry I hurt you. There's no excuse, so I won't justify it. But I really do regret it. I'd like to be your friend again, if you'd let me."

For the first time since the breakup, Melody smiled at me. It wasn't her full-force, gorgeous smile, but it was a start.

"Want to buy me a taco, Leon? We can walk from here."

"I'd like that." We stood up.

"Do you need to tell Johnny you're leaving?"

"I think he'd be happy never to see me again."

We walked on through the crisp spring night in silence. I couldn't remember ever feeling so relieved. Though she wouldn't take me back as a boyfriend, at least she'd forgiven me enough to be friends. It was a start . . . and an ending, it seemed. Dan had been right. Melody had passed through the fire. She was harder. Those special feelings she'd had for me were gone, and I'd have to accept that.

Then again, she was still holding my hand.

ALSO BY BRIAN KATCHER

Almost Perfect

Logan Witherspoon's new crush
is hiding a big secret.

AVAILABLE IN OCTOBER 2009 FROM DELACORTE PRESS